The ghost of her passed through the room, raising the hairs on his arms.

There she was, vibrant as though she was in the room with him. "Don't tell me you don't like it." She gave her new dress a twirl, barefoot and beautiful, all ready for a night out but for the heels she would wait to put on to the last. Her toe-nails were painted red. The arch of her foot flexed strong and graceful with the movement. Her blonde hair shone in the light of memory. She stopped short, the soft blue fabric swinging against her legs, and grinned at him.

It went straight through him. He raised the bottle to his lips, holding on to the vision. It wavered beneath the intensity of his gaze.

Then there was nothing on the floor but scuff marks and the shimmer of dust. His trainers, mud-caked from that morning's eight-kilometer run, took up the space where her heels should have been. He had almost forgotten the way she used to toe her shoes off, always sliding the left one off first for some inexplicable reason.

The wall was cold and hard against his back, the Scotch smooth and warm.

There was no other choice. He'd made his decision two years ago. It was time.

Tomorrow, he would commit murder.

Praise for Vanessa Westermann

"A riveting introduction to a charming, smart bookstore owner... *AN EXCUSE FOR MURDER* is original, compelling, and a lovely launch for a great new sleuth."
 ~*Carolyn Hart*

~*~

"*AN EXCUSE FOR MURDER* skillfully interweaves the elements of spy thriller and cozy to create an engaging story with emotional resonance."
 ~*M. H. Callway*

~*~

"A mesmerizing page-turner... Westermann is a talent to watch!"

~*Rosemary McCracken*

~*~

"Engaging characters, and an intriguing take on a classic murder mystery."
 ~*Sleuth of Baker Street Mystery Bookstore*

~*~

"A lyrical thriller that crackles with defiance, danger, and uncertain romance. Kate Rowan is the perfect heroine for our times: wit, charm, and spirit balanced by impressive skills in self-defense and lock-picking."
 ~*Barbara Fradkin*

An Excuse for Murder

by

Vanessa Westermann

This is a work of fiction. Names, characters, places, and incidents are either the product of the author's imagination or are used fictitiously, and any resemblance to actual persons living or dead, business establishments, events, or locales, is entirely coincidental.

An Excuse for Murder

COPYRIGHT © 2019 by Vanessa Westermann

All rights reserved. No part of this book may be used or reproduced in any manner whatsoever without written permission of the author or The Wild Rose Press, Inc. except in the case of brief quotations embodied in critical articles or reviews.
Contact Information: info@thewildrosepress.com

Cover Art by *Kim Mendoza*

The Wild Rose Press, Inc.
PO Box 708
Adams Basin, NY 14410-0708
Visit us at www.thewildrosepress.com

Publishing History
First Crimson Rose Edition, 2019
Print ISBN 978-1-5092-2517-0
Digital ISBN 978-1-5092-2518-7

Published in the United States of America

Dedication

For my family,
for encouraging me to follow my dreams,
and especially for my mom.
You inspire me, always.

Prologue

Gary couldn't stop thinking about the way her skin felt under his hands. How the curve of her shoulder had glowed palely in the dusky room that morning, the faint shadow of a bruise below her knee, the almost translucent skin on the underside of her wrist.

His concentration should have been centered on the parking lot, planning and scanning the premises, alert to potential danger. It was what he was paid for, what he was good at. One of the best, in fact. The sun, low and intense on the horizon, glared off car windows, in flashes of light that left dark imprints across his vision. Despite the glare, the air was damp and cool. If necessary, he could recite the license plates of the vehicles parked on the street in that London borough, but still, there were blind spots, and he knew it.

Tension shimmered like heat waves at his peripherals. His jacket collar chafed uncomfortably against his skin. There was an edginess in the air Gary couldn't explain. Something pressing at him, threatening. But still he could feel a smile lingering on his lips, warm as her hand resting on his arm.

"Did you read it?"

"Read what?" He looked back at her, an involuntary move, assuring himself she was there. It should have been another day like any other, but there was something in the details he couldn't grasp hold of, that felt wrong. It was just the faintest impression of fear, a tingle at the back of his neck.

"The book." She was insistent now, meeting his eyes with hers, and he found himself looking too long, caught again by that small brown fleck in the iris of her right eye. "The one I gave you?"

"You're like a cat," he laughed. "You only want my attention when I'm busy." He glanced at the sidewalk, at two passing pedestrians, white male and female, mid-forties, heads bent together with the easy closeness that years of marriage provided.

"That's not true. I always want your attention."

"Now if only that were true," he teased. "Your father hired me to protect you. Let me concentrate on the job at hand, and I promise you'll have my undivided attention later." What was it about her that always made him want more, even though it was wrong? "Don't worry, you're always on my mind. You're like a poison. I can't get you out of my head." The way she had led him in long strides through the Victoria & Albert museum earlier, past exhibits without so much as a glance for artwork, porcelain, and stained glass, until she stood in front of one cabinet. Floral marquetry of walnut, pine, oak, and ivory. Sprays of berries tied with ribbons, a central door concealing tiers of more drawers. Aged wood, birds rich with detail, and a prowling lion, claws extended had been caught in the passage of light, spilling dimly from the sloped windows above them. You can look and look, she'd said to him, and always see more.

Movement on their right had him pivoting, placing a hand beneath her elbow, pulling her closer to him. He searched for the source of the threat, scanning sidewalk, empty cars, opaque windows, skyline. Instead of a casual shift in their positions allowing him to shield her, his muscles had tightened, not with the useful surge of adrenaline, but with mindless and inexplicable dread. He resisted the sudden urge to rush her to the car, away from that space filled with too many unknowns.

"What is it? You're hurting me." She tried to pull her arm from his hand.

"It's nothing," Gary said, loosening his hold on her reluctantly. Just a door opening and closing across the street. Nevertheless, he couldn't shake the feeling that they were being watched. He glanced at Adriana's bent head, her features hidden behind a wash of pale hair, and pulled her closer to him. She was toying with the necklace he had given her, running her finger over and over the orchid impressed in the pendant. "I'd lose my job if your father found out about us."

She looked up at him then, with that serious expression he'd seen so many times before. "Is the job more important than me?"

"Of course not." He counted five empty parked cars, one of them a Ford Focus with a distinctive scrape across the passenger side door.

"So quit then."

"And let someone else protect you? The jealousy would kill me." The smile was for her, although he was looking away, toward the building on their right, the shape of the tree and the shadow beneath it.

He felt the movement of her body as she turned toward him. "I love you, you know."

Gary couldn't tell if he was walking or rooted to the spot. She was a client and he should keep his distance, at least until the assignment was over. But all he could see was the smile playing at the corners of her mouth, the softness in her eyes that was only for him. To hell with the rules. Gary knew he was grinning like a fool, quick and reckless and carefree. "Adriana—"

The pressure came from above his left shoulder, a sudden shift in the air. A whistle of sound past his ear. Her body jerked against his as she staggered. At first he thought the bullet had missed its mark. That sweet, heady gasp of relief.

His next instinct was to find safety, to clear the scene. His thoughts were already racing through the following stages. Make sure the shooter was no longer on the scene. Check for wounded, for injury.

She was sliding toward the ground. It was as though a weight was pulling her down, and him with her, until he was on the pavement next to her.

He pressed against the wound, blood running warm across his knuckles to pool on the ground, damp beneath his knees. He knew there was little to be done for a chest wound like this. The acrid-sweet metallic smell of her blood was nauseating and unforgettable, altering her familiar scent into the bitter stench of impending loss.

There was a surge of focused movement behind him, running footsteps, cries for help, a siren in the distance. Her heart beat beneath his hand, fainter each time. With each beat, she was slipping farther away from him, and all he could think about was finding the person who pulled that trigger.

Rage compressed within his chest, a cold force. Hatred pulsed in the sharp pain at his temples, in the clenched fingers of his blood-stained hand.

He should have moved faster, turned in time,

gotten her out of the way. He should have relied on his own instincts, instead of being distracted. Hell, he'd warned her against routine, but all it had taken for him to let her go to the museum was a touch of her hand against his and an unhurried kiss. If only the empty apartment and coffee with him had been enough. Instead, she'd wanted antiques and lunch, pasta and wine. As though nothing else existed.

It was his fault.

He could feel her last painful breath burn in his own lungs. He would calculate the exact trajectory of the shot. He would dissect that moment, tear it apart and find who did this. Hunt them the way they hunted her.

Dense impressions crowded his mind, clarifying and concentrating. The pavement grinding against his knees, the sun reflecting off her blood, steam rising, the weight of her in his arms, the wild arch of her throat, the curve of her cheek. The guilt aching like violence in his bones.

Chapter One

For a man who knew how to handle his liquor, Gary was two pints the worse for wear and on his way to finish off the job. His apartment was only a fifteen-minute walk from the pub. Cold night air rushed past him, a sudden gust that whistled down the alley farther ahead and had his ears buzzing. A cluster of teenagers jostled their way down the other side of the street. Gary heard a shout, followed by loud laughter as the tallest boy finished the joke he'd been telling, hitting the punch-line.

The shops in the pedestrian area were closed, the windows shuttered, while the pubs were coming to life. An empty crisp packet drifted past on a current of air. The wooden sign of the bookstore at the end of the street swung on rusted hinges. He was still too far away to read the sign, but it didn't matter. He'd seen it before, many times. *Fortune's Cove Books. Kate Rowan, proprietor.*

Adriana could never walk past a bookstore without going in. Hard to believe it was two years to the day since she died. He could almost hear her heels ringing against the pavement, feel her silver ring cold against his skin when he slipped his fingers through hers.

It would be easier to leave Caulden, but he doubted he'd be able to build another company as successful as Fenris Securities somewhere else. He had put everything he had into planning his revenge.

There was still a choice. He could stay home tomorrow instead. Listen to a live album, speakers turned up too loud, the bass pounding through the walls. Or he could go out, have a good time. Forget Adriana.

A door banged in the distance. A car drove past slowly, the tires rasping over the pavement.

A step fell in pace with his own.

Gary glanced over his shoulder but said nothing. He wasn't in the mood for company.

They continued in silence, the rhythm of their steps matched perfectly over the years. The man beside him began to whistle a minuet by Mozart. The sound was clear as glass. Gary's fingers tensed on a flash of irritation. He dug his hands into his pockets.

"Nice night, boss," Percival remarked in his rumbling baritone.

"Go away, Perce."

"Had a pint in the pub, eh?" The tone was easy, conversational.

It didn't take Sherlock Holmes to make that deduction. He hadn't hidden the fact that he had been drinking. Still, it seemed like Percy had spotted a weakness.

The familiar sizzle of violence began at the base of his skull and spread down his arms, through the tendons in his hands. His nostrils flared, his breath came fast. He was itching for a fight. "I mean it, Percival." His voice was dangerously calm.

Other men might have sensed something off, a quiver of tension in the air and nothing more, but Percival knew the warning signs. He could read them like no one else could. He should have walked away. "Buy you a coffee?"

Gary spun and dragged the man toward him by the collar until he could see the whites of Percival's eyes. The crisp fabric strained under his grip and cut into his palm. Percival outweighed him by a good two stones, but what Gary lacked in size he made up for in skill and the sheer muscle to back it.

Percival was impassive, infuriatingly patient. He grinned. "Round of chess, then?"

Gary let him go, exasperated. "Friday night maybe, but not now."

"All right then." Percival shrugged, his massive width straining at the shoulders of his tweed jacket. "A client came in today. Didn't like the security system we installed. Said it didn't suit his needs. I thought we'd covered all the bases, but people hide things, boss." It was said casually. "Sometimes you have to dig up the truth, no matter how deep it's buried."

Gary ignored the sharp taste of adrenaline at the back of his mouth. It could be small talk. There was a fine line between cautious and paranoid. Still, the shock of that one sentence almost had him sobered. He should have been prepared but, here he was, caught off guard. Another man might have come up with lies. Gary waited.

Percival looked up at the sky, now a bruised purple and dark with the promise of rain. "Then again, sometimes it's better if things stay hidden."

"So long as the client's happy. We'll draft an alternative system for him." Gary watched the bookstore's sign swing in the breeze, and he knew. He'd made a mistake somewhere along the line. "See you in the office Monday."

"Sir." Percival walked away, whistling softly to himself.

He had to be more careful. Even if he changed his mind, decided to wait again before making his move. He couldn't afford another mistake. Not before it was done and over.

****

The key scraped over the lock before sliding home. Gary rammed his shoulder against the door in one well-aimed move, applied just the right amount of force to release the latch, and entered his apartment. He had chosen the flat on the top floor, up three flights of stairs that creaked under the slightest weight, for the same reason he hadn't fixed the door. There was only one way in and one way out, and he wanted to know if someone was coming.

He stepped into the living room. A green light flashed beside the door. Gary punched in the code that disabled the security system he had installed himself. He didn't bother to turn on the lights. As he moved into the room, he was met with the stale scent of what had been an excellent Arabian blend. A mug half-full of yesterday's coffee was still on the end table in the living room.

A pockmarked wooden support beam was the only division between living room and kitchen. High quality speakers, powerful enough to spread the sound of classic hard rock through the apartment, were set up on a shelf full of vintage LPs. On a low table on the other side of the window was a wood carving of a dog and a marble chess set, the pieces laid out two moves into a five-move problem. The knight was next to play. The natural luster of the board was dulled by a film of dust. The walls were bare. He'd left them the same indeterminate beige the last bloke had painted them. There were no photographs, no pictures.

Gary headed toward the glass-fronted cupboard on the back wall. A section of an old copy of the *Financial News* slid to the floor as he passed. A stiff wind blew against the window, shaking the frame and rattling the panes.

The shadowy figure in the glass mirrored his movements as he opened the cupboard door. For an instant he met his own eyes in the reflection. He reached for the Scotch. Single malt.

Gary paused as he caught sight of the book on the top shelf. The color had faded around the gilded letters spelling out Lord Alfred Tennyson. He knew without touching them that the edges of the paper had softened, that they were no longer as crisp as when she had handled them.

He shook his head abruptly and took a swig from the bottle, drinking deeply. The slow burn of barley and honey had him gasping. Gary turned, his back to the wall, Scotch in one hand. He slid to the ground and let his head fall back. He rested the bottle on one raised knee and stared into the shadows. They shifted and gathered, clotting in the corners of the room.

The ghost of her laughter teased across his skin, raising the hairs on his arms.

There she was, vibrant as though she was in the room with him. "Don't tell me you don't like it." She gave her new dress a twirl, barefoot and beautiful, all ready for a night out but for the heels she would wait to put on to the last. Her toe-nails were painted red. The arch of her foot flexed strong and graceful with the movement. Her blonde hair shone in the light of memory. She stopped short, the soft blue fabric swinging against her legs, and grinned at him.

It went straight through him. He raised the bottle to his lips, holding on to the vision. It wavered beneath the intensity of his gaze.

Then there was nothing on the floor but scuff marks and the shimmer of dust. His trainers, mud-caked from that morning's eight-kilometer run, took up the space where her heels should have been. He had almost forgotten the way she used to toe her shoes off, always sliding the left one off first for some inexplicable reason.

The wall was cold and hard against his back, the Scotch smooth and warm.

There was no other choice. He'd made his decision two years ago. It was time.

Tomorrow, he would commit murder.

Chapter Two

"Where did you find the body?" Marcus Evans asked. The clipped phrases and lengthened vowels of his Eton accent resonated through the cell phone.

It was a familiar question and one Kate Rowan had even looked forward to, while turning the pages of a book late at night. As the owner of Fortune's Cove Books, she had a weakness for crime fiction and the means to indulge it. Now here was Marcus asking her that same question and she realized that all it took was two words to turn a man into an object, inanimate. *The body.*

"Sprawled at the bottom of the basement stairs." She could feel a frisson of panic waiting, one moment ahead.

The body was lying across the last step like a rag doll on a shelf. Kate stood at the top, looking down, and clutched the phone to her ear. A draft of cool air brushed against the back of her neck from the open door behind her. The paperback she'd been holding was lying splayed open across the dead man's chest where it had fallen. The pages riffled, a dry whisper of sound, stirred by the breeze. It could have almost been a final exhalation of breath. The words seemed to ripple across the paper, a flurry of black on white, as the page moved.

"What are you doing in the basement? Shouldn't

you be at work?"

"I wanted to bring my beanbag chair up from the storage room. I thought it would work well in the bookstore." A fragment of glass gleamed in the shadows of the unlit hall.

"Isn't that the dust-infested blob I carried downstairs for you last year, because it's so hideous?"

"I thought I'd take another look at it."

"As your best friend, I say this with the kindest intentions—it should be incinerated. Are you sure Mr. Wendell's dead?"

"Yes." Her eyes were diverted by folds of fabric, touched by the sunlight coming through the open door behind her. It was the little things she hadn't noticed at first, that she couldn't stop noticing now. Gray-cast skin. One claw-like hand clutching at his chest, calloused fingers stiff. Eyes torn wide. She met his gaze, resisting the urge to flinch. "Absolutely sure." The purple bathrobe, dark in patches, twisted beneath Mr. Wendell's legs.

"What happened?"

"I don't know." Taking a deep breath, Kate inched closer. She shifted, gripping the railing with her free hand for support, and peered cautiously down. Her sneaker slipped on the carpeted step. The next thing she knew, her knee connected painfully with the rough texture of the wall, her palm skidded off another surface and she was on the ground, her right hand planted in something sticky and wet. "Shit!" The word exploded on a breath.

She knelt face to face with Mr. Wendell and stared into his vacant eyes. Those filmed irises, with the barely visible lids and a feathering of pale lashes, seemed to take in everything and nothing at the same time. His lips were stretched tight in a grimace, an eerie imitation of a smile that shot a surge of pure terror through her. Not that she'd admit it for the world.

"Are you okay? What's going on?" Marcus demanded anxiously.

Kate scrambled backward, away from the body. "I'm fine." Her voice did sound fine. Strong. A line of blood trickled warmly down her leg from the tear in her jeans. "I slipped on something wet."

"Was it Mr. Wendell's blood?" He sounded a little too eager.

"No." Kate raised her hand to her nose and the harsh scent of vinegar assaulted her nostrils. She gagged, a reflex reaction that was all shock, even though she knew exactly what was coating her fingers with a wet sheen, pearly in the half-light of the basement. "Pickle juice," she managed.

"Oh, sure. Pickle juice." A pause. "Why pickle juice?"

"He loved pickles. Looks like he's crushed the jar beneath him." Kate pulled herself slowly to her feet. She winced as her knee smarted with the movement. "Based on the descriptions in crime novels and a couple of different TV shows, I'd say he's had a heart attack."

"Isn't it a bit risky, drawing conclusions on reality from fiction?" Marcus asked. "Oh, wait. That's the way you live your life."

"Thank you, Marcus." She rolled her eyes, taking a shaky breath of the too still air. The acidic scent of decay and fermented pickles caught at her throat. "Books teach people about life, offering experiences you can't have yourself."

"It's called entertainment, love."

"I don't have time to argue with you right now. Mr. Wendell wasn't the nicest person, but he didn't deserve to die like this."

"You're right." Marcus sobered. "Did you call 999?"

"Of course I called 999." Kate pressed a hand against her throbbing knee. "I'm not an idiot. It was the first thing I did."

"And here I was thinking I was the first person you'd ring upon stumbling across a corpse. How foolish of me."

"It's that ego of yours. What if Mr. Wendell didn't die of natural causes? What if someone killed him?" Her mind raced through the gruesome possibilities.

"Right." Marcus snorted on a laugh, which was surprising since he was normally too elegant to make such a crude sound. "As though Mr. Wendell could irritate anyone enough that they would make the effort to bump him off. Besides, things like that don't happen in neighborhoods like Willowsend. The most malicious thing anyone even thinks of doing is stealing someone's newspaper off their porch. 'Course, add twenty minutes travel time and it's a different situation. Caulden isn't exactly London, but statistically crime is more likely to occur in a city than in the suburbs."

"You obviously have no concept of the dark deeds that go on behind the white-washed walls and polished doors of suburban homes."

"The Victorian house you're living in, with its cracked façade, fairy-tale tower and generally ethereal appearance, simply cannot, and I repeat, cannot be compared to the average suburban home."

"That's true." In the years she had been away, the house had remained untouched. It had also been altered in details so subtle that the changes could startle her even now.

"How long has Mr. Wendell been down there?"

"It's only eight now. Elaina must still be sleeping or else she'd be knee-deep in the action by now." The basement, the house itself felt strangely empty. The only sounds were the repetitive high, thin notes of a goldcrest in the distance outside. "He must have been here a while. He's already starting to get stiff." Kate fought back a wave of faintness. "He isn't exactly dressed for company. The bathrobe is ancient...and seems to have loosened in the throes of death."

"That is too bloody much information." Crackle, crunch.

"Are you eating?"

"Mm, yes. Toast. Delightful."

"After I described Mr. Wendell's prone frame to you, bathrobe and all? You are one sick man."

"No, just hungry, and my imagination isn't as vivid as yours. However, there are houses waiting to be sold and I need to leave my flat to do so. Give me a ring after to let me know how it went. Keep your chin up. Maybe some gorgeous hunk of a man will wander into your bookstore today. You'll lock eyes over a tattered copy of *Enduring Love* and he'll sweep you off your feet. That would be quite the distraction. Death in the morning, affairs of the heart in the afternoon."

"That's wholly unrealistic."

"It would not be unrealistic if you looked more closely at the men around you instead of only swooning over the ones on paper."

"Tell me you could resist a handsome inspector with a sense of humor and apologetic ways." She looked down at the green and white cover of *Artists in Crime* lying open on Mr. Wendell's chest. The 1949 edition was a tight copy, with a slight lean to the spine and signs of ageing. The imagery in that last chapter was still fresh in her mind, the little scarlet thread of blood and the glinting hilt of the dagger. Kate could smell the chalk from the drawing and the dust beneath the throne, feel that delicious thrill of foreboding as though she'd been in that artist's studio herself. "Since *Artists in Crime* is on top of Mr. Wendell, I don't think I'll be finishing it."

"It doesn't seem fair that you've got the corpse, but not the inspector."

"I don't think we need a detective."

"If he's handsome—"

"Bye, Marcus." Exasperated, she hung up the phone. A square of light fell through the open door behind her, illuminating the body in a startling wash of daylight. Her silhouette was a dark shadow over the twisted figure stretched at her feet. She could have used a few more words of motivation. Kate suddenly felt terribly alone. "'Bollocks,' as Marcus would say."

Kate turned her back on the corpse and wiped clammy palms against her jeans. That was that, then. Vigilance be damned. She needed fresh air.

The outside door was heavy, a metal construction meant for safety. A residential door with a good lock. It felt as though she was sealing a tomb, when she closed it behind her.

Kate crossed the terrace and entered the house through the kitchen. Sunlight, deeply golden and belonging to summer, shone on red floor tiles and bruised corners with deep shadows. She steadied herself against the back of a chair, shut her eyes and tried to forget what she had seen.

The sound of heels clicking softly across wood, as though hesitant to disturb, came to her from the hall. Kate squared her shoulders, and turned to face Roselyn Marsh as the older woman entered the room.

"Oh! Good morning." Her great-aunt froze in the doorway. "I thought you'd be out already." She took in Kate's torn pants and the gash in her knee. "Have you hurt yourself?"

Roselyn Marsh was the epitome of a lady, if Kate had ever met one. She was refined and eloquent, and never had a silver hair out of place. Her rose-colored silk pants and matching blouse concealed the fact that she had been a devoted widow for ten years. Her hair was pulled back and wound into a tight bun, offsetting delicate features lined by time and emotion.

It was almost impossible to believe they were related. Seventeen years ago, Roselyn Marsh had smiled beautifully, handed Kate a cookie as she sat on the counter and told her stories in exactly the right intonation to distract a young girl from the sting of disinfectant being applied to a cut. The time apart had turned them into strangers. Great-aunt Roselyn had become Mrs. Marsh.

"It's nothing. I'll take care of it in a second. I was on my way out, but—" Kate searched for words, tucking a strand of hair behind her ear. Her earring was cold to the touch, chilled from the morning air. "Mr. Wendell…"

"Yes?"

"He's—he's dead."

A thin hand fluttered, rested briefly upon the regal neck. She stumbled back a step. Kate moved to take her arm, but the other woman shook her head and raised a hand in warning. "Dead?" The word was barely more than a whisper. She cleared her throat before trying again, more firmly. "Dead?"

"He's in the basement, but you don't have to see him. I've already phoned. They're sending someone over."

Mrs. Marsh grasped at the counter for support. In a barely audible voice, though steely in its intensity, she forced between clenched teeth, "There will be no more death in this house." Her carefully colored lips were a thin pink slash against white.

Unsure of how to react, not just to what Mrs. Marsh had said, but to the entire situation, Kate suggested, "I'll go out and show them where"—she hesitated—"he is."

Mrs. Marsh suddenly nodded decisively. "Yes." She straightened. "I'll get some coffee started."

"Are you sure you're all right?"

"I'm fine. There are more pressing matters at hand than a feeble old woman's sensibilities." She reached for the pot and began to systematically measure coffee. The metal spoon tapped against the edge of the plastic filter, a brisk, hard little sound.

Before she left the room, Kate glanced back. Maybe she had only imagined the desperation she had seen in her great-aunt's eyes. The uncontrollable anger.

"Not again." The fierce whisper pierced the air.

The door slid into the latch.

Chapter Three

A jolt of adrenaline woke Gary. He stretched one hand out, fingertips sliding over the blanket, a pillow. It took a moment to realize the space next to him was empty.

His eyes blinked open. The ceiling seemed to spin, one slow circle before settling. He'd stripped, thrown his clothes in the wash, and stretched out full-length on his bed. One glance at the watch on his nightstand told him that was hours ago. It had been a long time since he'd slept like that, down and out, without waking once.

Images drawn from the depths of sleep hovered before Gary's eyes. Disjointed fragments of memory. Moonlight glinting off distant windows. Rounding the back of a house that looked old, all brick and stones, like something from another time. Breath rasping in his lungs. Blinking against a bead of sweat. The sudden release of weight, dropping from his grip in a boneless heap.

Gary scrubbed a hand over his jaw, feeling the scrape of stubble.

"Hell." He groaned and sat up, planting his feet on the floor. He rolled his shoulders, stretching stiff muscles.

Gary reached for the photograph he'd left lying on the nightstand. A square slip of paper, wallet-sized, with a white border. Glossy, but not the best quality, meant more for information and a purpose than the kind you'd tuck away in an album for safe keeping. The upper left corner was torn, where it had been stapled to the file. He'd found it in his office yesterday, beneath a sheet of lined paper in the bottom of a drawer.

Gary held the picture facing him between thumb and fingers. He palmed it so that it was hidden in his hand, then flipped it, shifting it between his knuckles. The white backing, slightly yellowed from its time in the drawer, flashed, disappeared, and reappeared with the movement.

Despite the plain background and the professional smile, it was her, along with all of those details he'd forgotten. His memory had distorted her features, stylized them until they were reduced to bland adjectives that could mean anything. Blonde hair, green eyes.

Floorboards creaked in the flat below, loud as though the sound came from the next room. The sharp lines of the photograph pressed against his palm.

The body would be found. Soon probably. Maybe it already had been. It brought a little bit of pleasure, imagining it. His corpse laid out on a slab in the morgue. Investigated, possibly, but that was unlikely. In any case, there was nothing that could tie Gary to the dead man. Everything was too circumstantial. There was no connection to dredge up.

And that was the beauty of it. A death that had fate written all over it. There'd be no coroner's report, just a death certificate, recording the cause, the time, the date.

The photograph was almost in the bin before he changed his mind and replaced it on the table.

Gary threw back the blankets. He grabbed his track

pants off the back of the chair, dressing as he walked to the door. Tied his trainers with a sharp tug of laces. Then he was out and down the steps, his feet picking up the rhythm set by the beat of the song slamming through his earphones, loud and fast.

Pebbles skidded beneath the treads of his trainers. Sweat soaked his t-shirt, but still Gary pushed on, farther and farther, faster and faster. Blood roared in his ears. His feet pounded across the asphalt of the jogging trail. Sunlight seeped dark and red through the canopy of leaves above and stained the ground in front of him. The terrain changed quickly before his eyes. Stones at the edge of the path shimmered copper, gold, and rust. The filtered light created the illusion of unity until everything was the same. Oaks, sycamores, evergreens became trees; cornflowers, daisies, dandelions became wildflowers.

The only thing he saw was her face. A white-bordered image and the smile that was nothing like the one he remembered. Gary laughed, the sudden sound startling a falcon. It shot into the sky, its wings drenched in burgundy like everything else. It flashed and dipped before disappearing from sight.

He had used love as an excuse for murder.

His feet beat on relentlessly.

Chapter Four

The ambulance was in the center of the drive, planted like a strange growth of modernity. A man climbed out of the vehicle, medical bag in hand.

"You called it in?" He scowled at Kate. There was an edge to his voice, exasperation, a bit of swagger.

Kate held back a sharp retort. She hated being intimidated. "Mr. Wendell—the body—is in the basement, at the bottom of the stairs. If you go around the left of the house, you'll see the door."

A young man hopped out of the ambulance like a puppy let off his leash. When he caught a glimpse of the house, his jaw dropped. He stood still, staring in wonder.

"Boy!" The man barked. "Oy, lad!" No reaction. He waved a hand in disgust. "Useless anyway." The doctor growled in Kate's direction, "Keep your eye on him," before stalking around the side of the house and out of sight.

"This is it," the boy murmured.

"What is?"

He shot Kate a glance before rubbing a sheepish hand across the haphazard stubble on his chin. "The fairy tale house. Everyone calls it that. I've never seen it before, but it's just like they said."

Kate stood beside him and took in the old building, the sun in her eyes. "It's something, isn't it? It was built circa eighteen-ninety. Repairs and alterations have been done over the years, of course. I've even done a patch-up job here and there."

He nodded, his face turned toward the porch and the glint of stained glass. "It looks good."

"The tower would have appealed to Rapunzel, even though it's missing the thorns and brambles."

"You live here?" The boy tore his gaze away from the house.

"I rent a room on the main floor."

"Shit." The word was a sigh of awe. "What's she like?"

"Who?"

"The Eternal Wife."

"The what?" Kate eyed him warily.

"You know—the lady who owns the house and mourns her dead husband. Some people say," he added conspiratorially, "she walks the graves at night, weeping. And now there's been another death."

Kate frowned. "I don't know who you've been talking to, but I don't think they're all that reliable. Roselyn Marsh? She may have her eccentricities but she's not the Miss Havisham you seem to think she is." How many times had she heard a voice replying to a question that had never been asked? It didn't mean anything.

"The gaffer will be after me in a minute," he said, his eyes on the tower. "I'm Jeremy."

"Kate." She wondered how often Jeremy got called in to record a death. "I'm going to go check on the doctor."

"I'll be right there."

She left him looking up at the irregular roofline.

Reflections in the window shifted as she walked past. Leaves flickering, a sudden hot flare of sunlight, clouds.

The doctor straightened from his examination as she came down the basement stairs. The scene could have been an illustration in a penny dreadful. The gentleman doctor standing over the body of the tenant. Kate stopped a few steps away.

The basement had been a place for hide-and-seek, truth-or-dare, broken toys turned into treasures. A place they could leave if one of them heard a quiet rustle in the room. Leaping back up the stairs toward Orangesicles and sunshine.

The doctor gave the body a narrowed glare. "Where's the lad got to now?"

"I left him standing on the lawn."

The doctor rolled his eyes. "Boy," he growled as Jeremy appeared in the doorway, "if you want to learn, you have to be here when I carry out the formalities. I work, you watch."

"Sorry, Dr Garreth. It won't happen again." Jeremy squatted down next to the body and examined the pallor of the skin.

"This fellow," the doctor shot a finger at Mr. Wendell, "suffered a severe myocardial infarction. A heart attack in layman's terms. Death would have been instantaneous. We can keep the body in the hospital morgue for up to forty-eight hours but then you or another relative need to make provisions—plan a funeral or cremation."

"I'm not related to Mr. Wendell," Kate said quickly.

"A ladylove?" The doctor cocked an eyebrow.

"No!"

"You don't sound British."

Kate crossed her arms. "I'm half Canadian, half British. Does it matter?"

"That depends." Dr. Garreth rocked back on his heels comfortably. "Who is the next of kin?"

"I don't know. He's only lived here a couple of months...maybe three. You'd have to ask Mrs. Marsh, my great-aunt. She owns the house. Mr. Wendell kept to himself. I didn't see him much."

The outer door swung back on its hinges, slamming hard against the brick wall with a crack of noise. Elaina stood in the doorway, dark curls tumbling to her waist. The strap of Elaina's short black nightgown slid from her shoulder as she braced an arm against the door. Kate heard Jeremy gulp. Men had been known to fall in love with Elaina at a glance when she was fully clothed. Jeremy didn't stand a chance.

"What's with all the ruckus?" Elaina murmured, her voice rough from sleep and years of cigarettes.

"What is this?" The doctor turned to Kate. "Some sort of hippie commune?"

"Almost."

Elaina looked down at the obstacle at the bottom of the steps. "He doesn't look very good."

"You think?" Kate couldn't help asking.

Elaina shrugged. "Give me a break. I was up late last night, supposedly kissed by the muse." She rubbed a finger across the streaks of paint scarring her arm. "This morning I'm not so sure. It's difficult to be brilliant after only two hours of sleep."

"He's dead!" Jeremy blushed to the roots of his hair when Elaina turned her soulful eyes upon him.

"So Mr. Wendell finally kicked the bucket. Not surprising. He was out of shape and loved pickles far too much. Has anyone got a cigarette?"

"I don't think a doctor is going to have a cigarette—" Dr Garreth silenced Kate by pulling a pack of Marlboros from his chest pocket. He tossed it to Elaina, who snatched it deftly out of the air with one hand. "All right. I stand corrected."

Elaina shook back her hair, lit the cigarette, and inhaled deeply. Jeremy took a step closer, his eyes fixed on breasts straining against black lace. Kate grabbed his arm to stop him from crushing Mr. Wendell's hand beneath his shoe.

"I hate to bring up technicalities." Kate kept a firm hold on Jeremy, who seemed oblivious to everything and anything but the woman draped in the doorway. "But how much longer is this going to take? I need to get to work."

Dr Garreth jammed his fists against his hips and attempted to tower over her, although he wasn't a very tall person. "Everybody should get the attention they deserve, even in death. Now stop gawping, Jeremy, and get to work!"

Elaina watched the scene with a delighted grin. "You can go open the store. I'll take over here. I don't have to be at the pub until four."

Kate had visions of the whole thing going horribly wrong. Call it premonition, or just plain logic, but she had a bad feeling about this. "Could you keep an eye on Mrs. Marsh? She seemed shaken by what happened to Mr. Wendell."

"I will."

"And put some clothes on." Kate added as an

afterthought.

"Spoilsport!" Elaina screwed up her classic features and stuck out her tongue. Even that managed to look mysterious and attractive on her. Sometimes it took all Kate's effort not to hate her.

"Make sure nothing goes wrong."

"What are they going to do, Kate? Kill him a second time?"

"You never know."

Chapter Five

Gary shouldn't have been surprised to see her there.

Eyes still adjusting to the dim interior, his fingers tightened on the door handle as he entered the Old Firehall Café. Kate Rowan was sitting on a wooden stool at the counter, her back to him.

Gary stood in the doorway. Just an average bloke on a Saturday, debating what kind of coffee to buy. The first time he had come in the café, he had expected dainty tea-cups and pastel shelves. Not exposed brick and wide spaces. Tables arranged around a fireman's pole. Air thick with freshly brewed coffee. An undertone of something lighter, herbal. The place gave an impression of purpose, left over from its days as the local fire-station, that even a fresh coat of paint couldn't hide. That's what had him coming back.

"Mr. Wendell died this morning," Kate told Neil, the owner of the café, as he filled a sieve with loose-leaf tea. Her voice was quiet, but the acoustics were right. Low background noise, high ceiling. The place was still half-empty, only a few tables in use.

Kate toyed with the handle of the creamer in front of her, waiting as Neil prepared the take-out cup of tea. Gary caught a glimpse of her profile. Just the cheekbone, a corner of her mouth.

That sentence should have felt like gold. Any kind

of knowledge gave you an advantage, kept you in control. A first-hand account from someone living in the house? It was like being handed intel, gift-wrapped with a bow on top. So why was he suddenly wary as all hell?

Gary approached the counter. Neil glanced at him, nodded. The man had always been friendly. Gary tipped and never stayed long. But that shared camaraderie he'd sensed between Kate and Neil when he entered was gone. Their conversation wouldn't pick up again until he was well out of the way. Fine by him. He smiled, slow and easy.

"Medium coffee, two sugar, one cream?" Neil was already reaching for a mug. He handled the collection of pottery and bone china cups as carefully as a man half his size would.

"That's right. Same as usual." Today, he was sticking to routine.

The scent she wore was subtle. You had to be close before you picked up on the citrus. One strand of hair curled above her ear, twisting outward. She hadn't taken time over it. She smiled at Neil. There it was again, that flash of friendship.

It was only standing right next to her that he noticed how young she looked. The dash of freckles over skin, clear as a child's. Hands so small he could hold both in one of his.

"Thanks." He took the coffee from Neil, felt the heat of it through the stoneware. "Keep the change."

Gary sank down into a chair near the door, his back to the wall. Far enough away, but still close enough to catch every word, so long as the other customers kept their voices at that same low murmur. He pulled out his phone, always a useful prop. Idly scrolling through messages, he crossed his legs at the ankles and settled back. His heart was racing.

Neil wiped down the counter carefully. He was taking his own sweet time bringing the conversation back around. Long enough to have Gary thinking he'd lost the moment. Finally, the man tucked the cloth into his pocket and folded his arms across his chest.

"I thought there was something," Neil said to Kate. "You've been picking at your nails. Nervous habit. And you're drowning your Assam in milk."

"Am I that predictable?" She pushed the creamer away from her.

One of the women seated at the table nearby rose and approached the counter with the fragile steps of old age. There was a steady kind of intent about it. Gary could have cursed her for interrupting. In a surprisingly fluid move, she rammed her cane at an angle against the floor next to Kate. The plastic sparkled menacingly. "I'm takin' it ye'll be the lass who found the corpse." The woman's voice reverberated with a Scottish brogue.

He wasn't the only one who had been listening.

"I don't see how that's any of your business." She leaned away from the woman.

So Kate was the one who found him.

"Donna even try tae deny it. I know ye are." She wagged a finger at Kate.

Neil cleared his throat. For a man obviously comfortable around women, he often seemed overwhelmed by them. "Look, Penelope, let the girl fix her tea in peace. Let it go."

Penelope huffed. "I'm only askin' a question! Noo,

lass, how did ye find him? Did ye walk past and identify the shoes of the mangled body as belongin' to Mr. Wendell? How did he die?" She leaned closer, her nose only inches from Kate's.

Kate turned her head away. She didn't flinch, didn't draw back. That slight turn of the head was a motion of dismissal that had him thinking of women in old portraits, pale and aloof.

Her glance met his. Gary resisted the urge to look away. Secure in his position at the back of the room, it felt as though he'd suddenly been exposed. Had there been a flicker of recognition? The chair creaked beneath him, and he realized he was leaning forward.

She gave him a sidelong smile, sharing her exasperation with him. "I'm not saying anything." For one confused moment, he thought she was talking to him.

Penelope sucked in a breath. A sharp hiss that carried over the clink of cutlery. "All right. But mark my words"—the old woman glared at Kate—"this'll no be finished yet." She pivoted and limped past him, out the door. The scent of spearmint arthritis cream wafted after her.

The chattering of the women at the other table had become suspiciously quiet. Kate stood. "I'll tell you more about it later, Neil, when there aren't so many people around."

Gary stopped listening. All that build up, the air practically snapping sparks at him, and it led to nothing. His coffee remained in front of him, untouched. He wasn't in the mood for it anymore. The café suddenly seemed too crowded, the air sickeningly sweet.

It happened quickly. Gary pushed the chair in,

stepped back and, the next thing he knew, he was off-balance. It was a solid collision. Probably enough to knock the wind out of Kate. A cup fell to the floor. He adjusted his weight fast. Hands on Kate's arms to steady her. He loosened his hold when he felt the fine bones beneath the long-sleeved jumper. And felt like letting go entirely when he met dangerously narrowed eyes.

"Could you move?" she asked.

"I would, if I could," he said, amused.

"What's that supposed to mean?"

He held his hands up, palms out and glanced down.

"Oh." She uncurled the fingers that were clenched on the fabric of his shirt. His grin spread as her skin flushed pink. She picked the cup off the floor where it had fallen.

He bent down and used a napkin to soak up the spreading tea. "Let me buy you another."

"No, thank you. Look, I've had one hell of a morning and you're still in my way." She gestured impatiently for him to move aside.

He waited a beat, long enough for her to look up at him again. Frown at him, actually. Shaken, but not traumatized, then. It would show in the eyes, otherwise. "I'm sorry."

A glance, checking his face for sincerity. "No problem. It was like running into a wall, but I don't think there's any permanent damage." She brushed past him.

Gary was a pace slower leaving, had his hand on the glass, ready to push the door open, when Neil's voice stopped him. "If you want to have a shot with that girl who had you tripping over your feet just now, she's here most mornings. Normally earlier than this. I would avoid spilling her tea again, though."

Gary's eyes flickered dangerously. "I'm not sure what you're talking about, but I'll keep it in mind." Anything that drew attention was a risk. People began to make assumptions. Everything had to be calculated now and he couldn't forget that.

Chapter Six

Blood, that's what she needed.

Kate scanned the top shelf. There was room for one more book in her final display of summer reads for the season, and the cover had to be eye-catching. This time, she had arranged the books around a vintage carafe and glass set. The bay window showcased the hard-covered books and allowed a glimpse of shelves lining the space within. The design was close to perfect, but something was missing.

Extravagant characters in an exotic setting. A sensational illustration.

Her cell phone buzzed, vibrating against her hip. Kate jumped and pulled it out of her pocket. Looked at the screen. One new message. Ethan. Kate smiled at the sight of her brother's name. She scanned the text. *Found a body? Somehow not surprised. A wish fulfilled or nightmare? Mom says, "Just goes to show you shouldn't have moved to England." Assumption of high death rate must be caused by reading Agatha Christie. Call soon or guilt trip will get worse. Also, need Cadbury's. Situation dire. When are you sending next parcel?*

Kate shook her head. News had always travelled fast through the family grapevine. She'd call as soon as she got the chance.

Her thoughts drifted back to the café. The jar of

collision. The silver line of a scar beneath the shadow of stubble. There was something about the way he moved, the width of the shoulders, tilt of the head. Some vague memory at the back of her mind. Probably a four-sentence description, a fragment of dialogue. It had happened before. A line, so certain it had been a part of a conversation, when all it had been was words on a page.

The bell above the door chimed as someone entered the store. "Kate?" A familiar voice called from the doorway. "Where are you? Show a sign of life, a hand, anything!"

"Over here, Marcus!"

Marcus breezed around the corner on a whiff of expensive cologne. He was impeccably dressed in a designer suit. A plastic bag, weighted down by the contents, in his hand. "There you are! There are far too many angles to get lost in, in this labyrinth. Sometimes I'm positive you designed it purposely to baffle." Marcus pressed an affectionate kiss to her forehead.

"What are you doing here?"

"What about, 'Thanks for coming, wonderful to see you, you're looking positively dashing?' You're welcome. I'm touched you noticed."

Kate rolled her eyes. "Do you need a partner for that conversation?"

"I've brought dinner. Chinese." He held the bag up.

"From the place we like?"

"Only the best. I was showing a two-bedroom garden flat around the corner, and thought, why not?"

"Fantastic, I'm starving. Let me just prop a window open, so the store doesn't end up smelling like a restaurant." A glance at her watch, past seven now.

She flipped the store's sign to closed.

"Much as I love coming by, I think we should revert to telepathy." Marcus dropped into one of her worn leather armchairs, careful not to wrinkle his trousers. He brushed an offending piece of fluff from his sleeve. "It would save so much time."

"We're merely a step away from telekinesis as it is. Plates?"

"Yes, please." Marcus shifted a stack of books out of the way and began unpacking the cardboard containers, arranging them on the table next to his chair. "We could enter into a marriage of convenience. We'd live together in blissful harmony until death do us part."

"You're actually quite annoying." Kate ducked behind the counter, grabbed two plates off the shelf. Blue china, cracked and a little faded. A fork for herself. No point in trying to maneuver with chop sticks tonight. Tap water in wine glasses. The beat of the song on the radio had her pausing. Distorted guitar tones, rough vocals, electric down the spine. Late sixties. She turned the volume up, quick twist of the dial. Just enough to pick up the rhythm, pleasantly scratchy through the speakers.

"Really? I do have some flaws. I keep having inappropriate thoughts about that man I showed a flat to last week. So it's probably for the best." Marcus accepted the plate from Kate with a grin. "How are you doing?" His eyes held hers.

She sat in the chair next to him, took a sip from her glass. "I've never started the day by finding a dead man before." She still felt edgy, off. Her hands were steady though. She wasn't one to give in to jitters.

"If you have, you've hidden it well, and you'll have to forgive me if I no longer spend time alone with you." Marcus pretended to shrink away from her, shielding his face with one raised hand.

Kate laughed, took a heaping fork full of rice. Shrimp, soy sauce, mushrooms. Still hot, sizzling on the tongue. "Don't worry, it wasn't murder." She leaned back in the seat, curled her feet beneath her. "Mr. Wendell died of a heart attack. The doctor confirmed it. He said it was quick."

"I can't believe he's dead. Gone, like that." Marcus snapped his fingers. "I hardly knew the man, but still." He shook his head in disbelief. "He was, what, forty-six? It's enough to have a person pondering their own mortality."

"I lived in the same house with him, and I don't know much more." A question, some small talk, that's all it would have taken. Easy, afterward, to dwell on the what ifs. "Mrs. Marsh never complained about him. I'm assuming he paid his rent on time. He worked at an office and dressed the part, suit and all, but I have no idea what he did there. I don't even know if he has family." She thought back. "He was in and out at strange times." An arc of light across the window, late at night. Tires, crunching on the drive, heard through a dream.

"We can't know everything about other people. Just because you don't know his favorite color, doesn't mean you're a bad person."

"The only thing I can think of right now, is Mr. Wendell shuffling through the kitchen in worn sweats, eating pickles straight from the jar and listening to his MP3 player. You still think that doesn't make me a bad person?"

"No worse than anyone else. Everyone has something to hide." Marcus shrugged. He leaned forward, chose a spring roll from the bag. "Everyone lies."

"Even you?" Kate raised an eyebrow.

"Even me," Marcus replied solemnly. "Plum sauce?"

"Here." Kate nudged the plastic cup toward him.

"What happened after our phone call this morning?"

"Not much. The doctor came to pick up the body. I had to open the store, so I left Elaina in charge."

Marcus choked. "You left—" He swallowed, tried again. "Elaina in charge? Do you think that was wise?"

"Let's just hope they didn't drop him in the hydrangeas. When I told Great-aunt Roselyn, she said"—Kate dropped her voice—"'There will be no more death in this house.'"

"'No more death.'" Marcus considered the phrase, chop sticks hovering over his egg noodles. "Did her husband die in the house?"

"I think he had cancer and spent the last month in the hospital. It's not on par with a sudden death at the bottom of the basement stairs."

"She may have been referring to a relative who died in the house long ago. Not something recent."

"I suppose. But who?"

"Much as I'd love to don the deerstalker with you and solve the mystery right here and now, I doubt we'd have much luck." Marcus looked up from his plate, frowning at the shelves around them. "Right, I can't stand it anymore. What is that humming sound?"

"Humming sound?" Kate blinked and looked around. A whirring, low and steady, under the music. "Oh, that humming sound. It should stop soon. If not, I'll warn you. You'll have more than enough time to duck for cover."

"I hope you're joking. Is that coming from your computer? You should get that fixed."

"That takes money. Are you going to finish that?" Kate gestured at the remaining noodles on his plate.

"Be my guest." He pushed it toward her. "Will you be safe?" Eyes slanting, smile playing at the corners of his mouth. Half-serious, half-joking.

"Of course."

"No need for heroics?" Quirk of a brow.

"None."

"So disappointing. May I give you one final piece of advice?"

"If you must." Kate copied his posh accent, putting the emphasis on *must*.

He tapped the tip of her nose. "Leave that box I see discreetly tucked next to the shelf. Unpack it in the morning. The books can wait." He gathered their empty plates. "Go home, get some rest."

"Have a G and T?"

"Yes, that would work, too." Marcus laughed. "Open that bottle of gin I gave you. Put your feet up." He pulled her close in a one-armed hug. "Don't be stubborn."

"I'm never stubborn." Her voice came out muffled against his shirt.

An Excuse for Murder

Chapter Seven

Percival was nursing a grudge. Gary's office was warm, a fan in the corner working hard to circulate what little air there was. Percival sat across from him, in one of the two chairs facing the imposing oak desk, unobtrusive despite his size. Percival had hunched his shoulders slightly to squeeze his width between the armrests. The chair sagged and his knees had risen in consequence. His hands rested loosely on his thighs. He waited patiently for Gary to speak.

The sawing of traffic and general din of nine a.m. sounds coming from the open window increased. Gary stood, jiggled the top half of the window, hit the frame sharply with both fists. Nothing. He sat back down. Even with the hum of the fan and commotion from the street, the silence was pricking at the back of his neck. Percival hadn't whistled a single tune since he entered the room. No Bach. No Mozart. No Schumann. Not even a G minor scale.

A conference table large enough to seat eight stood on one side of the room, along with a whiteboard, still streaked with the traces of previous notes. Hanging on the wall across from the pebbled glass door was a canvas. Some sort of modernist painting meant to impress the hell out of visitors. Blocks of colored squares that looked like it had been done by somebody's five-year-old with finger paints and a box of crayons. Maybe it had been. He had no clue where it had come from. One day the canvas had just appeared. He'd gotten used to it.

Gary leaned back in his chair and tossed his pen on top of the clutter strewn across his desk. Organized chaos. Better to have a hard copy to markup than to spend the day staring at a computer screen. "I'm going to need you to go out to Graylenn's tomorrow, get the security system installed. Run through it with them and go over the grounds, make sure we haven't missed anything."

Fenris Securities provided protection to local and national companies from small office complexes to high-rise towers, as well as covering residential properties. They designed and consulted on customized security systems from access control card systems to wireless technology alarm systems and trained staff to make sure the security system was effectively implemented.

"Can't we get someone to fix the damned window?" Gary asked, irritable. You looked at a view, you shouldn't hear it.

"Ask Elspeth," Percival rumbled. His bovine features were stoic, his eyes lidded. The corners of his lips were pulled down. "I can't," he said suddenly.

"You can't what?" Gary slid a sheaf of papers into the left-hand desk drawer.

"Go to Graylenn's."

"Why not? Got plans? I could send someone else instead."

"No need." Percival slumped forward, frowning at his knuckles.

"What does that mean? I'm going to need more

words here."

"We lost the account."

Gary leaned forward. His eyebrows rose. "We what?"

"Lost the account." Percival blinked at him.

"Reason?"

Percival shrugged. The chair creaked ominously. "Said that a Mr. Harris had advised them to go a different way."

So that explained it. Adriana's father. It had happened a few times over the years, clients mysteriously deciding that Fenris Securities wasn't for them. Just a little reminder, a prod at old wounds. It wasn't over. It wasn't forgotten. This was the first time his name had cropped up, but Gary had always managed to trace the connection.

"Well, that's their decision. We cater to the fundamental need people have to protect what they love most. We'll always have business."

"Can't believe people pay for fancy alarm systems. Bloke I know grabbed a nine iron and went after the intruder himself. Scared him off." This was a long speech for Percival. He looked appropriately solemn.

"Some people avoid brute force." Hypocritical. "But that's what we're here for. Percival—" Gary paused, awkward. He hovered on the crest of an apology. He shouldn't have snapped the other night.

The door that led to the hallway burst open and Elspeth crossed the room, carrying a tray. She was wearing jeans with a bright red jumper, sleeves pushed up to her elbows, red on her lips, too. Spirals of wiry gray curls had sprung free of her ponytail. Her eyes were deceptively gentle.

Elspeth dropped a bowl in front of him, filled with something resembling bird food. She set a plate of sliced apple down next to it, so firmly it clattered against the desk for a moment. A blueprint wafted toward him.

Gary looked up at her. "What's this?" He prodded at the bowl.

"A nutritious start to your day. If you're not going to sleep, you might as well eat right."

Gary fought the urge to yes ma'am her. He picked up the plate, tilted it and peered at the contents. The apple was peeled. He cleared his throat and slid a document from beneath the bowl.

Elspeth nudged Percival with her hip. "Sit up straight, Percival. You're slouching."

Percival turned a red that matched his hair and tried to maneuver his bulk into what might be loosely defined as good posture.

Elspeth nodded, her lips pursed primly.

"How's Jeremy?" Gary asked politely. Not at all desperately.

Elspeth glowed with the pride of an indulgent grandmother. "Peachy. He's a bright boy. Told me a grand story about a call he and Dr. Garreth responded to at the fairy tale house. Something about death and a woman in black lingerie." Elspeth waved her hand vaguely. "Pickle juice."

An apple orchard. The slide of a syringe into flesh.

"Oh, I don't know." Elspeth pushed up her right sleeve. "He's happy and that's all that matters. You had a phone call from the police," she added benignly to Gary.

Gary willed his facial muscles to be still. "What

did they want?" Carefully relaxed. No hesitation. Good. His heart was pounding.

"Complaint about an alarm that keeps going off. He didn't sound happy."

Relief spread through him, thick and sweet. "Address?"

"In Willowsend. Residential. Penelope… I'll have to double-check the name."

Gary nodded. "Probably forgot the passcode. I'll send someone out to reprogram it."

"Can't," Percival said.

"What now?"

"Everyone's busy. Mobile patrol. After-hours security escort. Installing that glass-break sensor. The motion detector."

"Fine. I'll take care of it personally, then."

"Wonderful." Elspeth smiled at him. She picked up his mug and headed for the door.

"Hey!" Gary jolted upright. "I wasn't finished with that."

"I'll bring you a glass of water," Elspeth said over her shoulder before pulling the door shut behind her.

"You didn't ask her about the window," Percival pointed out.

"No." They looked at each other. "Remind me again why I hired her?"

"You said you always wanted to have a Miss Katherine Climpson."

"So I did." Silence. "She's better than the alternative, that twenty-year-old with the crop top who answered the phones sounding like she was one step away from an orgasm. Elspeth swayed me by being able to remember the callers' names. A feat in itself apparently. She helps maintain our professional image."

"Hank was okay."

Gary quirked an eyebrow. "Hank had a basic knowledge of security procedures, could handle violent behavior and non-defensive communication. He was not able to handle private and confidential information with discretion. In other words, he thought with his dick."

Percival guffawed.

Gary grinned. He reached for an apple slice. Took a bite. Pulled a face.

Percival picked up a file and pulled out a pair of slender spectacles from his pocket. He propped them on his nose, twinkled at Gary over the rim before beginning to read with great concentration.

If Gary wasn't wrong, Percival was whistling a '70s rock song.

Chapter Eight

"Maybe Kate killed somebody." Two eight-year-old boys jostled their way into Kate's bookstore, staring intently at the Y-shaped stick one of them was holding. Bright spots of excitement glowed in their cheeks. They were bundled up in jeans jackets, colorful scarves wound tight around their necks.

"Or it's wrong," Will added, eyes never leaving the stick. The forked branch twitched.

"It's not *wrong*." Tim snorted in disgust at his friend's ignorance. "There are loads of dead bodies in a bookstore, stupid, they just aren't real."

"Or it's because she found that guy—Mr. Wendell."

Tim sighed. "Not in the store. Honestly, Will. And that was a heart attack."

"If it isn't my two favorite customers." Kate put down the book she had been shelving. "What's the stick for?"

The boys stopped abruptly. Will gripped the back of Tim's jacket. Tim stood in front, arm outstretched, stick clasped firmly in his hand. "It's a dividing rod," Tim said.

"To separate things with?"

"No." Tim rolled his eyes. "To find things with."

"Ah." Kate smiled. "A divining rod."

"That's what I said."

"You can find anything you want with it," Tim explained knowledgeably. "That's important, because there's no mystery if you can't find the body. It really works, too."

A figure at the edge of Kate's vision had her turning. A customer stood between the shelves. Probably a business man from one of the offices nearby. The man's clean-shaven features were all sharp angles and lean planes, his lips thin. His fingers were clenched around a book, the pages bending inward beneath the pressure. His stare was like something physical, cutting. Kate took a step back.

Kate turned her attention back to the boys. "What are you two doing, searching for corpses in my store?"

"Have you got any?" Tim asked, surprised.

"I hope not."

"It's probably better if you don't," Tim told her. "They get moldy."

"They what?" Will turned to look at him, shocked.

Tim shrugged. "They rot, which is why we have to hurry when we get a reading on the divining stick."

Will thought about that. "That's gross," he decided.

"You just point it around until the stick starts to shiver," Tim explained. "Then you know you've found something really good."

"Can I try?" Will asked.

Tim looked at Will doubtfully. "I don't know... It isn't as easy as it looks."

"I just filed some new books from the Everly Boy Detective series on the shelf there, Tim," Kate interrupted, before they started their search. "I think there are a couple you haven't read yet, if you want to use your detective skills to solve fictional cases instead."

"Cool!" The boy's features lit up. "Have you got *The Mystery of the Mayan Warrior?"*

"I might. If not, someone brought some books in yesterday. I haven't shelved them yet. So, if you don't see it on the shelf, I can go on the hunt." This was her favorite part of her job, helping kids find books. Stories weren't just an escape from everyday duties but complete worlds they lived and breathed in. The books they read at that age came to life for them. The characters were their friends, real people, not just fiction. Kate would pull all the strings she had to get them the books they wanted.

The man moved toward them, skimming books with his eyes as he approached the counter. His expression had smoothed over. Had the contorted features been a trick of the light? The corners of his mouth imitated a smile that didn't reach his eyes.

He dropped the paperback next to the cash register. Kate glanced at the cover, read the title. "Death is often the punchline of life."

"Excuse me?" The man asked, startled.

"It's a line from the book. Well, paraphrased. Nabokov writes convincingly about loving someone and not being loved in return. Life ending in disaster."

"I've read it before."

"Then I'll stop waxing poetic." She flipped to the first page, checked the penciled price.

"Kate knows about the stages of decomposition," Tim whispered to Will solemnly. "Since she found the body. I'll bet the flesh flies were already circling."

"Sometimes, Tim, you can tell that your father is a cop. That's four fifty," Kate told the man, glancing up.

His jaw was clenched tightly, a muscle jumping beneath his cheek. She could smell cigarette smoke on him like cinders. Coins clattered loudly onto the wooden counter. Kate handed the book over. "Have a nice day."

The man paused on his way to the door. "You know, the easiest way to find a corpse is to kill someone," he informed them blandly.

Kate resisted the urge to clamp her hands over the ears of the nearest boy. "No, it's not! That's not a good idea, got it?"

"Kate." Tim looked at her pityingly. "I'm eight. I know what corpses are and I know that only bad guys kill people. Right, Will?"

"Right." Will nodded, looking at Tim with hero-worship in his eyes.

"Come on, Will. I want to show you something really awesome." Tim tore off to the back of the store, Will close on his heels. Books shuddered on the shelves as their feet rounded the corner. How could such small feet make so much noise?

"Why would you tell them that?" Kate asked the man, flinging her hands out in exasperation.

"I thought they should know what they're looking for," he replied and stepped out onto the street.

Chapter Nine

Gary knocked on the door again, louder this time. Two houses down from the scene of the crime. Only he knew that.

Same smell, faint on the breeze. Sun-warmed apples.

He glanced behind him. Just a strip of lawn between where he was standing and the road. A tree. A tire swing. Beyond that, the street, straight down far as the eye could see. Two properties in between here and there.

You'd drive past and never even notice the old building. Maybe a glimpse of brick above the hedge, if you looked hard enough, caught the right angle as you were passing by.

A woman in a blue dress stepped off the curb to his right, moving toward the trees at the edge of the property, toward the old house, hidden from view. That familiar lift to her step. It hit him like a fist to the solar plexus. The swish of fabric over her hips, sunlight catching on the ends of her hair. Face turned away.

The street was bare and bright. Sound of kids playing in the distance. Five steps, maybe six, and she'd be within reach. He'd see her face.

"Ye're late," a voice said behind him.

Gary spun toward the door, now open. Checked his watch. "It's only half past five." He looked back. The street was empty. The trees were a tangle of branches, shadows, and leaves. Flicker of blue. Just a flash, then gone.

"How do I know you're who ye say ye are?" Penelope asked, suspiciously.

He dug out his wallet.

She studied the ID closely, turning it this way and that. Then handed it back to him. "The boss man hi'self." Penelope moved into the house, leaving him to catch hold of the door before it closed. "Ye were in the café yesterday, back o' the room." Shrewd eyes over a shoulder.

No point denying it. "Yes, I was. The coffee's good." It was cooler inside the house. Sunlight fell across dark wood. Papers, heaps of them, were spread across a desk in the entrance. Uncapped ball point pens. A pencil on the floor. There were no candles or vases. None of those porcelain figurines with full skirts. A sheet of lined paper, torn from a spiral notebook, was tacked to the wall above the desk. Math sums, then a drawing of a bicycle done in biro and highlighter. Loose, childish lines. "Interesting drawing."

"My grandson's."

Gary looked at the keypad in the entrance. It was blinking, like it should be. "You've had a number of false alarms."

Toss of the head, impatient. "There's somethin' wrong with it."

"I'll change the backup battery for you and set up a new passcode. See if that fixes the problem." Hard to remember the last time he had personally reset an alarm system. "I'll need to access the main control panel."

"It's downstairs." Gary followed her down a

narrow hallway. "Useless thing." Fast mutter, beneath the breath, and hard to catch as she moved ahead of him. "Doesna stop people from stealing off your verra lawn."

She moved quickly, despite the limp. The stairs were steep. The turn halfway down had him angling his shoulders. A strand caught the light and he brushed a hand at the spider web, flicking it away from his face. "You've had a theft?" That indentation in the ground beside the mailbox. He'd noticed it when he arrived. Something had rested there so long the soil had sunk. Then been removed.

"Cowards. Then that figure in the night. At the fairy tale house." It sounded like a curse. The grin crinkled her eyes as she looked back at him. "I saw him, from my window, upstairs." Penelope flipped the switch, casting light from a bulb on the ceiling. "Your height." She considered him. A long, hard stare that was unsettling. "Then a deith. Sirens at the crack o' dawn. Ay, three things." She leant on her cane and held three fingers in the air, throwing a shadow across the gray carpet. "Theft, a figure in the night, an' deith." She counted them off. "Never ignore things that come in threes. It's close tae the end then. Here it is."

"Here what is?" His head was reeling.

"The control panel." She tapped the box with the end of the cane. She took a small key from her pocket. The panel creaked on rusted hinges. She moved aside.

The ceiling was lower there. He had to duck his head, hunch down, as he disconnected the power and the back-up battery. The wall he faced smelled of metal, dampness. Water gurgled through exposed pipes. The control panel wasn't hard-wired. Good. Cutting off the circuit breaker would have slowed things down. He could feel her close behind him, watching. "I'll show you how to power up the system and then reset the passcode. This man you saw at the house, what was he doing?"

"Sneakin' around the way people do when they don't want tae get caught." So close her breath brushed his shoulder.

"I wouldn't think you'd be able to see the house from here." The night had been his. Fireflies winking. The give of the ground beneath his feet. Darkness all around. He'd have known if someone was watching.

"Ye can see the orchard. Enough o' it anyway. He was there. Crouched." Her hand tightened on the cane. Veins blue beneath thin skin. "Watchin' the hoose, at half-four in the mornin'."

The timing could be right. He had to plant a seed of doubt. "It must have been difficult to get a good view, from that distance, in the dark. Hard to tell a tree from a man, if the angle's right."

"Only a fool would mistake a tree for a person," Penelope snapped. She stepped toward the stack of storage boxes leaning against the wall, gray with dust. Opened a lid, peered inside. "Kitchen cloths. That's richt. The first time was different though."

"The first time?" Gary turned to her, put his hands in his pockets.

"A night or two earlier. He was movin' fast between the trees, low tae the ground."

"You saw the same man twice?" His tone was sharper than he'd intended. "In the orchard?"

"I'm just after tellin' ye, aren't I? Movin' toward the fairy tale hoose," she said, a hard glint in her eyes.

"Fast too. Then I went off to bed."

He had been there only once at night. "Sometimes the mind plays tricks on us." He thought of the woman in the blue dress. "I wouldn't worry about it. You have a good alarm system. It'll alert you if someone opens a door or a window."

"The Eternal Wife has to fill the hoose wi' strangers tae keep the ghosts at bay." Penelope pulled her sweater closer around herself.

"Roselyn Marsh?" Gary turned back to the panel. "It must be hard, living with a legend of undying loyalty."

"The Eternal Wife has little to do wi' the love of a husband and everythin' wi' deith." There was bitterness there, hardened over time.

"I see." He glanced at her. "Let me show you how to reset the passcode. It helps if you choose numbers that have a meaning for you. Something you'll remember."

"There is nothin' wrong wi' my memory."

"Of course not. Sharp as a scythe, you are."

She laughed. A young sound that had him thinking of the children he'd heard playing in the distance. "True enough." She looked at the boxes again. "'Tis easy tae keep secrets. Things ye've heard or seen. Stowed away tae use when the time is richt."

"Or take them to the grave. Whose secrets are you keeping, Penelope?" Gary bent down, said it low, "I don't think you've told anyone about what you saw in the orchard."

"Och well." Her lips quivered, hovering on the verge of a smile. She wagged a finger at him. "Just reset the passcode. We'll be safe as houses then."

Chapter Ten

The stone stairs in the tower trembled beneath Kate's feet with the deep bass. Turpentine and oil paint fumes burned her nose. Elaina was painting. This was unusual. She should have been at work by now, serving shots of tequila and pints of beer to woebegone characters in the pub downtown, wearing burgundy lipstick and a heart-stopping outfit. Instead, Elaina was in the tower, blaring rock music.

Kate paused on the circular landing. The door to Great-aunt Roselyn's rooms was tightly sealed as always, to block the draught that seeped into the tower through cracks in the mortar.

The stairs narrowed. Through the archway ahead, Kate could see Elaina shaking her hips to the music, while streaking a paintbrush across the canvas in front of her. "Elaina!" Kate shouted over the sound of wailing guitars, as she came into the room.

Large, rounded windows circled the space. It felt as though they were standing in the center of the clouds. When the sky became dark, the walls of the tower took on a green cast. When rain lashed at the glass, the many windows cast shadows of streaking water across the ground. The tower seemed to always be waiting in anticipation for the wind to batter and ravage it once again.

Elaina twirled to the music, scattering splashes of

blue around her in the process. Kate moved around palettes and splotches of wet paint, trying to get within Elaina's line of vision. She didn't want to startle her and risk ruining the painting.

Elaina bobbed her head and gave a shimmy to the beat. It looked like she was doing the nineteen-sixties twist. The floor around her resembled a Jackson Pollock painting.

Elaina spun and finally caught sight of the intruder. She waved, then swirled ochre paint from her palette. Kate moved closer and looked over Elaina's shoulder, watching the minute brush strokes. She breathed out a sigh of jealousy. Yeah, Elaina was good.

Even unfinished, the portrait was stunning. Rain smudged in angles, dark and glistening, across the background. The woman's face was the focal point of the picture, set slightly off-center and unnaturally pale. Reds and greens and yellows gave the image a surreal quality, the lights and the darks enhanced. Behind a veil of white lace, careful shading drew attention to the passion blazing from blue eyes. She seemed to be looking out of the painting at something in the distance, above Kate's shoulder. The force of the woman's gaze was almost physical. The features were there, from the narrow jaw to the fine wrinkles, but it took Kate a moment to recognize her great-aunt.

Elaina had trapped secrets in oil and canvas. The pain that lay hidden beneath a tranquil surface. Kate shivered as a breeze drifted across her bare arm, raising gooseflesh.

Moving quietly, Kate left Elaina to continue uninterrupted and turned her attention to the loose sheets strewn across the table nearby. The edges were rough, as though they had been torn from a sketch pad. Among the collection of scattered drawings, one caught Kate's eye. She carefully lifted it free of the others and held it up to the light. The sketch was done in brown charcoal and lacked the detail Elaina had given the others. It looked as though it had been done spontaneously, on a wave of emotion, only to be tossed aside just as quickly. Yet the image was striking.

The man seemed to leap from the paper. His features weren't classic, they were too rough for that. The interest came from a sense of captured movement, even though he was standing still. His face was alive with laughter, the wide grin reflected in his eyes. But his shoulders were half-turned, his back to the viewer. He seemed to be about to leave the page. As though he had told one last joke, given one last devil-may-care grin before walking away.

"Who's the looker?" Kate teased. Her voice was loud in the sudden silence between songs.

The brush clattered to the floor, splattering paint across Elaina's bare feet. "What?" Her face was void of expression, her eyes blank. Suddenly, anger flared, contorting her features. Blood rushed to her cheeks. "Give that to me!" Elaina lunged and tackled Kate.

They crashed to the ground in a heap of tangled limbs. The cold floor was hard against Kate's spine. Elaina's elbow dug into her ribs.

"How dare you?" Elaina tore the sketch from Kate's grasp.

"What is wrong with you?" Kate rammed her fists against Elaina's shoulders and, with one heave, shoved her to the side.

Elaina lifted the sheet and tore it into scraps. Kate

watched in stunned amazement. The pieces fluttered one by one to the floor. Kneeling there with her hair waving wildly around her shoulders, her cheekbones sharpened by the dim light, Elaina looked like a triumphant warrior. "You had no right," she said and let the last shredded corner fall.

"No right to what? Look at your art? You've never been bothered by that before." Kate pressed a hand to her aching side. It was disturbing to see Elaina shaken.

"Some things are personal." Elaina stood.

"What are you doing here anyway?" Kate got to her feet as well and glared at the taller woman. "Shouldn't you be at work?"

"I was painting. Liz took my shift." A smile tweaked at the corners of her mouth, spread, and turned into a chuckle. "You're covered in paint, Kate." The chuckle became a fit of giggles. Elaina doubled over, holding her sides.

Kate could feel her shirt sticking wetly to her back. "How much of this is oil paint?"

"Don't worry, it's mostly acrylic," Elaina gasped and wiped tears of mirth from her eyes. "A good laugh is just the thing to restore the karma. Drive out the ghosts. If left too long, these things can cling to the walls."

"The only thing clinging to the walls is the nicotine from your cigarettes." Kate rolled her eyes.

"Don't be so tetchy."

"You knocked me over." Kate swiped her hair away from her face, and hoped she hadn't just spread more paint across her cheek. "You think the house absorbs the events that take place inside it?"

"Not just events. Generations later, perceptive

souls can sense if the previous owners experienced emotional or physical pain while living in the house. There's an aura that lingers on, especially if a sudden or violent death occurs on the property."

"Have you been watching late night shows on paranormal activity again?"

Elaina ignored that and picked up a paintbrush, a finer one than before. "Mrs. Marsh wants our help to box up Mr. Wendell's things."

"Shouldn't his relatives do that?"

"I don't think she wants to wait. She'd like the room cleaned out on Sunday."

"I hope he wasn't a messy person." Kate didn't want to spend the weekend rooting through mold and dirty socks.

Elaina narrowed her eyes at the canvas, considering the painting. "We'll have to break through the lock on his bedroom door first. Mrs. Marsh hasn't been able to find the key."

"That's odd. What did he have to hide?"

Elaina shrugged. "That's what we're going to find out. I'm pretty handy with an axe. I could take the door out." She paused, reflectively. "Or we could call a locksmith."

"I imagine Great-aunt Roselyn wants the door to remain intact," Kate pointed out dryly. "Maybe I can have a go at it. I've always wanted to pick a lock. It can't be that difficult to do." She could see herself already, kneeling in front of the door, tools in hand; hear the click of the lock as it opened. Taste the satisfaction of the triumphant sleuth. "I'm sure Marcus would get a kick out of it, too."

"Yes, but if you manage to open the door, will he

help us with the boxes? Somehow I can't imagine Marcus getting down and dirty."

"You'd be surprised." Marcus could handle anything when it came to going through someone else's closets. "I do love snooping." Kate grinned.

Elaina nodded absently. Her attention was on the canvas, and the haunted eyes of the woman she had painted. Kate recognized the intense focus. Elaina's moments of inspiration resembled a trance more than anything else.

Twilight had descended outside. Clouds drifted past the windows in gossamer wisps. Kate left Elaina to her work. She'd grab a book, a Victorian mystery of some kind, and while away a few hours in the company of her fictional heroes.

Who was the man in the sketch? Kate exited the tower and let the heavy door slam shut behind her. She made her way across the lawn, toward the French doors that led into the kitchen. The wide orchard behind her pressed closer. A sibilant whisper slid between the trees. It might have been the wind or the spectral remains of a ghost searching for pickles. Kate stepped into the kitchen quickly, closing out the growing darkness.

Maybe the man in charcoal was a musician who had performed at the pub one night. Eyes meeting across the smoky, crowded room while he strummed a love song on his guitar, melting Elaina's tough façade like ice cubes on a summer day. Elaina would have fallen head over heels for the first time in her life. Kate sighed and pressed a hand to her heart.

But why had Elaina reacted like that?

Perhaps Marcus was right. There were always

things kept hidden, truths untold.
    Locked doors.

Chapter Eleven

Kate knew it was a dream but it all felt so real, from the cold metal of the doorknob in her hand to the pavement beneath her feet. It felt as though she was standing on solid ground. Then she glanced down and saw only dizzying turquoise space that went on and on, the sky mirrored beneath her in endless depths. The inverted sky was clear as a summer afternoon, while the world around and above her was shadowed by dusk. She was standing outside her bookstore.

There was only one thing to do.

Kate turned the knob and stepped inside her store. The oak floor was lustrously golden, while the rest of the space was dimmed and hazy. The only light seemed, in fact, to come from the floor. A sheet of gold.

Kate stood within the doorway and looked at the figures waiting inside. She blinked and glanced behind her, but the door was closed. Something wasn't right. She should leave. But she was curious now.

In the center of the luminescent ground was a man, waltzing in slow circles around and around, his arms framing an invisible partner. He hummed gently to himself, supported by the soft padding and sliding of the soles of his shoes as he went through the steps. A frown of concentration puckered his brow. He was good-looking in a clean-cut, pleasant way. He was wearing a cutaway tailored coat over a waist-length satin waistcoat and dark breeches. The outfit looked as though it had come straight from the late seventeen-eighties.

Behind the dancer, a teenager in Elizabethan garb was sitting on her counter. His chin was propped on his fists and he was staring moodily at his dangling feet.

Kate caught sight of the third and final member of the patch-work party. He lounged tall and handsome against a bookshelf. Shadows half obscured him, when suddenly he glanced up and met her eyes directly. His frank stare and haughty expression sent a jab of shock down her spine. A well-cut dark coat hugged his shoulders, while pale-colored trousers reflected what little light there was in the dim room. She recognized the kind of top boots country gentlemen wore in the eighteen-hundreds from the covers of her historical novels.

They were being sported in her bookstore like the average Nike sneaker.

What was this? Reunion of the time travelers?

"Who are you?" she stammered into the stillness.

The boy raised his eyes. He smiled slowly. "It is my lady, O, it is my love!" His voice was rich honey, pure velvet, and satin. "O, that she knew she were!"

"What are you doing here?" Kate fumbled behind her for the door, which seemed to melt beneath her grasp. His words seemed familiar.

"She speaks yet she says nothing, what of that?" The boy shook his head, teasingly. "O speak again, bright angel!"

The eighteenth-century dancer continued turning in slow, steady circles, unfaltering. He glanced at her furtively.

"Stop speaking in riddles and rhymes. Give me a straight answer and tell me how you got in here! I'm this close to calling the cops and having you kicked out." Kate scowled at the familiar strangers.

"Can I go forward when my heart is here?" The boy sighed.

"And what's with you?" Kate fumed at the man watching from the corner. "What are you staring at? Trying to figure out how to break into the cash?"

He chuckled quietly and crossed his arms. "Your conjecture is totally wrong, I assure you. My mind was more agreeably engaged. I have been meditating on the very great pleasure which a pair of fine eyes in the face of a pretty woman can bestow."

"You can't be trying to flirt with me?" Kate's thoughts were reeling.

On the dancer's second solitary turn around the room, he smiled at her sweetly. "A dance would honor me greatly, madame." He paused in front of her and held out his gloved hand in invitation.

"No, I'm not going to dance. I can't dance." But before she knew what she was doing, her hand was in his, her feet falling into the pattern more naturally and easily than they had ever done before. She wasn't a dancer, but suddenly she was spinning around the room like she had never done anything else.

"Ah, I have found true love." Her partner declared softly.

Kate snorted. "Kind of jumping the gun, aren't we?"

"Stony limits cannot hold love out." The youth remarked. "And what love can do that dares love attempt."

"Come Darcy," her partner called over his shoulder as he spun her gracefully, "dance with us!"

The man leaning against the shelf shook his head. "You are dancing with the only handsome girl in the room."

"Darcy?" Kate repeated disbelievingly. Had the characters come to life? "Mr. Darcy?" She looked more closely at the boy perched on her counter. She should have recognized the iambic pentameter. "Romeo?" She fixed her attention on her dancing partner. "Who are you?" She demanded.

"It has flown my mind while in the presence of so delightful a countenance."

"Do you have to be so charming?" she groaned. "Charming?" She narrowed her eyes at him. "Prince Charming?"

"At your service." He bowed his head and spun her in yet another dizzying circle.

Suddenly, the door chimed and a customer entered the store. What was a customer doing in this collection of living, breathing, flirting fictional heroes? She shook off Prince Charming's hold and ran forward. She didn't get far, but instead bounced back off an invisible wall that separated her from the woman.

"Ouch!" She stumbled back.

Kate pressed her palms flat against the cold surface. It stretched on and on, separating Kate, Romeo, Mr. Darcy, and Prince Charming from the rest of the world. She was locked in with her books. Kate stared at the woman as she walked the slender alley between the glass divider and the open doorway.

Fear clenched in her gut. "Let me out!" Kate gasped wildly and beat her hands against the wall.

"This isn't right!" The customer walked the length of the store, staying near the open door, and apparently completely unaware of anything else.

Kate could feel the romantic heroes ghosting toward her, closer and closer. Mr. Darcy brushed dry, papery fingertips across her cheekbone. Romeo wrapped a possessive arm around her waist and Prince Charming reached for her hand, smiling.

"In vain I have struggled," Darcy whispered to her. "It will not do. My feelings will not be repressed. You must allow me to tell you how ardently I admire and love you." He seemed completely sure of himself, calm, and matter of fact as though there could be no doubt of her answer.

Did she have a choice?

"You know the slipper fits." Prince Charming pressed.

"Why can't she see us?" Kate asked.

"We have night's cloak to hide us from her sight," Romeo explained.

"What do you want from me?" Kate leaned her forehead against the cold, transparent partition.

"The exchange of thy love's faithful vow for mine," Romeo said.

The other two men nodded in solemn agreement.

"My life were better ended by their hate, then death prorogued, wanting of thy love."

"Midnight will never come," Prince Charming told her. "There are no obligations. Stay with us. You're safe here. You belong here."

"I'll still stay," Romeo murmured in her ear, "to have thee forget, forgetting any other home but this."

"I don't belong here!" Kate shook her head

wearily, knowing it was futile.

"Stay," they breathed as one. "Stay with us. Love us."

"O blessed, blessed night!" Romeo fluttered a kiss against her neck. "I am afeard. Being in night, all this is but a dream, too flattering-sweet to be substantial."

Kate caught at that. "It isn't substantial! You have to believe me. This really is just a dream! I'll wake and everything—"

Prince Charming pressed a hand against her mouth, stifling her words. "It is more real than anything you've ever experienced," he told her gently as he lowered his hand again.

Tears pricked at her eyes as she stared at the blinding sunshine cascading through the door. She thought she caught a glimpse of a shape, momentarily silhouetted against the light. Could they help her? Could they rescue her from the heroes of her dreams? But it was only fleeting, and it might have been anything. "I don't want this."

"Of course you do," Mr. Darcy said simply.

"We are all you have ever desired." Prince Charming smiled.

"We are perfection," Romeo added.

Slowly they stepped together, blending, creating a single man. His features were blurred, undistinguishable, but stunningly, heartbreakingly beautiful. They were right. He was what she had always wanted.

"I will protect you, save you, love you." His voice hummed with the strength of a bass trio, richly layered and resonant. "You will have everything you ever wanted here. After all," his voice changed pitch, echoed eerily, like a chord hitting the wrong note, "love is but a dream within a dream."

Kate faced him fully now, her eyes suddenly dry. "No. That's wrong." She could feel her strength of will returning, her confidence building. "None of you ever said that. That's a line by Edgar Allen Poe, and love isn't a dream within a dream." Kate awoke with a start. She clutched the sheets to her chest, gulped and finished the quote aloud in the silence of her empty bedroom, "All that we see or seem is but a dream within a dream."

Chapter Twelve

This was a bad idea.

Stopping at the hardware store on his way home had been a spur-of-the-moment decision. Now Gary was staring at paint swatches. He gave up looking at the cards and picked up a tin of blue paint. If he chose to put his flat on the market, a fresh coat of paint would up the resale value. He rotated the tin to read the name.

"Made your choice?" A sales clerk asked cheerfully on his way past.

"Not yet." What the hell was he doing, holding a tin of Stunning Cyan paint? He'd need brushes. A roller. Primer.

"We have a visualizer app online, if you need help finding a color palette."

"Right." Spend an hour fiddling about with a virtual room and paint samples? Not likely.

"Let me know if you have any questions." The sales clerk continued down the aisle, straightening tins as he went. "We'll be closing soon."

"Yeah, thanks." He'd have to remove the old paint. Get the loose flakes off. Tarp the furniture. It would be a good weekend of work, if not more.

Fall into bed exhausted and he might sleep. Gary could still feel Adriana's blood on his fingers from last night's dream, coating the skin like a film. He put the tin back on the shelf.

What did it matter if someone had been in the orchard, one step ahead of him? The old woman could have been imagining things, alone in the house. That fast mutter on the stairs, words circling in on each other. The sign of a mind slipping. Or fear.

If someone else had been there, covered the same ground, it would be easy to spot. Gary dug his hands in his pockets. There'd be evidence, even now. He could go back, search the area. For fibers snagged on a branch. Prints with any luck.

It would be a risk. Maybe even a waste of time.

Past the greens and he was heading into the browns and the same beige his walls already were. Pick that shade and he might as well not bother. The yellow caught his eye. Adriana's voice in his ear. *Just imagine, yellow walls on a rainy day.*

Gary reached for Stonewashed Blue. He could live with that color.

There was movement at the end of the aisle. Gary looked up. Framed by the shelves, head down and intent on the bag slung over her shoulder, was Kate Rowan. She should look out of place. Five foot nothing, delicate features and power tools on the wall behind her.

Gary propped a shoulder against the shelf beside him and crossed his arms. She hadn't seen him yet. A square of paper appeared from her purse, and a bite-sized chocolate. Kate popped the candy in her mouth and strode out of sight, unfolding the paper as she went.

Gary left the paint and followed. A second too slow rounding the corner. She'd disappeared. Walking between the aisles, he glanced down each side. Past electrical and plumbing. Seasonal. It was with the hand tools and carpentry supplies that he found her. Stretched up on her toes, reaching for the shelf a good two feet above her head. Fingers just touching the edge and missing by a long shot.

"Need any help?"

Kate jumped and whirled around. Dark hair sparking like copper under the overhead lighting. Startled, she let out a breath when she recognized him. Smiled. Not full-on, but polite. "That'd be great."

"Which one did you want?"

"The slotted screwdriver. The small one." Kate pointed at the one she meant, and glanced again at the paper in her hand. A list. Hard to read from his angle.

"There you go." Gary weighed it in his hand before passing the screwdriver to her. Hardened steel blade. Length sixty millimeters. Tip width two point five millimeters. Good grip. Small all right. "Anything else?" Up the charm a bit. Lean closer. It wasn't often you were given a second chance. Play things right and the encounter could work in his favor.

Kate hesitated, scanning the selection of tools. "The four-piece awl, pick and hook set."

He took it down for her. "Got a project lined up?"

"Recreational locksmithing, in fact." Kate started toward the cash.

Not what he'd expected. "Lock picking? Planning a heist, are you?" He lengthened his stride to keep up with her.

"Would I tell you, if I was?"

"You have just told me you're going to pick a lock," he pointed out. "You'll have to buy my silence and cut me in now. I'm Gary, by the way." She turned back to look at him. "Partners in crime should be on a first name basis." He held out his hand.

She took it. "I'm Kate, but I won't be cracking a safe. Or pulling off a diamond heist." She stepped back with a rueful smile. "My great-aunt can't find the key to unlock one of the bedroom doors."

Not one of the bedrooms in use. They'd call someone if that were the case, get the door open fast. There was no guest room. Wendell's room? Must be. If they got in, what would they find? Blink, miss one thing, and you could lose everything. "You can order lock pick sets online."

"This is more fun. I'll try to jimmy the lock with the pick hook and a bobby pin. If that doesn't work, I'll remove the handle with the screwdriver to get at the locking mechanism. It'll be embarrassing if neither of those attempts gets the door open." She frowned.

"Can I ask you something?"

"Sure." She laid her purchases on the counter.

"Do you always have chocolate in your purse?"

Kate glanced back at him and grinned. "Sometimes it's crisps."

"A well balanced diet. If you'd like something more nourishing, we could grab a bite to eat. My treat. Unless you've got pizza in there too."

"Pizza would be far too messy." Kate took her bag from the cashier. "Weren't you going to buy something here?"

"Changed my mind." Gary sped up to get to the door first. He held it open for her. Kate stepped onto the street ahead of him. It was darker now. The setting sun reflected off the glass in the door as he closed it behind them.

He asked again, "So, what do you think? Fish and

chips at the pub?" A glass of wine, a sympathetic ear and the story would come pouring out. How she found the body. The doctor's verdict. What she thought Wendell had been hiding behind the locked door. "I knocked you over and spilled your tea the other day. It's the least I can do."

"I do love fish and chips." She looked down the street, emptier now that the shops were closing.

"But? Sounded like there was one at the end of that sentence."

"You got me." Kate laughed. "I've been unpacking boxes of books for the last few hours. All I really want is to go home and put my feet up."

"We can get a table for four. You can prop your feet up on the extra chair. If anyone asks, we'll tell them we're waiting for Dana and Gene."

"Dana and Gene?"

Gary shrugged. "First names that came to mind. Dana Andrews and Gene Tierney." He paused. "It's a win-win situation for you. Dinner at no cost to you. A spot to rest your feet. I'm the one at risk here. You appear to have a criminal mind and I've told you my name."

"I don't know your last name."

"That would be easy to find out. A woman skilled at recreational locksmithing would know how to do the research."

"I could just ask."

"True." He waited.

"It's tempting, but I'd rather not go for dinner."

That was blunt. He didn't think she'd say no. "Another time?"

"I'm not sure you'd find it worth the effort."

"Why not?"

"I have high expectations." Kate added lightly, "and a reputation for demanding perfection."

"I'm not perfect." Far from it.

"Not many people are. It's disappointing." Kate began walking, turning around to face him. "Thanks again for the help." She held up the bag from the hardware store.

"Is your car parked far away?"

"In front of the bookshop." She pointed at the car parked on the other side of the street from them. "I own Fortune's Cove Books."

"I'll watch, make sure you get there safe."

"The traffic is treacherous." There wasn't another car in sight.

Gary laughed. He watched her cross the road and wave when she got to the car.

He'd always liked a challenge.

Chapter Thirteen

The banister glinted, leading up into darkness. There was no welcoming glow from the second floor. No strains of Debussy drifting downward.

Kate thought of her sneakered feet resting on a seat reserved for the late Dana Andrews and grinned. It was good she hadn't agreed to fish and chips. She really was tired. She should have waited to try out the tools tomorrow.

"Great-aunt Roselyn?" Kate's voice echoed back at her. She placed the pick hook and the screwdriver on the side table. Carpeted stairs creaked beneath her feet as she walked up them.

The sitting room was dark. Kate slid her hand along the wall, searching for the light switch.

Someone was standing in the corner of the room. A woman wearing a wide-brimmed hat. It was angled low, hiding the woman's face. Fabric fluttered in the breeze.

The window was open. As Kate glanced toward it, the shutter cracked against the brick siding of the house. Swung closed again, clattering against the frame.

Kate found the switch, turned on the light. Just the old dressmaker's dummy. Not a woman. Relief weakened her knees. The hourglass figure of the padded torso was visible beneath the shawl. Her aunt must have moved the dummy. Added the hat. Fine straw and handmade roses. Another hat for her collection.

"It's me," Kate called. Was she ill? Or not home at all?

A damp draught spread from beneath the door to the tower. Kate moved around the roll-top desk, the rosewood rocking chair. She yanked the window up higher, straining against the heavy glass. Caught at the shutter, latched it to the hook on the wall. A gust of wind pulled at her hair, whipping it into her eyes.

Something pale moved amid the apple trees below. A figure in white.

A woman in a nightgown. Cap sleeves, bare arms. The fabric billowing behind her. Orange-hued light flickered against the silhouette. A candle cupped in the woman's hands. A small flame within glass. Gray hair hung loose to her shoulders. Too difficult to see the face, from that distance, lit from below. Shadows hollowing the eyes. But Kate knew who it was.

Why was she outside, dressed like that? What was she doing? "Aunt Roselyn!"

The figure disappeared beneath boughs heavy with ripening fruit. Insubstantial golden light filtered up between the leaves.

There she was again, at the back of the orchard. A vivid specter against the trees. The woman turned, moving across the grass. Slowly, at first. Then more quickly. The dress flowed around her, catching at her legs. The flame flickered with the motion. Suddenly, it was gone.

There was only the night now. Heavy, opaque, and filled with things unseen.

Kate lowered the window. The mannequin swayed

on its wooden stand. Kate turned, found the stairs, took them two at a time.

She went to the kitchen and grabbed a glass from the cupboard. Filled it from the tap and gulped the cool water.

The French doors opened. Her great-aunt stepped inside. Strands of wet grass clung to her feet. The hem of her nightgown was damp and streaked with dirt. Hair hung in tendrils over her shoulders, clung to her temples and neck. Splotches of bright color marked her cheeks. She still held the extinguished candle in her hand, a pool of gold wax in the holder. Kate caught the scent of beeswax.

"Oh, hello, dear," Great-aunt Roselyn murmured. It might have been a meeting at a garden party.

Kate set the glass down carefully. "Are you all right?"

"Naturally." She looked down at herself ruefully, and smoothed the fabric with her free hand. "I suddenly had the urge to get a breath of fresh air. I didn't realize the ground would be so damp. Sneaking out to walk the grass barefoot. I felt like a girl again. So exhilarating." She smiled and moved past Kate toward the hall. "I'm embarrassed you caught me indulging my whim. I hope I didn't give you a fright."

The woman who normally conformed to all the rules, all the conventions, suddenly decided to traipse the orchard alone in her nightgown? "Of course not," Kate said.

"Now I really shall retire to bed." Roselyn walked across the tiles, leaving dirty footprints in her wake. She paused, turned back. "It's hard, Kate, finding the empty shell of a human being. I know that only too well." Light caught the curve of a wistful smile.

"Who did you find?" Kate waited. Her heart beat against her ribs.

"It was long ago, but you never forget." Her aunt's gaze was lost in the darkened orchard outside. "Love is what it is. You'll learn that in time."

"The person who died, was it someone close to you?"

Great-aunt Roselyn turned abruptly. The glass Kate had been drinking from was at the edge of the counter. Her wrist grazed the side and the glass tipped. Water spread across the counter, dripped onto the floor. "Oh dear. These slender glasses get bumped so easily."

"Here, let me." Kate took the tea towel off the rack beside her. She sopped up the mess, lifting a ceramic bowl filled with berries to sweep beneath. The china felt delicate in her hand. There was already a chip in the floral chinoiserie border. Something soggy and tangled caught Kate's eye. She lifted it by one end and held it up. "What's this? A shoelace?"

Great-aunt Roselyn nodded. "Elaina found it outside, caught on one of the bushes by the terrace. Is it yours?"

Kate shook her head. "It looks like it belongs on a dress shoe, or a man's business shoe."

"Possibly." Great-aunt Roselyn looked doubtful. "Do you think it belonged to Mr. Wendell?"

"I would bet my edition of *Four Faultless Felons,* in the Arthur Hawkins art deco dust jacket, that the man didn't go a day without trainers."

"It must be the doctor's then."

"I suppose." Kate draped the black shoelace over the edge of the sink to dry. She could have sworn the doctor had been wearing loafers, but she could be wrong.

Isra slid from the shadows and wound between their feet. Roselyn reached down to stroke the Siamese cat absentmindedly. Almond-shaped blue eyes narrowed to contented slits. The cat purred.

"I went by the hardware store and got the tools to open Mr. Wendell's door." Kate leaned back against the counter. "I couldn't resist. I went downstairs and tried it." Rocked the hook up and down in the keyway, gently at first. Arms already aching from moving books around. Applied pressure, adjusted the pick hook painstakingly until she felt the pins give. "It's unlocked." The door had swung upon. "I glanced inside, but that was all."

"You unlocked the door?"

"I think it was brute force rather than skill, but it worked."

"Nobody seems to know if the man had family." Roselyn frowned. "I tried calling the number he gave me for the offices he worked at, but they had never heard of him before. Can you imagine?"

"You mean, he lied to us?"

"I should have checked up on him more thoroughly, but he was very polite. Perhaps the mystery will be solved when we clean out his room."

"Just wait. We'll go into that room tomorrow, and all secrets will be revealed."

"Nothing scandalous, I hope. I'm going to bed. Sleep well, dear."

"Good night."

Great-aunt Roselyn turned and began to make her way upstairs. A current of cool air swept across Kate's ankles. Where had it come from? All the windows were closed. Isra arched her back, her eyes narrowed and feral.

The door to the orchard. It was open. A narrow gap. Enough for a person to slide their fingers in. Grasp the edge. Push it back. Enter the house.

Isra gathered her muscles and leapt through the opening, out into the night. The hunter now, intent on her prey.

Kate closed the door and secured the lock. The wings of a moth thrummed against the glass, seeking the light.

The only scandal was her aunt walking the orchard at night. Barefoot. In her nightdress. If anyone heard about this, the rumors would spread. If someone had seen her, it would be worse than before. She wished she could phone home. Mom would know what to do. But she'd be at her book club now. She wouldn't be home for hours yet, not with the way that group could talk when they got started. The five-hour time difference made spontaneous calls across the Atlantic impossible, and sometimes that was harder than Kate wanted to admit. Made the distance seem farther.

She rested her forehead against the glass and listened to the moth. The rain began to fall.

****

Gary listened, head tilted, every muscle held still.

It was dark, well past ten now. He should have waited longer, but the rain would have washed away any traces. Not that he had found any. A few blurred footprints. Barefoot, too small and more recent, heading to the house. A broken twig. Lichen scraped from the trunk of a tree at shoulder height. Without the beam of a flashlight, he'd searched carefully, thoroughly. He found nothing. No proof that another man had been in the orchard before him.

Tiny noises echoed in the space around him, hard to pinpoint. Scrabble of a rodent. Hoot of an owl, somewhere above. A latch catching.

Gary looked toward the house, through the tangle of greenery between. A light in the kitchen. The silhouette of a woman. She was standing, her fingers pressed against the glass of the sliding door.

She couldn't see him. The yellow circle of light touched the terrace and not much farther beyond. Kate should have been asleep, or reading a book in her room. Not standing in the kitchen, looking out at the orchard.

Something leapt out of the hedgerow beside him. A breath escaped between his teeth. Slanting blue eyes, like chips of ice. The Siamese cat. She wound through his legs, warm fur against his jeans, and he bent to stroke her head. She purred, rubbing against his fingers.

The damp was beginning to soak through to his bones. Get in, get out. Tidy up the loose ends. Then he'd be done with it all. Gary straightened. The kitchen was empty. The light off.

He eased between the trees, to the basement door, staying well away from the thorns of the climbing rose. The flowers gave off a strong smell of musk and myrrh.

Gary glanced over his shoulder. Not a sound now. A few deft movements, and he was in.

He paused. His damp shoes would leave prints on the carpet. He slipped them off, carrying them in his hand. Moved soundlessly down the stairs. The third step creaks, he reminded himself. Slow and steady.

Gary dropped to one knee in front of the door. He

pulled on the surgical gloves he'd brought with him and took a leather pouch from his pocket. The Bogata rake would do. The keyhole was large enough. No need to worry about security pins on this door. He gave the handle a twist. Always worth a try.

The door swung inward.

One second to process it. Kate. She'd gotten there first. Had unlocked the door. Been in the room.

Gary stood, stepped inside. An undercurrent in the air, stale and vacant. Across from him, a pinprick of light flashed in the dark. A laptop or phone charger. The blind was down. He could hear the rain against the window, heavier now. Gary slid the pouch of tools back into his pocket. He nudged the door closed behind him.

The penlight would have to do. He swung the small beam, brightest setting but still not strong enough, around the room. Heaps on the floor. He bent down, careful not to touch anything. The light picked up plaid print, checkered squares. Discarded clothes. Unwashed, from the smell of them. The bed was unmade, one pillow on the floor.

If only he knew what Kate had seen already. How thoroughly she'd gone through the dead man's things when she opened the door.

He kept moving, searching for anything that might reveal who Chris Wendell really was. For any items that needed to disappear.

He shifted his focus to the desk, and the blink of yellow. He resisted the urge to power the laptop up. Kate and her friends would never get past the security.

Glint of gold on the dresser, dead ahead.

Scrap metal stored in an empty tin of travel sweets. Bought once a month, like clockwork. Faint scent of caramel and barley sugar rose as he tilted the tin, shone the light on the contents. Two dental crowns. A bracelet, small, broken at the link. A tangled necklace.

It was the glittery strand that knocked the breath out of him. The last time he'd seen something similar, it had been around Adriana's neck.

He lifted it out. The chain dangled off his hand, swinging in the air. The pendant turned on the end of the chain. Fourteen karat gold. An orchid on one side. The impression made from a Victorian era wax seal.

A flower that can survive the powers of my black thumb! That giddy lift to her tone. The smile that was better than winning the lottery. *It looks like something from another time. Can you just imagine, using this image to seal a letter? Who do you think used it? A lady of the manor, before sipping her afternoon tea.*

He'd gone over that street, again and again after she died. Looking for the necklace.

And the bastard had it all along. He must have picked it up off the pavement. Her blood still fresh on the ground. Too fucking scared to sell it. Stored away in a collection of old and broken metal, to be melted down. Cash for gold. His hand fisted on the necklace.

It was evidence that could tie him to the dead man. But it was more than that, too. It was hers.

The pendant lay in the palm of his hand.

Gary closed the door, retraced his steps up the stairs and out to the orchard, into the rain.

Chapter Fourteen

Kate half expected the door to bump into the edge of the wine cabinet the way it used to, on the far-off cry of *tag, you're it!* Of course, there was no cabinet now. No dusty bottles. No trunks stacked in the corner.

"I can't believe you picked the lock last night. Well done." Marcus was dressed for the job at hand, wearing beige slacks and a blue polo shirt. Casual for his standards.

"The lack of faith." Kate shook her head at him.

"After you." He stepped aside to let her into the room first. Elaina and Roselyn Marsh followed, carrying cleansers and packing boxes.

In the light of day, the room looked just as neglected as it had last night. And just as ordinary.

The sheets on the bed were swirled into a heap. A white blind covered the window. Stained at the corners. Clothes everywhere. A gym sock caught in the drawer. A fly buzzed around the mug on the desk.

"Everything must be spotless." Great-aunt Roselyn looked down at the scratches on the hardwood floor. Immaculate as always and nothing like the woman Kate saw walking the orchard last night. "I'll be letting the room again, as soon as possible."

Elaina picked up an empty crisp packet from beneath the bed. Potato dust sifted to the floor. "I don't know if spotless is possible."

Marcus went straight to the wardrobe. "I'll go through the clothes."

"Why doesn't that surprise me?" Kate pulled on a pair of disposable rubber gloves with a snap.

"Absolutely no idea." Hangers rustled. "Ah, spider!"

"Oh, the horror!"

"You try battling an eight-legged fiend, while swathed in the arms of a polyester robe. Take that!" A thump. "It's still alive." Marcus's voice was muffled.

"Try not to think about it and you'll be fine." Kate deposited a wad of take-out napkins in the bin.

Elaina grabbed a towel hanging off a lampshade and revealed a poster of a voluptuous blonde with blood-red silicone lips, leather bikini bottoms and a whip. "Urrgh!" She reeled back.

"Are those nail holes?" Great-aunt Roselyn moved closer to examine the wall.

"Does anyone else feel strange about this?" Elaina asked.

"Worried about ghosts with pickles on their breath?" Kate teased.

Marcus gave an eerie howl from within the wardrobe.

Elaina lobbed a rolled-up sock in his direction. "Going through his things like this, it feels odd."

Marcus groaned. "It's what any decent private investigator does for a living. The police do the same with a search warrant, and most people are alive to witness it."

"We couldn't have left it as it was," Roselyn Marsh reasoned. "The room has to be cleaned. And no one else seems to want the job."

"Has anyone else noticed that there aren't any photographs?" Kate looked around.

"Some people don't like mementos. I don't." Elaina tossed a vest into the box.

"It isn't just the photos. Where are the opened bills, the office documents?" Kate moved to the desk. "No notes. No shopping lists. Just a laptop. A used cup. It's like a stage set."

"Says the girl who devours mystery novels stacks at a time," Marcus said. "He may simply have kept electronic files and managed his accounts online." Loud zip of the packing tape as he sealed a box.

"Maybe." One of the desk drawers was open a crack. Kate tilted her head and squinted at the desk. Something about the height and depth of the drawer didn't match up. She pulled the drawer out farther and peered inside. Staples, a broken pencil, and a short length of twine. The space was shallow, the base a good five centimeters higher than it should be. Custom made?

"Looking for something, Kate?" Marcus asked.

"I don't know." Kate slid her fingertips over the rough surface of the wood, testing for unevenness or gaps. Her index finger ran over a circular indentation at the back of the base. She gave it a tug. With a scrape of wood, the base slid back.

Marcus leaned over her shoulder.

"It takes a certain amount of courage to stick your hand down a dark trap hole." Kate could feel Marcus's breath against her neck.

"Like the Mouth of Truth in *Roman Holiday*."

She glanced at him. "Do you want to do it?"

"The honor is all yours, Kate." He nudged her. "Go

ahead."

"That's what I was afraid of." Kate gritted her teeth and carefully worked her fingers into the slot. She touched something cold and smooth. Sucked in a breath. She maneuvered the small rectangular object until it fit through the opening.

Lying in the palm of her hand was Mr. Wendell's MP3 player. Kate pressed a key and the screen lit up. Instead of a colorful image of the album being played, the display was simply black and white. The last played song untitled. The MP3 player was surprisingly low-tech, without internet connection or flashy widgets.

"Did the man have such an eclectic taste in music he felt the need to hide it in a secret drawer?" Marcus wondered.

Kate shrugged. "Only one way to find out." She unwound the headphones coiled around the device. Grimaced and stuck the headphone buds into her ears, trying not to the think about the last place they had been. "What's the worst that could happen? A playlist consisting of '90s pop songs on repeat?" She pressed the Play button.

They stared at her expectantly.

Silence. If she strained her ears, she could hear a faint electronic whirr, but nothing that could be described as music. Kate gave it a few seconds, then shrugged. "Nothing."

Marcus frowned. "Really? Nothing at all?"

Static crackled through the headphones. "Hold on." A rhythmic creaking sound, a male grunt. A whimper. Kate's eyes widened. Moans, then a breathless, throaty female voice, "Yes. Yes. Oh, *yes*!" Kate yelped, and yanked the headphones out.

Elaina and Marcus each took an earbud. Kate heard a muffled scream. A wide grin spread across Marcus's face. "This gives a whole new meaning to oral sex."

Elaina doubled over with laughter. "This is priceless!"

A shudder ran through Kate. "He listened to that thing at the breakfast table!"

"He had a strange taste in audio books."

Great-aunt Roselyn frowned at the device. "This is shocking."

"I don't think it was an audio book." The sound hadn't been clear enough. Nothing like the full-cast radio dramatizations Kate kept on stock at the store.

"No wonder he hid it." Marcus chuckled.

"Mr. Wendell, the man of mystery," Elaina summed up in a smoky voice.

"Mr. Wendell, the peeping Tom," Marcus corrected. "It does seem odd when you consider the camera, the telephoto lens and the Dell laptop." He picked up the camera and zoomed in on a bird outside the window. "High resolution. Lovely." He swung it around and pretended to take a picture of Kate.

"Mr. Wendell never struck me as computer-savvy."

Marcus shrugged and put the camera back on the desk. "This stuff definitely takes some expertise."

"You can always tell the techno-fanatic," Elaina said knowingly, "and Mr. Wendell wasn't one."

"Technology these days is so complicated." Great-aunt Roselyn frowned. "I don't know what any of it is good for."

Marcus shrugged. "My line of expertise runs more to shoes and trousers, but I'd say this is either the property of an avid hobbyist or the tools of a professional. What did Mr. Wendell do?"

"I have no idea," Great-aunt Roselyn admitted.

"I suppose they could be prototypes." Marcus took the floor. "All right then. What do we know? Mr. Wendell was a chap who worked at a company dealing with technology, but didn't fit the label of what an electronic genius is supposed to look like." He counted the points off on his fingers. "He was an avid bird watcher, hence the lens—" Marcus pointed at the camera Kate had replaced on the desk—"and kept no personal hardcopy files on hand. He had a strange sex fetish. His door was always kept locked, with good reason when the MP3 player is taken into account. He was a slob, which Kate here thinks was a deliberate ploy. A typically optimistic sentiment, in my opinion." He winked at her. "Ergo, he must have been a corporate spy or a thief. Am I missing anything?"

"The pickles," Elaina said. "Don't forget the pickles."

"Right. And an abnormal fondness for pickled cucumbers."

"As well as a tendency to hoard gold," Kate added.

"What?" Marcus stopped pacing and turned to look at her.

"In this tin of travel sweets." Kate went to the dresser. "Do you remember, Aunt Roselyn, the mixed berry drops you used to put out for us? In that beautiful bowl."

"Yes, I do." her aunt said dryly. "I remember you broke it."

"Did I? Are you sure it wasn't Ethan or Chris?" A vague memory rose in her mind of a lecture on manners, made more intimidating by her great-aunt's crisp diction. *One can be a lion tamer, but not near the Waterford crystal.* "Never mind. I suppose I did. But that's why I noticed the tin yesterday. You used to have three or four of these stacked on a shelf in the pantry."

"Out of reach, or so I thought."

"It was like a treasure hunt."

"Sugar drops as jewels in the rough?" Marcus grinned.

"Exactly. And now here's a tin, being used to store actual gold." Kate picked the tin up, metal clinking within. "Well, just bits and bobs really, but a pretty necklace, too. Like an enchanted talisman in a book—" She stopped mid-sentence. There was nothing in the tin but the dental gold and the broken bracelet. "It was here last night." She'd held it up to the light, watched the pendant swing from the chain. For a moment, she'd been tempted to take it. To keep it safe. But she'd put it back in the tin. She was sure of it. Had it fallen on the floor?

"What did it look like?" Elaina asked.

"Gold. A pendant like a wax seal with an impression of an orchid on it."

"An orchid?" Great-aunt Roselyn echoed. She was surprised into a smile. "Sunday orchids," she murmured beneath her breath.

"Pardon?" Kate looked at her aunt, surprised.

"Oh!" She startled. "Well." Great-aunt Roselyn seemed flustered. "It's nothing really. Just that," she lowered her voice, "whenever he could, Frank, your great-uncle, would bring me an orchid on Sundays. He'd say—" A blush spread across her cheekbones— "'The most elegant flower for my elegant Rose.'" She trailed off, lost in the memory. She blinked and shook off the reminiscence abruptly. "Anyway, I haven't seen it. I don't know why Mr. Wendell would keep a necklace in a tin. It seems highly unpractical. Perhaps it's time for a break. We should give Elaina the chance to have a cigarette, for our sake."

"We all have our vices." Elaina shoved a box out of the way with the toe of her shoe, clearing a path to the door. "Mine just happens to be cigarettes."

"Mine is tea, and I could murder a cup right now." Marcus straightened and arched back, arms above his head, to stretch his spine. "Magpies must have stolen the necklace, Kate, or a master thief." His eyes twinkled the way they did when he played along with her stories.

"Maybe." It hadn't been a trick of the light or an over-active imagination. Kate remembered the sugary scent of the old tin as she replaced the necklace. The liquid feel of the chain as it slid through her fingers.

Chapter Fifteen

"Tastes better than it looks." Percival glanced at the fish Gary had ordered.

The air in the pub was sweet with the smell of spilled alcohol, sharpened by the tang of vinegar rising off the fish and chips in front of him.

"Don't rush a man enjoying a pint." Gary tipped his glass at Percival.

He should have left off the alcohol. He needed a clear head. He needed to sleep. Music pounded from the speakers in the corners of the ceiling. Something with a hard beat, more guitar than vocals.

"A goal like that is about the opposing team." Percival nodded at the Manchester United match playing on the screen above the bar, raising his voice to be heard. "The next move." Percival lifted the bun off his burger and spread ketchup across the charbroiled meat.

"And here I was, thinking it was about the players." Gary took another long draw from his glass, reached for his fork. The haddock was like butter. The batter crisp and golden. The fish was good. Really good. He hadn't realized how hungry he was.

"Pretty girl," Percival remarked.

"Someone caught your eye?" Gary grinned. He rested his arm on the back of the chair and swept his gaze around the room. Slow and easy, not bothering to hide it, knowing it would annoy the hell out of Percival.

"Sitting at the bar."

The pub was crowded. A man in shirt sleeves was standing, eyes on the screen, blocking Gary's view of the bar stools.

"Seems like it might be time for you to make your move." That, he'd like to see.

"I doubt it." Percival picked up a chip. "She's been looking at you for the past twenty minutes."

The man moved and Gary had a clear view of the woman sitting at the bar. She crossed her legs, displaying long, toned limbs. The hem of her skirt rose higher. A flick of hair to catch his eye, followed by a confident smile.

Percival raised an eyebrow.

"Yes, I see." He thought briefly of Kate and how quick she had been to turn him down. "But I'm not interested."

"In this one in particular, or blondes in general?"

Gary shot him a look. "There was someone. She's hard to replace." He could almost see Adriana at the bar, ordering a drink. She'd get come-hither eyes on a vodka and orange. "She was stubborn as all hell. Didn't give an inch. Always had to have her way."

Percival ate and listened.

Gary took another bite of his fish and leaned back. The necklace was a dull weight in his pocket. "She had a way with words." Gary swirled his glass, watched the foam creep up the sides, the blond at the bar forgotten. "You'd relax, just listening to her. You'd give her the world, without realizing it."

"Sounds dangerous to me."

Gary laughed. "She was. In an argument, she'd use

those words like throwing knives. Perfect aim, straight to the heart, every time."

A near goal was deflected. Gary looked up at the screen. Overly confident after the first-half goal, the red shirts were missing a sense of purpose. They were making mistakes.

"I take it you're going to let the blonde go then?" Percival's eyes twinkled.

"I believe I will."

Normally riveted by a solid right foot strike, Percival absently pushed the remaining chips around on his plate. Beneath his breath, he whistled three disjointed notes. "Something on your mind, Perce?"

"You always tell us to pay attention. To make the connection."

The fish suddenly tasted tough and dry. Gary forced the bite down with a swallow of beer. He pushed his plate away. "Right." The words twisted, low in his gut.

"I looked up this Mr. Harris." Percival rested his elbows on the table, leaned forward. "A bit odd, that."

"How so?" The voices around them were cheerful and loud. Peanut shells on the floor cracked beneath the soles of shoes. The air in the pub seemed to be getting hotter, seemed to be closing in. A line of sweat ran down his back.

"He advised Greylenn to cancel our contract with them."

"I remember you told me. That does happen, now and then."

"It's good business sense to know why," Percival said gravely. "To prevent it happening again."

"Yes, I suppose it is." His glass was empty.

"Nothing much there to discover. Successful CEO of a multi-conglomerate. Nothing to do with security. Not competing with us. That surprised me." Percival folded his napkin into a neat square, creasing the edges. "There was one article that was more interesting. His daughter died." Percival looked up, met Gary's eyes.

"How long ago was this?" Ask the right questions. Give nothing away.

"Two years ago. A few days after the anniversary of her death, Graylenn got their phone call from Mr. Harris. I wondered why."

"What did the article say?" Not too quick. Casual curiosity, that's all.

"Adriana Harris—"

The sound of her name and he was building up his defenses before he knew it.

"She was killed. Shot in London. Location unspecified. There was mention of a bodyguard, but no names given. Her security failed to react quickly when the shot was fired. The delay cost her life. The bodyguard's speed was questioned, and his effectiveness."

Accurate, yet vague. The whistle of air as the bullet past his ear was loud in his head, mingling with Percy's whistled tune. His pulse throbbed.

"So I thought," Percival said slowly, "maybe her bodyguard is working for us now."

Relief made his head swim. "And that's why Harris is holding a grudge? I'll check up on it. Thanks for looking into it, Perce." Gary laid several bills on the table, enough to cover his share and a generous tip. "I think I'll call it a night." He stood.

"I'll stay for one last pint. See if they recover."

Fifteen minutes left on the match. "Suit yourself."

"See you tomorrow, boss."

Outside, Gary dragged fresh air into his lungs. It was foggy now. The street was thick with it. He began to walk, at a pace that might burn off the adrenaline flowing through his veins.

No pointless lies, that was the most important thing. Wait it out.

Vengeance. It was hard to blame a man for that. Adriana's father had the right to turn away clients and far worse. He'd deal with it as it happened. And if someone discovered a connection between him and the dead man? Well, he'd deal with that, too.

A woman appeared beneath the streetlight up ahead. She froze in the light, glancing around, then stepped forward, into the shadows. Even with the distance between them, the haze rolling across the pavement, Gary recognized her easily.

Kate was moving quickly, avoiding the streetlights.

Gary knew her routine. He knew when Kate left the store. She rarely parked in front of the bookshop. Kate used the parking lot nearby and left the street space available for customers. He knew the route she normally took to get there. He knew how long it took her to walk to the parking lot and this was no short cut. What was she doing there?

People were creatures of habit. They didn't alter their routines without reason, especially when the old ones made sense. So what had changed?

Gary's eyes narrowed. This street was better lit, more populated than the one her shop was on. Lights glowed from office buildings, whereas the stores would be closed by now. And yet, she was trying to stay in the dark.

Why did she decide to add ten minutes to her walk?

Then he saw and he knew.

He wasn't the only one watching her. Someone was following her.

****

The soft slide and scrape of soles against pavement continued. Closer now. Almost behind her, and still Kate couldn't see through the fog.

She made her way past empty store fronts, past office buildings. It was only eight thirty, but it might have been midnight. Kate pulled her cardigan closer. The short skirt fluttered against her legs as she walked. Kate wished she had worn something warmer. The click of her heels against the pavement echoed loudly. She'd forgotten about the cobblestones. The uneven ground slowed her down.

Ever since she left the store, she'd sensed an additional presence behind her. Now she was sure of it. She could feel eyes watching her, tracing her steps, even though she had altered her route. Her skin prickled under the unseen gaze.

Her heart beat faster. Kate took longer strides, not quite a run. She was careful, knew the rules. Leave before dark. Don't park too far away. Safety first. But parking in front of the store meant losing out on business.

Footsteps ebbed, rose and fell, like waves behind her. She looked back, but all she could see were clouds of mist, indistinct shapes.

It might just be a late shopper or one of the other store owners going home. Someone leaving the office.

A coincidence that they seemed to be moving with her, at her pace.

Knee, shin, groin. Kate ran through the list of weaknesses, the ones she'd aim for if she had to. Gouge the eyes. A palm rammed into the nose from beneath, fracturing bone. Crush an instep.

Almost there now. So close, she could see the darkness leading down between the photography studio and apothecary ahead. Toward the stairs that would take her to the parking lot and to her car. She had forgotten how dark it was here. Across the street, lights were on in the office building, but she was walking away from it, into darkness. She should have taken the shorter route.

Kate stumbled over the first step. Her feet hurt. She hadn't intended to walk this far, not in these shoes. Clutching at the handrail, she hurried down toward the flickering light below, fumbling in her purse for the car keys. Her fingers searched for the familiar round plastic shape, for the metal key ring. She glanced behind her.

A black figure stood at the top of the stairs. A living shadow, sprung of the night and the mist.

A man. He was watching her, hands in his pockets, feet spread firmly on the top step. The light reached up toward him and fell short. Dress shoes gleamed. His features concealed.

Kate stood still, her hand clutched convulsively around the cold metal railing. Her fingers numb with fear. The muscles in her legs quivered with adrenaline. She should run. She'd make it. She had the keys in her hand now. But she couldn't move.

As she stared, he bowed his head and lifted one hand in greeting.

The moment seemed endless, extended to the breaking point as she stood, transfixed. There was something cruel about that wordless motion, that raised hand.

Kate turned then, and ran.

Someone grabbed her arm, jerking her to a stop. She swung out blindly with her free hand and her knuckles connected with his jaw. Kate heard his teeth clack together. The jolt of impact shot up her wrist. She sucked in a breath, ready to scream.

"Ow! Kate, stop."

The voice was familiar. She gave up struggling and took a closer look at him. "Gary?"

"Yes." He sounded exasperated. Light from the lamp above them slanted over his face. Gary swiped at the blood seeping from his split lip.

"Why would you grab my arm? You scared the living daylights out of me."

"You were about to run into me. Again." He seemed to be scanning their surroundings, focusing on the darkened corners, the shadows between parked cars. "I'm starting to think it's become a habit."

"The first time, you ran into me," Kate pointed out.

"Pedantic. Besides, you just punched me. That's a powerful right hook you've got there, by the way."

"Sorry. I thought you were—" Kate looked back to the stairs, but there was only darkness now. The man was gone. "Never mind. Here, let me." She dug a fresh tissue out of her purse. She rested the fingers of one hand lightly against his jaw, angling his face toward her so that she could see better. Gary stood still as her fingers brushed over his skin.

She dabbed carefully at the wound. He winced.

Kate shot him a look. "It's not that bad. It's almost stopped bleeding."

His face was close to hers. She could smell his aftershave, scent of sandalwood and herbs.

"Thank you."

"First turned down, then punched. I think I'm losing my touch."

"Stop smiling. You're making this more difficult."

"No, this would make it difficult." And his mouth was on hers. His lips were warm and gentle. It was quick, just seconds, before he stepped back. He looked as surprised as she felt. "Are you going to hit me again?" He asked warily.

"Not right away, anyway."

"Thank God for that." Gary rubbed a hand over his jaw. "How's your hand?"

Her knuckles were aching. "Fine." There was a pause as she thought of something else to say. "Is your car parked here?"

"No, I'm walking. I usually come through the alley"—he pointed to the entrance on their left—"and cut through the lot to get to the next street. It makes the walk five minutes shorter. Isn't this the longer route from your shop?"

"After being in the store all day, the fresh air was nice."

"And the fog?" Gary raised an eyebrow.

"Atmospheric."

"So you're a recreational locksmith who knows how to throw a punch and enjoys a stroll through the fog."

"And sells books," Kate added.

"Be careful. It's a long, dark walk on your own."

The warning was sudden, his tone serious.

She shivered. "I'm always careful."

"How did it go with the lock picking?"

"It was very successful."

"I'm assuming the diamonds have been sold by now?" He asked, more lightly.

"Naturally."

"Well," he looked around the empty lot. "I'm going to go home and get some ice."

Kate laughed. "You do that." She walked toward her Mini.

"You're not going to get very far without these." Something small and shiny swung from his fingers. Her car keys. "You dropped them during the skirmish."

Kate took her keys from him. "They might be useful."

"Of course, you could always show off your lock picking skills." Gary grinned.

"Too little light." She hit the unlock button, and opened the door.

"Kate?"

She turned back.

"I might ask you for dinner again one day." He stood there smiling at her, his hands in his pockets.

"One day, I might say yes." She got in the car. Gary waited for her to lock the doors. In the rearview mirror, Kate watched him jog across the street. Just before he was out of sight, he glanced back in her direction.

Kate started the car and pulled out of the lot. Her lips tingled. She shook her head and concentrated on the drive. What she needed was a pack of red licorice, a soak in the tub, and a relaxing book.

She had bolted, as simple as that. The man on the stairs could have been a regular customer, another shop owner. It might have even been the vegetable man she bought cucumbers from in the market. But he should have said something, instead of just standing there.

A sign for Maple Road appeared ahead, suspended in the headlights, and Kate turned onto the familiar street.

The house rose up out of shrouds of fog. Birds gusted over the chimney, around the tower, and between the trees. Their cries echoed through the orchard. Light from an upper window spilled to the ground. The rest of the house was dark.

It made Kate think of the email Mom had sent yesterday. *There have always been ghosts in that house. That's why I tried so hard to convince you to change your mind about staying there. My mother never told stories about their childhood, and she left Willowsend as soon as she could, got as far away as she could. I always felt there was a reason she did. Roselyn was the one who inherited the property. Kept everything the same. My mother once said taking care of that house was Roselyn's atonement, or a part of it anyway. Wish I could tell you more but, as you know, your grandmother never liked to talk about the past.*

With those words echoing through her mind, Kate parked the car and grabbed her bag. Something rustled in the weeds at the side of the drive, scurried in the darkness. Gravel crunched beneath her shoes as she walked up the path to the porch. She dug in her purse for her house key and almost tripped over the sneaker that appeared in front of her.

Kate froze. Her key fob, in the distinctive shape of

a tiny book, slipped from her fingers, disappearing into the depths of her bag.

Chapter Sixteen

A dead body. Not again, Kate thought.

She took a closer look at the long shape lounging on the steps. The sneaker twitched.

Kate decided to take that as a sign of life. "Who are you?"

The man jumped to his feet, unfolding gangly legs from the darkness. White teeth flashed in a rakish grin. "I think the doorbell's broken. I saw the light, but no one answered. Figured I'd wait." A faint accent added an irregular cadence to his words. She had the impression he was used to slipping between languages.

"Who were you waiting for?" Kate stepped past him. A large duffel bag was blocking a good portion of the front door. She maneuvered around it and turned on the porch light.

"Ah, see, if I could have found that—" He met her slightly hostile stare and trailed off. "I, er, wouldn't have had to wait in the dark," he finished. He stooped to pick up his bag and grinned at her over his shoulder. "Don't get me wrong, I don't mind waiting."

The light hit him, and a jolt of recognition ran through her. The tousled hair, the wide grin. The confident, energetic movements. "The man in charcoal," Kate murmured. Elaina's sketch come to life. Looking only slightly scruffier in person.

He gripped the heavy bag easily in one hand and

blinked at her. "Excuse me?"

"Nothing. Never mind." So he did exist.

"I was passing through and decided to stop by. Elaina isn't expecting me. It was a spontaneous decision. I sent an email, but I wasn't sure if I'd be able to make it."

If he had told her he was thinking of visiting, Elaina hadn't been overjoyed by the news. Kate would have noticed. It was hard to miss when Elaina was happy. "Passing through on your way to…?"

"The Middle East." He rubbed a rueful hand across the back of his neck. "All right, so it's not exactly on the way."

"Soldier?" The sneakers, tattered laces and cargo pants didn't suit her idea of a returning soldier.

"Travel writer," he corrected. "I'm writing a piece on Sharm el-Sheikh," he explained. "Willowsend is slightly off the beaten path but, if you've got the time, you have to seize the opportunity. Do you know when she'll be home? I'm Ian Kale, by the way." He held out his hand.

"Kate Rowan. Nice to meet you." His grip was firm. "Elaina won't be back until late, but come on in." Kate unlocked the door. "You can wait in the kitchen. It's more comfortable than the porch."

"I'm sure." Ian grinned, toeing his shoes off inside the door.

"You've been here before."

"A while ago."

Kate led the way to the kitchen. He strolled down the hall behind her in his socks. Piano music drifted down to them from upstairs. The dreamlike notes rose and fell in melancholy spirals of sound. It was no wonder Great-aunt Roselyn hadn't heard the doorbell.

"Is someone else at home or do you always have Debussy playing in the background?"

"My great-aunt must be upstairs."

"It's been a while since I was here, but the place hasn't changed. Frozen in time, like Sleeping Beauty's castle." He glanced at Kate. "I guess my last visit must have been before you moved in."

"Over two years then." Had it been that long since he'd seen Elaina or only since he'd last been to the house? "Can I get you something to drink?"

"Green tea, if you have any." Ian slouched into the chair, long legs sprawled beneath the table. He leaned forward and grinned, laugh lines crinkling around his eyes. "Sorry for startling you before, by the way. It must have been a shock, finding someone on your porch."

"Just a little," Kate said dryly. She poured boiling water over the tea bags and brought two cups to the table. "How long have you known Elaina?" She wrapped her hands around the thick mug, warming her chilled fingers.

"Close to eight years now."

"Really? That long? How did you meet?"

"Elaina doesn't talk about me much, does she?" Ian swirled the tea in his cup, a wry smile on his lips. "That's okay," he said when he saw her expression. "You don't have to answer that. How we met… I'd just gotten my first assignment and was going to meet some friends in front of the anthropological museum to celebrate at a café nearby. Elaina was studying art at the college. She was my friend Brandon's date."

Kate laughed. "I see."

"She walked up to the museum steps wearing this short dress, killer heels and dark lipstick that stained her cigarettes red. She had this fuck-off attitude that got everyone's attention. I think I was the only one who saw through it." He grinned at the memory. "To make a long story short, she left the café with me. I haven't spoken to Brandon in eight years. Not a huge loss. We never had much in common. Well, until that night."

"I could give Elaina a call at work, let her know you're here."

"I don't mind waiting."

He looked comfortable and fully prepared to wait as long as it took. "I'll let her know anyway. It won't take a minute." A lot could happen in two years, no matter how much he seemed to want to think time had stood still. Elaina deserved a warning.

Ian sat at the kitchen table in a pool of white light from the lamp above, his back to the door. Kate grabbed the phone and dialed the number of the pub. A mixture of canned music and crashing glasses sounded through the line. "Elaina? It's Kate."

"What's up?"

"Don't sound so excited."

"I forgot my pompoms." A blast of noise filtered through the line. "You're cut off!"

"The connection seems fine to me."

"What? No. This guy is so far gone, his tie is soaking up the rest of his whiskey. Look, was there something you wanted?"

"Ian is here." Silence. "I found him on the porch when I got home."

"Shit. Just what I needed." There was a pause. "Okay, tell you what. Give him the bottle of vodka in the fridge. Hopefully then the last thing he'll want to do when I get home is talk. And, no, I won't be leaving work early just to see him. Someone has to break it to him that the world doesn't stop turning just because he decides to show up again. Narcissistic—" A round of raucous cheers drowned out the rest of her description. "Thanks for the call." Elaina hung up.

At least she'd gotten a thank you.

"There's a bottle of vodka in the fridge," Kate told Ian.

A gasp from the doorway startled her. Great-aunt Roselyn stood on the threshold, pale and wide-eyed. "It's not possible," she said, her voice raw with shock.

Ian swung around to see what Kate was looking at.

As he turned, Roselyn's fingers unfurled from the white-knuckled fist her left hand had formed. Her expression changed to one of relief. "I seem to have gotten lost in the past." She stepped into the room. "For a moment, you looked like someone I used to know, a long time ago. It startled me. Ian, how nice to see you again." Her voice was calm now. Pleasant and welcoming and, Kate thought, viciously controlled. "Elaina will be pleased. Has Kate been a good hostess? Can I offer you anything? I have a tin of biscuits somewhere."

"I'll pass right now, but thanks." Ian rose to greet her. "I hope you don't mind that I showed up like this. I didn't come empty-handed." He dug in his bag and pulled out a small package. "Goda Masala. I hope you like Indian food."

"Spices are a lovely gift." She set the packet down on the counter. Were her fingers trembling?

"It's the least I could do. If it's all right with you, I

think I'll wait in Elaina's room." Ian turned to Kate. "I will take you up on your offer, Kate."

"Sure." Kate got the vodka from the fridge, her eyes on her great-aunt. It was the expression, the sudden flash of confusion, that worried her. She had begun to recognize it, that loss of focus, and to dread it.

Ian took the liquor from Kate. He examined the label and grinned his appreciation. "Trust Elaina to get nothing but the best." He slung his duffel bag over his shoulder. "Nice meeting you, Kate. Goodnight, Mrs. Marsh, and thanks for putting me up."

"Of course, Ian."

He walked down the dark hall, the bottle of vodka dangling from his hand, the worn bag at his side.

Out of the corner of her eye, Kate noticed Great-aunt Roselyn move to the French doors. One arm was wrapped around her waist. She was absorbed in some unseen reality. Or the past. Her features wavered in the reflection, distorted in the glass.

Lonely, Kate was surprised to catch herself thinking. Her great-aunt looked lonely.

And here she was, nursing sore knuckles and thinking of a kiss beneath the glow of a streetlamp.

****

The kiss was a mistake.

The lamp at Gary's elbow buzzed and flickered. He reached for his coffee. No mystery why the office at the back of his flat smelled like a strong dark roast. The guitar-driven sound of blues rock was playing on the stereo, turned down low. A faded green sofa, sagging in the middle, leaned against the wall. Far past its sell-by date, it was the most comfortable piece of furniture he owned.

An Excuse for Murder

The bruise on his jaw throbbed. For a little thing, Kate could throw one hell of a punch.

Her lips had been soft, though.

Gary took a sip of coffee and scalded his tongue, felt the caffeine hit his system. He reached for the remote and turned the volume up until the music filled the room.

Kate had been scared. That much was obvious. The man had followed her at a distance, kept her in his sight and slowly closed the gap between them.

What would have happened if Gary hadn't cut through the alley and gotten to her first? And taken a punch for his efforts, he thought ruefully.

At least he had gotten a good look at the man. Pausing next to a Jag parked on the street, he'd let the man pass and used the opportunity to take in the details. Suit and tie. Expensive leather briefcase. Too thin, gaunt even. Clean looking. Someone you'd assume followed the rules. Showed up at work on time, paid his bills. But appearances could be misleading.

The man was already walking away when it hit him. Gary had seen him before. But where? Gary picked up a pencil and tapped it thoughtfully against the edge of the table. The beat picked up the bluesy rhythm of the song.

Wink of gold on the man's ring finger. That was surprising. A married man would think twice about following the next pair of hips that swung past. Didn't chase after just any pretty face. Not if it meant risking the wrath of an angry female. And he certainly wouldn't be wearing his wedding band to go on the prowl. That ruled out attraction as a motive.

Where had he seen him? Gary ran through a mental

line-up of faces. The pub. No, not there. A client? Doubtful. He had an almost photographic overview of the workings of Fenris Securities. Nothing missed, nothing forgotten. Maybe it was the briefcase. That was it. Something to do with that briefcase. The connection lay there. He could see the man exiting a building. The pencil rapped out a faster beat. The subwoofer amplifying the rapid roll of the drums.

He stopped, the pencil poised in the air. The song ended. And he had it.

The memory was there, sharp and detailed. Swing of glass doors. The man exiting the building at a fast clip. Key card dangling off a lapel. That building. Shit.

Tech companies had numerous employees. 'Course they would. Employees ensured continued growth. Even comparatively small ones like this, focusing on software rather than hardware. It might be a coincidence that it was the same one that had, for a time, employed Derek Wendell.

But coincidences set off his radar. Made him suspicious. It wasn't the caffeine that filled him with energy now. It was the hunt.

Gary turned to his laptop. Gave the company name in the search bar, pulled up the website. All those handy icons right there on the homepage. He grinned. Don't be afraid to share. Isn't that what they said? You had to love social media. So much information, just a click away. He scrolled down, skimming past links to articles on troubleshooting, updates on new releases, infographics. It was a name he wanted. He refined the search.

And then, there it was. A picture. The photograph even had its own headline, documenting corporate philanthropy. Volunteer work at a shelter to encourage camaraderie. And in the background, the man he was looking for.

Gary zoomed in. Forced smile, but it was him all right. Not looking too pleased about taking part in building morale. Not a team player then, are we? Ryan Delaney. The name, black on white. It didn't ring any bells. Gary copied the image and the accompanying status update. Stored it in a secure file.

Now to dig a little deeper.

With a few practiced moves, Gary pulled up what he was looking for. His eyebrows rose and he whistled through his teeth. "Now this is interesting."

Occupation, sales manager. In comparison to Delaney's position, Wendell had been a rodent, an underling. Still, it was something to keep in mind.

Thirty-nine years old. Married for ten years. Delaney earned a decent yearly salary, plus bonuses and commission. Very comfortable. Enough to keep Mrs. Delaney in all the Jimmy Choos her little heart desired.

But that didn't help him figure out why the bastard was tailing Kate. What he wanted. Still, it was a start. It wouldn't take much to find out more. A few well-placed questions. An open wallet.

Gary leaned back. The chair bobbed pleasantly beneath his weight. He propped his feet on the table and stared at the ceiling, his thoughts circling around the details. He picked up the pencil again, turning it over in his hands.

It broke in half with a satisfying snap of wood.

Chapter Seventeen

"Kate, love," Marcus said as he entered the bookstore, "you look like a faded rose."

"Lack of sleep will do that." The computer was slow to restart. The monitor still dark. Kate put down the cloth-bound edition of fairy tales she was holding, ready to catalogue.

"Something on your mind?" Marcus slid the fairy tales toward him and thumbed through the illustrations. Delicate pen-and-ink figures seemed to dance across the pages.

"The usual. Finding a corpse. Worrying about Great-aunt Roselyn. She's started misplacing things more often. She sets something down, then forgets where she's put it. I think it upsets her more than she lets on." Kate hit a key and looked at the screen. Still nothing.

"At least it's a becoming pallor. More pre-Raphaelite than Victorian consumptive." Marcus closed the book. "Have you spoken to your mum about Roselyn?"

"She called the store about half an hour ago. I couldn't talk long but it was a nice surprise. She and Dad have been looking at flights. They're thinking of visiting over Christmas."

"Good. Then you won't have to deal with it all on your own. Busy today?"

"It's been quiet for a Saturday morning. I'm expecting a collector later, though."

Marcus leaned against the counter, and crossed his legs. "Did you hurt your hand?"

Kate glanced down. Tinge of blue across the knuckles. "You should see the other guy." She grinned.

Marcus chuckled, then stopped when he saw her face. "Hold on, you're serious? You punched someone?"

The bell above the door chimed. A customer. "Hold that thought." Sun in her eyes, spilling through the open door. A man, features a dark blur with the light behind. Not tall, but broad shouldered. Her skin prickled. The next second, he'd turned to leave.

"He saw you, now he's fleeing," Marcus observed. "Was he the one you hit?"

"It must be the pallor."

Halfway out the door, the man turned back.

The glare faded and a jolt of recognition hit. Last time she'd seen him, he'd been standing over Mr. Wendell's body. "Dr. Garreth?" He was walking toward them with a determined stride. Flash of a morgue through her mind, a medley of voices discussing stomach contents, blood samples. Something read and forgotten.

Marcus shot her a glance. "A doctor. The pathologist that issued the death certificate?"

She nodded.

Marcus stood. "How do you do?"

The doctor looked Marcus up and down, from his carefully pressed shirt sleeves to his leather brogues. "The wife wants some books."

"You've come to the right place." She gestured at

the shelves. Just books then, not questions. For now, anyway.

The doctor took in his surroundings. The same careful precision he had applied to the examination of human remains. "I've seen corpses that deal with death better than my wife does with a common cold. I've got a list." Some customers saved lists on their phones. The doctor pulled a scrap of lined paper from his pocket. "Not the kind I'd buy."

Bodice-rippers? The writing was neat, each line spaced carefully. Five titles in total. Chick lit. Most were in stock. "Let's see what I can find." Kate took down a copy here, a copy there until she had a stack in her arms. She set the books down on the counter. All paperback.

He looked at them, then back at her. "This one is pink!" The jacket blurb had him rubbing his forehead. "Shopping, affairs. Jesus."

Marcus choked on a chuckle, turned it into a cough.

The door opened and a woman entered the store.

"Welcome to Fortune's Cove Books." Kate smiled her shopkeeper's smile.

Dr. Garreth turned too quickly, his elbow brushing the stack of books. It wobbled dangerously. He flushed crimson.

"Which ones would you like?" Kate waited.

"These two." He pushed them toward her, shifting to block the counter from view.

Kate turned to her computer to enter the first ISBN. The screen was black with white text. Operating System not found. Not found? She clicked the mouse. Nothing.

Marcus looked over her shoulder. "Problem?"

She gestured at the screen. "Any brilliant ideas?"

"None. On the plus side, it doesn't sound like it's going to explode."

Soon she'd splurge for something shiny and new. And compact.

"I could give you a name," Dr. Garreth said. "For a discount."

"A name?"

"Someone who could fix that." He nodded at the computer.

"I could just call a technician."

"Mine's cheaper."

"What kind of a discount?"

"Ten percent."

Kate did a quick tally. The profit margin was high enough. "Deal." She took out a calculator and wrote up a sales invoice. Pen and paper never failed. "Tell me the name and you'll get your discount."

He smiled. "The lad who works for me paid his way through med school fixing computers."

"Jeremy?"

"Talks binary code on the weekend, blood and tissue samples during the week. Charges less than an expert." He jotted a cell number on the back of his wife's list and handed it to her, along with the money owed.

It wouldn't hurt to save the service fee. "If he can't fix it, I can always get a professional to look at it. I hope your wife enjoys the books." He didn't leave. "Was there something else?" A cadaver on a slab. Shears opening the chest cavity, laying organs bare.

"A bag." He pointed at the multi-hued books, the

shoes and slender cartoon girls.

"Right." She chose one from beneath the counter. Shoes. A floral motif. The shoelace in the kitchen. "Are you missing a shoelace? We found one in the yard after you left." Near the house. In the bush by the terrace.

"Never wear laces on the job." He took the bag from her. "Don't want them trailing over the ground, soaking up blood and bile." He stepped back and she caught sight of his shoes. Sensible loafers.

"It was just a thought." The door closed behind him. If the lace wasn't his, whose was it?

Marcus took her hand and studied the bruise again. "Why, if I may ask?"

The steep stairs. The sudden hold on her arm. "He startled me."

"Poor soul. Him, not you."

"It felt like I was being followed." The footsteps echoing behind her.

"Kate." Marcus shook his head. "This is a sign you should intersperse crime with romance."

"I assume you mean genres?"

"Do I?" He raised an eyebrow.

Kate laughed. "You're—"

"Wonderful?"

"Incorrigible."

"So who was your victim?"

"Gary Fenris."

Marcus thought for a moment. "Why do I know that name?"

"The security company."

"Oh yes. Fenris Securities." He whistled through his teeth. "And you got a punch in? Not bad, Kate."

"Thank you." It was the kiss she remembered.

"Speaking of chiseled features," Marcus drawled as he threw himself into an armchair. "I had the most delicious encounter yesterday while I was showing an, in my opinion, overpriced apartment. Do you want all the gory details?"

"Spare nothing." Then she'd dial the number Dr. Garreth had given her.

Chapter Eighteen

He should let it go. But where would be the fun in that?

Gary walked into the bar. A high-end cocktail bar in London. By his watch, five minutes after the door swung closed behind Ryan Delaney. In his experience, data on a screen never gave you a true impression of a man's character. Data could be manipulated. Micro expressions, on the other hand, they never lied.

The sound hit him first. Pulse of live jazz in the floor beneath his feet. Crack of billiards. Gary paused and looked around, loosened his jacket. It was warm inside. Deep armchairs, railway carriage booths, billiard tables in one long, narrow room. Low ceiling. Red lights on the walls, red lipstick on the waitresses. Waiters in vests. Everyone and everything designed to impress.

A tray went past. Four cocktails on it. Liquid glowed beneath the crisscrossing beams of light.

He touched the waitress's arm. She looked back. Then looked a little longer. "What can I get you?" Husky voice, pitched just right to be heard over the wail of the sax.

"Scotch and soda," Gary said.

"Of course." She turned on skinny heels, balancing tray and drinks with ease. A glance back at him, an extra smile.

Down at the end of the room, Delaney was chalking a cue. Shirtsleeves rolled up. Two men at the table with him, carrying on a quick exchange. Gary was too far away to hear what was being said. That would change soon. One of the men was over six feet tall and heavily built. The second one rangy, a light-weight. Wiry arms. Both of them gym-toned, if Gary had to wager a guess. Soft hands, probably. Expensive jeans.

Gary took his drink from the waitress with a clink of ice, hardly noticing the brush of fingers over his, the promise in her eyes.

He watched, one minute longer. The Scotch was good, smooth, and cold. Hint of oak and honey. He'd make it last. He wasn't there to drink.

Delaney was in charge. That much was obvious. The tall one, he was eager to please, shooting jokes, trying for a laugh. Lounging against the wall, beer in hand, content to watch the others play. Relaxed slouch to the shoulders. Business associates? Mid-forties, maybe late-thirties. Like Delaney.

Hungry glint in the eye of the smaller man. Focus centered on the table, he was lining up for a shot. Called it. Took his time, aiming carefully. Sank the four ball in the corner pocket. He straightened, pleased with himself. Delaney shook his head, said something, arguing. Pointed at the table, marking out the route of the ball. A foul? Gary raised an eyebrow. He hadn't spotted it. A push shot?

The tall man shrugged, shook his head. Not taking sides then. Wise man. Flash of temper on the little guy's face, angry twist to the mouth, you could spot a mile away. One hand curling into a fist, white knuckles. Gary rested an elbow on the bar, and waited.

But the guy backed down. Let Delaney take over the play. Delaney cleared the balls in quick succession, no hesitation, and closed the game. Leaving Gary with a sudden urge to wipe the smug smirk off his face.

Gary stood, made his way over to them. Trying to look like someone who spent his Saturday night networking in a high-end bar. Like them. Gary grinned, nice and easy. "Mind if I play?"

The tall man said, "Have at it." His finger moved against the glass, in time to the swing rhythm of the sax.

The little guy looked at Gary thoughtfully. "Loser picks up the tab."

"Fine by me."

Delaney handed Gary a cue. "I'm hard to beat."

"I noticed. You know who you remind me of? The guy from *Wing and a Prayer*."

"Never seen it."

The little guy scrutinized Delaney. "Dana Andrews?"

"No, William Eythe. It's the jaw mostly." Gary set his drink down. "Shall I take the break shot?"

"Go ahead." Delaney stepped back.

Last time he played, he'd watched Adriana lean over the table, wielding the cue like a pro. Jeans tight enough to distract him when it was his turn to play. Laughing as she made the shot. Gary broke cleanly, sank a ball. The solid colors were his. He circled the table, called the shot. "So what do you gents do?" The cue following the ball like a magnet. Ricochet off the rail and into the corner pocket. Gary straightened. Nice to know he still had it.

Delaney watched the play with narrowed eyes.

"Marketing manager. Matt and George are in sales."

"Sales manager," the tall man corrected.

"I've never seen you here before," Delaney said.

"First time." Center spot to side pocket. Easy. "I'll be coming back though. The waitresses are a sight for sore eyes."

"Curves in all the right places," Delaney agreed.

"Look too long though, Ryan," the smaller man said, "and Holly will have your eyes."

The tall man grinned. "Only if she finds out, Matt."

Delaney shrugged. "A quick roll through the sheets isn't worth the risk."

"That depends on the woman, doesn't it?" Gary said casually. Stoking the fire.

"Are you a cheating man?" Delaney leaned on his cue. Anger? No, just curiosity.

"I think"—Gary lined up the next shot—"promises are meant to be kept."

"Wears his heart on his sleeve, he does," Matt said. Sarcasm there.

Gary glanced up, caught Delaney watching him. And drove the ball to the pocket.

Delaney stepped forward, fast. Hand on Gary's shoulder, a hard grip. "That was a double hit." The bulb above the table swung, throwing shadows.

The hell it was. "I don't think so." Gary rested a hip against the table, folded his arms over his chest. Smiled.

"That shot's a foul. Right, lads?" Delaney turned to the others.

"Sure." Disinterested.

Matt shrugged, drained his glass.

Gary smiled. "Easier to call a foul than it is to play,

isn't it, Delaney?"

"Watch it." Delaney flushed. Tightened his hold on the cue. A perfect weapon. One more step forward and Gary was hemmed in between the wall and the table. Delaney shifted, adjusted his balance, but his feet were flat on the floor. Torso angled wrong. "What was your name again?"

"Gary."

Lower, "What are you trying to say, Gary?" Sneer on the name.

The other two were watching the scene unfold with interest.

Gary put his cue down. In the close quarters, there was no point using it. He'd rather have his hands free. The bartender looked their way. Gary would let Delaney get in a swing first. There were plenty of witnesses to confirm self-defense when he fought back. If it came to that. Gary moved forward. They were standing toe to toe now. He had an inch on Delaney. On the small stage at the other end of the bar, the drummer changed the rhythm, speeding up the pace. "Seems to me you like to pick the easy way out. Matt" —eyes on Delaney—"did you shoot a foul last game?"

A muscle twitched in Delaney's jaw. "Are you calling me a liar?" Breathing slow. Trying to keep his cool. But he was on the brink.

"'Course not, mate." Gary grinned. "But I think Matt is."

Matt spread his hands, eyes wide. "I didn't say anything."

That glance over his shoulder was a mistake. Delaney turned his head to look at Matt and Gary had the cue out of his hand before he knew what happened.

Gary returned it to the holder on the wall. "We'll call it a foul. The game is yours. But let's end it here, shall we? Before things escalate."

"Afraid to finish the round, are you?"

"Let's just say, you are hard to beat."

"I don't like to leave things unfinished."

"I prefer a fair game." It made winning that much more satisfying.

Delaney started to reply, but saw something in Gary's eyes. Something that stopped him from taking that next step. "Have it your way." Delaney moved aside.

Gary took his jacket from the chair, shrugged it on. Finished the last of his drink, taking his time about it. "Since I forfeit"—he set the glass down—"I'll cover the tab."

"Cheers," George murmured, avoiding Delaney's eyes.

Gary got the waitress's attention and settled the bill. Not as bad as it might have been. Only a drink or two each. "Thanks for the game." It was an education.

"Maybe next time, you'll have the guts to play it through to the end."

George spoke up then. "Let it go, Ryan." Quiet voice.

Gary nodded at them, brushed past. Walked down that long, narrow room and out the door.

He stepped onto the street, into the quiet. The air cool now. Beat of the jazz still throbbing in his ears.

That went well. No broken nose, for one thing. And he had gotten an impression of Delaney's character. Delaney was a ruthless opponent. Intent on establishing rank. Ready to gain the upper hand through lies. Through violence. In love with his wife. Or, more likely, afraid of facing the wrath of a woman scorned. There was history there. That comment about fidelity, that had set Delaney off. Changed the tone of things.

Gary tossed his keys in the air as he strolled to his car. Chink of metal when they landed in his palm.

That short fuse, the simmer of violence, was worrying. Delaney had followed Kate. Kate lived in the same house as Wendell, had found his body. Delaney and Wendell worked in the same company, in the same building. There was a connection. He just didn't know what it was yet.

Gary started the engine. Adjusted the temperature, turned on the heat.

He'd keep an eye on Ryan Delaney. For Kate's sake.

Chapter Nineteen

"You can't make these kinds of promises when you know you're not going to keep them. I don't want to hear it, so don't bother."

At the sound of Elaina's voice, Kate slowed.

"I don't know what you want from me." Ian, this time. "Something's changed."

"Oh, and it's my fault?"

The door to the kitchen was open a crack. Light spilled into the entrance, onto the carpet. Thick enough to muffle her steps. Pretend she hadn't heard, that'd be the polite thing to do. Give them privacy. Kate draped her jacket over the banister and thought of thick slices of rye, cheddar, and chutney. Her stomach tightened. A light lunch was all she'd had, hours ago.

Politeness be damned. She sucked in a breath and pushed the door open.

Elaina was sitting on a chair at the table, one knee pulled up to her chest. Ian was leaning against the counter. A bottle of red on the table, two glasses down. Chianti. Neither looked happy. Beyond the glass doors, dusk softened the forms of apple trees, turning them to ghostly shadows. Isra was dozing on the windowsill, next to the dish detergent. The refrigerator hummed loudly.

"Hi," Kate said.

Elaina smiled briefly, closed-lipped, in greeting.

Ian nodded.

"Sorry to interrupt, but I'm starving." Kate went to the pantry. Basket from the shelf. Empty. None in the bread bin either.

"On the counter," Elaina said. "I bought a loaf of ciabatta. Help yourself."

On the board, cut side down. Lean and crusty. Kate's mouth watered. "You went grocery shopping? I'm shocked. Flabbergasted. In case you hadn't noticed," she said to Ian, "this isn't a normal occurrence."

"I figured as much." He carried his wine glass to the sink. Ran the tap and rinsed the dregs down the drain. "Seems Elaina was so eager to see me, she stopped by the grocery store after work. At one a.m."

Elaina tossed her hair over her shoulder. "There were things I needed to get. I swapped my shift today, didn't I?"

"Yes, and so far you've spent the whole evening arguing with me."

The serrated edge of the knife broke through the crust, scattering crumbs. Waft of warm yeasty scent. "Did you see the spices Ian brought Great-aunt Roselyn from India?" Kate sampled the bread as she went to the fridge. Heaven.

"India?" Elaina turned, arm draped over the back of the seat. "When were you in India?"

Ian shrugged. "A while ago. I told you about it." Voice clipped and bordering on the limits of patience.

Kate selected the cheese and tried to pretend she wasn't listening.

"Maybe it was in one of your articles. You seem to get confused between what you write in the occasional email to me and what you write to your editor. One-line texts don't count."

"I'm sorry. I do occasionally forget where I've written what, but I like to think you might actually read my articles. Most of them are online. It doesn't even involve a trip to the news stand, if that takes too much effort."

"I have other things to do besides reading about your adventures, Ian."

Onion chutney? The jar behind the butter. Kate reached for it.

"There are things I don't tell you either." Elaina shrugged. "Someone died in this house. Kate found his body."

"What are you talking about? Someone died?" Ian looked from one to the other.

"My laptop today, too." Time to change the subject. Kate layered hunks of cheese with chutney.

"Mr. Wendell died." Elaina turned to Kate. "In fact, why don't you just use his laptop? It's there and he's not. Mrs. Marsh spoke to the lawyer and there is no will, and there's no contact information for next of kin. Since we don't have anyone to give his personal effects to, you could use the computer."

Jeremy had said it could take him a few days before he had time to come by the store. "Wouldn't it be password protected?"

"Could be a guest account you could access." Elaina poured more wine into her glass.

"It's gruesome, but not a bad idea." It might be a quick fix. Something she could use in the meantime. Internet orders needed to be taken care of and shipped. "Maybe we'll find an address or a phone number for a relative saved under his contacts. If we can get in, that is."

"I think I missed something." Ian rested his hands on the counter behind him and looked at them. "Who died?"

"The man who rented the room in the basement. Kate found him on the stairs. Heart attack," Elaina summed up.

Ian crossed his arms over his chest and whistled low between his teeth. "That must have been a shock."

"It wasn't what I'd call a highlight." Kate saw again the body on the stairs. The eyes torn wide, the emptiness behind them. She took a bite of the sandwich. The cheddar lodged in her throat, the caramelized onion sharper than she remembered. She swallowed hard.

"You should have told me." Ian stared at Elaina, like he was trying to read her mind.

"If I'd had your address, I might have."

Kate picked up her plate. "I'm going to talk to Great-aunt Roselyn about the laptop. See what she thinks. Thanks for the idea, Elaina."

"I saw Mrs. Marsh this afternoon at some point. She went upstairs, said she had a headache."

"I'll see how she's doing then." On the windowsill, Isra blinked and yawned, giving a glimpse of sharp teeth, a pink tongue.

Candle flickering on the side table at the top of the landing. No light on the stairs. Kate took several big bites of the sandwich on her way up. Left the plate with the rest on the table, next to the tea light. Pretty glass holder. Kate touched the rim. The wick was nearly burned down and safe enough. Scent of blossoms in the air, faint but there.

The door was open. Kate stepped closer. The standing lamp was on in one corner of the room. Great-aunt Roselyn was sitting at the vanity table. Something flashed in her hand. A silver-backed brush, gliding through her hair in slow strokes. Longer than Kate remembered and streaked with white. Youthful, but for the color. The reflection in the mirror seemed paler. No touch of pink on the lips. A nightgown, the color of cream, tied high at the neck. Bare arms, bones sharp beneath the skin.

Kate knocked lightly against the doorframe. Great-aunt Roselyn whirled around. The hand resting on her lap darted to cover something on the table. "Oh, it's you, Kate."

To the left, the curtains billowed, swelling. "The window's open. It's so cold in here." Like ice.

"Is it?"

"I'll close it, shall I?" Kate was already walking across the room. The fabric was sheer. Hardly enough to block the draft. She pushed the folds aside and latched the window.

"Where did all these wrinkles come from?" The meditative voice was quiet, had Kate turning. The familiar intonation a signal, and a warning. This was not the time to mention the laptop.

She took the brush from her great-aunt and began to softly run it through the woman's hair. Fine, like silk, it clung to the bristles. Natural boar to bring out the luster.

Eyes on her reflection, Great-aunt Roselyn said, "I remember when Frank and I went to one of his business parties. I waited in a corner of the room while he talked to this important person and that one, sipping at pink champagne. And looking at all those women with their diamonds"—a hand touched an invisible brooch at her throat— "and their swept-up hair." She pressed her lips together, remembering. "Suddenly, Frank slipped his hand in mine and whispered in my ear." Her eyes looked into the mirror, into the past. "'You are the most beautiful woman in this entire room.'"

"That's a wonderful story." Soft, so as not to break the spell.

"He could be charming." Rueful curve to the lips.

"Do you miss him very much?"

Downstairs, the grandfather clock struck the hour. The sound rich and deep and sudden. Roselyn jumped. The brush in Kate's hand jolted, snagged. The single square-cut diamond glinted as Roselyn rubbed gaunt fingers across her features. On the table, where her hand had been, was an envelope.

Kate set the brush down, curious. "A recent letter? It's still sealed."

Roselyn moved to reclaim it, clutching too hard, mangling the fragile paper. "I might not know what they whisper, but I can hear them." Sharp hiss. Anger flaring. "The murmur of their voices like the wings of a humming bird at the feeder. Incessant. Thrumming."

"Oh, Roselyn." Kate knelt next to the chair. She knew what they said. The eternal wife, losing her mind.

Fingers softened, unfurled on a sigh. "No, it isn't recent. Frank wrote it. Before he—" She opened the top drawer of the vanity, blue felt lining within, slid the envelope inside. Locked it with a small key. "I could never—I keep it, in case I have the courage to open it."

"You've never read it? Don't you want to know

what he wrote?"

"What he might have said, the beautiful words and phrases that could be. They're so much more. Once opened, all that will be gone." She replaced the key on a chain around her neck. Wedding band shining. She selected a wire pin, u-shaped, from the dish and secured her hair, twisting it into a tight knot. She touched Kate's cheek with cool fingers. "Don't worry, dear. Though it's sweet of you to do so."

The surface beneath the paint, Kate thought. Chipped perfection. How long could it last?

Chapter Twenty

Sunday morning. Gary was standing outside the bookstore. The sun was out, chasing away the chill that had crept in last night, warming his back. A few questions, that's all. Enough to fill in the blanks, some of them, at least. If anyone had the answers, it was Kate. Gary could see her inside, talking to two boys. An earnest conversation, by the looks of it.

Gary pushed the door open. Only a single cylinder deadbolt with a one-inch throw to lock it. Too simple. Brass handle polished to a gleam. Heads turned in his direction. Startled expression from Kate. She was surprised to see him. "I hope I'm not interrupting." The room smelled of books, and that same citrus scent he'd noticed standing next to her in the café.

Kate smiled. "Please do. I seem to be getting the third degree."

One of the boys was holding a small, spiral-bound notebook and a ballpoint pen. "We're carrying out an investigation." The boy looked up at Gary from beneath the brim of his baseball cap. The cap was too large and slipped down over his eyes. Emblem of the local police force on the front of it.

"An investigation? Into what?" Knickknacks above the shelves. An inkwell and quill. A small ceramic vase, flowers painted on it. An old mantel clock, hands stopped at quarter to twelve. By the cash, a dish of gold-wrapped chocolate coins. And a laptop. Gary zeroed in on that. He'd seen it before. What the hell was Wendell's laptop doing in Kate's bookstore?

"A murder."

A jolt beneath the skin. A thousand volts or more. The kid had a determined set to the chin and sharp eyes, beneath that cap. Gary would bet he didn't miss much. "A murder?"

"It's pretty gruesome."

His friend nodded.

"The body was found beneath the tire swing yesterday afternoon. Throat slit."

"The victim," Kate clarified, "was Penelope's garden gnome." Amusement in her eyes, but not a trace of a smile in her voice. She was good. "They think I did it, because the crime required a certain amount of imagination."

Penelope's garden gnome. Gary thought of the indent he'd noticed in the grass. Something stolen, she'd said. "I see." Gary took his cue from Kate, kept his voice serious.

"Sleepy was stolen and ransomed," Kate told him. "Missing for a week. Tim and Will finally found him with their divining stick, but it was too late. The gnome was murdered. And now, he's sleeping the big sleep."

"I told Grandma not to pay the ransom," the boy said, with the hardboiled tone of a weary detective. "I didn't think it would end like this. I didn't think the perp had it in him. Or her."

"Perp?" Gary asked.

Kate smiled. "Tim's father is a cop."

"That explains a lot. Is Kate a suspect?"

"We're not sure yet," the boy's friend replied.

"I don't want to obstruct official business. I'll wait until you're done." Take a look around. "If you need a lawyer, Kate, let me know. I'll make a call for you."

"You have the right to remain silent," Tim informed Kate, "but it looks fishy."

"I wouldn't want to look fishy." Kate thought it over. "I'll cooperate for now, see where the questions lead."

"Very wise." Gary nodded.

The boys consulted their notebook. Kate shot Gary a grin over their heads.

"Go easy on her, boys." Historical fiction. Far enough to give them space, but close enough for him to listen, and watch. Gary strolled over and studied the shelves. Rows of books, neat, but not perfect. Tempting customers to touch them, take one down. He skimmed the titles.

"The perpetrator"—the boy's friend stumbled a little over the word—"left a smear of blood from the mailbox to the swing to make it look like the gnome dragged himself toward the house."

"Blood?" Kate paled.

"Made from golden syrup. The syrup makes the blood nice and thick, but the ants were swarming. It was a mess." The boys looked at each other and grinned, delighted.

"I'm sure it was."

Lots of patience there, Gary thought.

Pen poised, the boy squinted at Kate. "Where were you between four and five p.m. yesterday?"

"One question first." Kate held up a hand. "This doesn't have anything to do with what that man said the other day, does it?"

"Who?"

"The—" She tugged a hand through her hair. "The man who suggested killing someone if you want to find a corpse. You didn't off Sleepy so that you'd have something to investigate, did you?"

"You have a dark mind, Kate." Tim shook his head sadly.

Gary stifled a laugh, turned it into a cough.

"Is that a no?"

Level gaze that cut to the quick. Tell a lie and she'd see straight through it, make you wish you'd never told it in the first place. Gary felt sorry for the boys. For their sake, he hoped they were telling the truth.

"Look here, Kate." Tim flipped back a page in his notebook, and stood hip-shot. "We're placing the time of death between four and five. Michelle was playing in the backyard with the babysitter until Mum got home. Mum picked up Sarah from school. Sisters, they're a hassle and a half. When Mum and Sarah got home, there was nothing there. No gnome."

The ornament had been stolen from Penelope's property and returned to Tim's yard. Kate was right to be suspicious.

"When Mum and Sarah got home, everyone went inside to have milk and cookies in the kitchen. Oatmeal raisin. The backyard was unwatched from four o'clock on."

The kid was good.

"And where were you?" Kate studied him.

"I went with Will straight to Grandma's house after school and was there until four forty-five. We had chocolate cake. Beats out oatmeal cookies hands down every time."

"Definitely," Will agreed.

"We walked back to my house together afterward. It took the usual ten minutes." Tim spread his hands. "Since the crime was discovered at five o'clock, it couldn't have been me. Or Will."

Kate leaned back against the counter. "Any theories?"

"We don't like to talk about an open case."

"Of course."

"So, where were you?"

"At the store."

Will studied Kate suspiciously. "Did anyone see you?"

"Mrs. Sulley came in, along with a handful of other customers."

Tongue caught between his teeth, Tim made a careful note. "Okay. We'll check up on that. Don't leave town. We may need to ask you some more questions."

"I was thinking of taking a holiday, but—" Tim shot a glance at Will. "I'm joking. I'll be here."

Tim flipped the notebook shut. "We should move on. Long list."

"Chocolate for the road?" Kate held out the dish.

They each selected one solemnly. "Thank you." They left the store, hands tucked into their pockets in identical poses. Looking like the weight of the world was on their shoulders. The door slammed shut behind them.

"You survived the interrogation." Gary returned the volume he'd been thumbing through to the shelf.

"I have a feeling it was just the first of many."

"You may need that lawyer after all. Wait until they uncover your lock picking skills."

"I hadn't thought of that." A pause. "How's the glass jaw?"

He grinned. "Much better."

Kate reached up and touched his jaw. The move caught him off guard. Sent a current through him, a slow sizzle this time that didn't let up. "Looks better."

He watched her lips curve and felt a slow tug low in his belly. "So tell me"—he stepped back, put distance between them—"what did you find behind that locked door? A guest room, covered in cobwebs, neglected for years?"

"A secret drawer." Same delight in her voice as was in the boys' when they were talking about murder. "And a disappearing necklace."

No time to brace for the shock. He went still. She'd seen the necklace. And then he took it. Shit. "Sounds like something in a book."

"It does, doesn't it?"

Gary propped a shoulder against the bookshelf, watched her carefully. What the hell was that about a secret drawer? He hadn't seen anything. "Was the necklace in the secret drawer?" Kept his voice relaxed, light.

"No, the necklace was in a tin of travel sweets."

"Then what was in the drawer?" Careful, now. Keep it easy. Like it doesn't matter one way or another.

"An MP3 player."

"That's an odd thing to hide." He'd missed it. Gone back and missed it anyway.

"The audio was a recording of a man and a woman having sex."

Now why would Wendell have something like that? It didn't jibe. "And that was in a secret drawer in the guest room? Who did your great-aunt invite to stay?"

"He wasn't a guest, he was a tenant. Mr. Wendell rented the room from her. Then he died."

And there it was. The in he'd been waiting for. "He died?" Gary raised a brow. "Are you sure you're not making this up?"

"I found the body."

"That must have been a shock. Where did you find him?"

"On the basement stairs."

He hadn't gotten far then. Hadn't taken long to die. "How did it happen?"

"He had a heart attack."

Sadness there, sincere. And wasted on Wendell. Gary knew he was on the edge of safe ground. Like one of the characters in her books, he was almost out of questions. One more though, one more couldn't hurt. "What happened to the necklace?"

"I don't know. I saw it, held it in my hand." She looked thoughtful. "The next day, it was gone. It's a mystery."

A mystery he hoped Kate wouldn't solve. Gary had some of the answers he wanted. He could buy a book now and leave. Pretend that's why he'd come. Stay away from her after that. But then, there was still Delaney. And Wendell's laptop on her counter. Loose ends. "I said I'd ask you to have dinner with me again, Kate."

Quick look up at him. "You did say that."

"How about tomorrow?" His palms were damp.

Heart slamming in his chest. Jesus Christ, he was nervous. Gary dug his hands in his pockets.

"Pick me up at seven?" Kate turned, reached over the laptop for a yellow post-it note. Wrote down the address he already knew and handed it to him.

211 Holly Road. "I'll be there."

Chapter Twenty-One

There were gaps. Books leaning here and there, spaces in between. Kate stood next to the bargain bin on the sidewalk, arms full of paperbacks, some more worn than others. Tried not to think about what she'd wear for dinner tomorrow. She'd said yes. Kate shook her head at herself.

Fast beat of footsteps from the right, coming closer, speeding over the ground. She glanced over, toward the sound, registered gangly limbs.

"Watch out!" Someone was running toward her, full tilt, a blur of motion.

There was no time to move. Nowhere to move to. Cars on the road, the bin beside her. Kate braced herself and waited for the impact.

Sneakers skidded, tripped over the pavement. Came to a stop. A laptop bag swung against her leg, one corner rapping against her knee. "I almost killed you," Jeremy gasped. Tufts of hair, quivering from the motion, added to his shocked expression. The last time she had seen him, he'd been kneeling beside Mr. Wendell's dead body. She could only hope he was as good at fixing computers as Dr. Garreth said he was.

"You're standing on my toe."

"Sorry." He moved back. "Running a hundred and fifty minutes a week can lower the risk of heart disease, reduce blood pressure and strengthen your bones."

Jeremy caught his breath.

He was heavier than he looked. Kate wriggled her toes in her shoe. Everything still worked. "Check my blood pressure. You'll find it's off the charts."

"Maybe you should take up jogging."

"I thought you'd be by later. I really hope you're here to look at my computer."

"That's the plan." He stretched his arms out and cracked his fingers. "Where's the patient?"

"Inside. Does Dr. Garreth let you wear that to work?" Kate gestured at the slogan on his jumper. *It's Only A Flesh Wound*. Red letters on black fabric.

"What?" Jeremy looked down at his chest. "Oh, that. Today's Sunday." He shrugged.

"Right. Do you think you could take a look at another laptop for me while you're at it?" Kate held the door open for him. "The laptop's…well, daunting. Do you think you could set it up for me to use? Or access the contacts? Only problem is, there's bound to be a login password."

"And you don't know what it is?"

"No," Kate admitted.

"That might be a problem. Depends what kind of security we're talking about, but I could take a look. Nothing's impossible." He dropped his backpack on the floor, and a binder popped through the open zipper. His laptop bag was lowered more carefully to the ground.

"Thanks for coming by. I really appreciate it."

"I live for this stuff." His eyes slid toward her computer, checking out the model the way other men would look at women. By the way his features fell, she assumed hers didn't impress.

Kate pulled out her desk chair, brushed a few bread

crumbs off it. Offered it to him. "The seat of honor is all yours."

Jeremy took a pair of silver-rimmed glasses from his pocket and slipped them onto his nose. They gave him a more studious appearance, balancing out the lightning-bolt effect of his hair.

"Would you like something to drink?"

"Nah. I'm sorted." Jeremy yanked a one-and-a-half liter bottle of cola out of his backpack and set it down next to him. "Do you mind?"

"So long as you don't spill it, no." Kate moved her empty tea cup, making space for him. Beneath the table, his knee jiggled up and down as he reached for the keyboard. There was a stain in the denim, about a quarter inch in diameter, uneven edges. A few more droplets trailing down the leg, becoming smaller. "That isn't what I think it is, is it?"

"Hmm?" Eyes on the monitor, the error message.

"The marks on your jeans. Please tell me it's paint."

Jeremy looked down. "No, that'd be blood. Damn. Protein's a bitch to get out of fabric."

Kate stared at the spots darkening his jeans.

"Good news and bad news, Kate." Jimmy stated, turning from the screen.

"A verdict?" Kate blinked. "Already?" She thought he'd have to take the machine apart.

"Yeah, piece of cake. Your hard drive's damaged."

"Can you fix it?"

"No. After a certain number of read-writes, the head wears out."

Kate's heart sank. "I'm hoping that was the bad news."

"Don't worry, it is. The good news is that all you have to do is buy a new one and replace it." Jimmy shut the computer down. He pulled out his own laptop, opened the internet browser. His fingers flew over the keys. "I suggest you pick from one of these." He angled the screen so she could see. The price was well within her range. Lower than she thought, actually. "You don't need anything high-capacity, so these are fine. Order now, and the hard drive could arrive in three or four days."

"I'll pay you for your time, too." It sounded too easy. There had to be a catch. "What does replacing a hard drive involve?"

"Swapping out the hard drive is a five-minute job. Installing it can take a couple of hours. Now let's take a look at that laptop."

"I was hoping I could use the laptop in the meantime, until my computer works again. Would I be able to use the internet on the laptop, maybe even access saved contacts?"

"If I can get into it, yeah."

Kate lifted the laptop and passed it to him. Jeremy's eyes widened. "This is some equipment, Kate," he murmured. "Not new, mind."

"Should I leave you two alone?" Kate laughed.

"Would you?" He turned the laptop on.

She wasn't sure if he was serious or not. "No."

"Too bad." He took one look at the screen, nodded, and scrounged through his bag. "I have a copy of Con-Boot burned onto a CD. You boot up from the CD, and get into the windows password screen. It bypasses the authentication process." Jeremy inserted the disc and moved back. "Here, take a look."

Kate looked over Jeremy's shoulder. "But it's still asking me for a password."

"With the CD, all you have to do is press Enter to bypass it, no password needed." He hit the key. "And hey, presto, you're in. The CD circumvents the login password, but you won't be able to access any protected documents."

"I was expecting columns of green figures, hours of slave-labor and furious typing. It's slightly unsettling that this was so easy. Makes you consider going back to lock and chain."

Jeremy shrugged. "You've got to know what to do. The only thing is, you're going to have to keep using the CD to get in. You can't set up your own password because we don't know the old one to change it. Just leave it in the CD drive and you'll be fine."

Kate studied the screen. Everything looked vaguely similar to her own, only sleeker. The desktop wallpaper was of stars, night sky, black trees. Depths that seemed to move, even though they weren't. "I can access the files, too?" Kate hoped she hadn't just made Jeremy accessory to a crime. Cleaning Wendell's room was one thing. Going through his laptop another. They still hadn't found a relative to contact. Maybe there'd be something, a phone number, a name, saved on the laptop that would help.

"You should be able to."

Kate clicked the address book icon. Scrolled. It was empty. There were no contacts. Not so unusual. Some people chose to save addresses in their e-mail accounts. She opened Windows Explorer. Kate double-clicked on a document titled 'Notes.'

Password protected. It looked like death wasn't

going to stop Mr. Wendell from keeping his secrets. "Can I use the CD to get around this password, too?"

"Con-Boot only allows you to access the system or create a new 'root' account. It won't work with this. But you can access the internet, sort your online orders, create new documents."

"You're a life saver."

Jeremy rammed the plastic soda bottle, now a third less full, into his over-full bag. "A computer god?" He grinned as he hefted the bag. The contents rattled mysteriously.

"Let's not get carried away."

"Let me know when the hard drive arrives and I'll try to come by after work to install it. And, if you don't have time, it would be okay if your friend was here. The woman with the dark hair. From the house." His ears were turning red.

"Elaina? I'm sure I'll be here."

"Right." He backed toward the door. "I just meant, if she's around." He trailed off. "Right," he said again. "Bye then." And left.

Poor Jeremy. Elaina always made an impression.

Kate turned to the laptop. Stars blazing on the screen. She pulled up the web browser, checked her emails. Took note of new orders, typed up the invoices she'd written by hand.

The cursor blinked. Kate moved it back to the folders, clicking through the files. Most were .jpeg files. All required passwords.

Suddenly an image appeared on the screen. The picture was grainy and dark as though taken at night from a distance. Odd tilt to it. The view seemed to be through the first-floor window of a building. A house?

Rows of books visible through one of the windows. Not a house. The architecture was too elegant, too expensive. A library? A door showed at the edge of the picture, marble columns. One of the windows was shielded by curtains, but the fabric wasn't drawn closed, not completely. The space between yielded a glimpse into the room within. And the face of a girl. She was looking out from behind the glass, half-turned and caught by surprise, as though she had caught a glimpse of the photographer positioned outside.

Nymphet. The word leapt into Kate's mind. Lashes thick and long and dark. Irises almost black, though that could have been caused by a trick of the light. Pale blue blouse, buttoned to the neck. Lips tinted red, conveying a sensuousness far beyond her age. Features like that of a porcelain doll. A girl-child. But it was the expression in her eyes that made Kate think of Lolita. That girl with her knowing gaze, caught from that voyeuristic angle, trapped behind glass. Like an object of obsession. It was unsettling.

Kate shuddered. According to the details on the file, the image was created over a year ago. Who was she? And why was there a photograph of her saved on the laptop?

Chapter Twenty-Two

"Mr. Harris is here to see you."

Gary glanced up from the blueprint. Elspeth was standing in the doorway to his office. "Excuse me?"

"Mr. Harris is here. He's early." Elspeth pursed her lips with disapproval.

It was a common name. It could be anyone. Gary realized he was on his feet and Elspeth was looking at him. "Who arranged the meeting?" Early implied he had an appointment.

"Percival. He wanted to take it himself."

"He isn't here." It had to be Adriana's father. Of course, Percival would call him in. Ask questions, take the direct approach. Gary should have seen it coming. Maybe it was better Perce wasn't here.

"The meeting was supposed to be tomorrow."

"Never mind. I have time. Show him in." Gary looked around the room. This was his office, his territory. Soundproofed. The situation could be controlled. "And bring us coffee, Elspeth. Not herbal tea. Coffee." It came out sounding shorter than he'd intended.

"I'll be right back." Elspeth picked up the nearly full cup of chamomile tea sitting on his desk, cold by now, and frowned. But she had the sense not to comment as she took the cup away with her.

Sun streaming through the windows. Gary's

thoughts raced. Face Harris from behind the desk? It would look like he was on the defensive. They'd sit at the conference table. Gary chose the chair facing the door. Footsteps coming down the hall. The same long decisive steps, bordering on impatience. Gary sat, leaned forward, and rested his elbows on the table.

Oliver Harris walked in. It was like being wrenched into the past. Adriana's father hadn't changed. Harris still had a presence that demanded respect. The same ease, same control. Gary stood, held out his hand.

Harris ignored it. Fair enough. Harris looked around the room, one long hard glance, longer at the desk. At the solid carved oak, the embossed leather insert. The carpet. The painting on the wall. Then he turned to Gary, taking in his suit, the watch, gold and steel.

"What can I do for you?" Gary gestured to the seat across from him.

Harris remained standing. So Gary stayed on his feet. Their eyes met and the force of the anger in them took Gary aback. "You've done well for yourself."

Harris was thinner. Shadows beneath his eyes. More lines. Gray at the temples. Two years had left a mark. "We've been lucky." Careful.

"Lucky, yes. I'd say you have been. So far." Harris picked up a glass paperweight, turning it over in his hand, watching the play of light. Below the surface, surrounded by pearled air pockets, blackberries were suspended within. "You are aware that I advised Graylenn to cancel their contract with you."

"You were also responsible for the loss of the Berkely account, McConeray Systems, to name a few, and I'm sure many more as well."

"Ah, you drew the connection." A smile now, pulling at the corner of his mouth.

Gary kept his tone neutral. "But my colleague arranged this meeting."

"A request from you, I assume." Fingers tightening on glass. "Let someone else take care of your problem. Such a weak response."

Gary checked his temper. Smiled instead. "It was his own initiative."

The glass sphere tilted, reflections fragmenting. Blackberries remaining frozen, static. The set of Harris's chin was like Adriana's when she got the upper hand. "Isn't Graylenn why I'm here?"

"I imagine that is why he called you, yes."

"To ask me to stop?"

"To ask you why."

That had his attention. "He doesn't know?" Amusement flickered.

No lies. Gary owed Adriana that. "He thinks Adriana's bodyguard works for Fenris Securities. He believes that's why you're turning away our clients." Draft on the back of his neck again. The muscles were starting to cramp.

The laugh shook Harris's shoulders. A hard sound. "And that makes it easier, doesn't it? No awkward questions. No guilt. No justifications." That last word ground out between his teeth.

"I'm sorry." Gary rested his hands on the table. "If I could turn back time, I would."

The paperweight fell to the floor, as Harris brought his fist down on the table with a crack. "Sorry is not good enough!" The surface of the table reverberated beneath Gary's palms. The paperweight rolled over the carpet, flashing with each rotation, until it settled against the bookcase. "You told me you'd find the person who killed her. But he's standing right in front of me. She's dead, because of you." Finger trembling as he pointed. "You made a mistake. You failed. And yet, here you are." Harris spread his arms wide, taking in the space around them. "Living your life. Successful. Well off."

"I would have done anything for her."

"You should have taken the bullet."

Yes, he should have. "What do you want?"

"I want you to suffer." Harris leaned closer, tobacco on his breath, voice lowered to barely more than a whisper, "I want you to never forget."

"Trust me, I haven't."

The door opened and Elspeth entered, carrying a tray. "Coffee, as requested." Reproach in her voice. She moved between them, oblivious to the tension, setting out cups, saucers, spoons, sugar.

"I won't be staying." Harris straightened, adjusted his jacket. "You can continue telling lies, Fenris. But it's going to get harder. You can be sure of that." He selected a cookie off the plate, sugar coating his fingertips. Bit into it as he strode out of the office, leaving a trail of crumbs in his wake.

Elspeth set down the pot of coffee she'd been about to pour. "What was that about?"

Gary waited until he was sure Harris was gone before answering. "The past, Elspeth. It was about the past."

Chapter Twenty-Three

He was ten minutes late. Kate dabbed perfume on her throat and wrists, and tried to ignore the jittery feeling in her stomach. She was going on a date. Small talk, good food, wine. And she liked him. So why was her heart pounding? Kate pressed a hand to her side and took a deep breath. It didn't help.

The sound of an interweaving melody drifted down from the room above. A deep, swelling vibrato-filled tone of a solo violin. Bach, one of Great-aunt Roselyn's favorites.

Elaina's voice, raised in anger, came from somewhere deeper in the house. "Do you have to keep saying it?"

"That's what I am." Taut control strained Ian's voice.

"Just dropping by like always. Here now, gone tomorrow. I'm tired of it. I'd rather have you than some postcard."

Kate set the bottle down, was tempted to close the door. But then she might not hear the doorbell.

"Then ask me to stay!" It sounded like a challenge. The argument was getting louder.

"You wouldn't stay, even if I asked." Elaina's voice carried through the walls. A timer beeped. What were they cooking again? Some kind of pasta.

"Do you want me to stop travelling? To stay here,

with you?"

"You know that wouldn't work. You wouldn't be satisfied. It wouldn't be enough."

Where was her compact mirror? Ah, there, glint of silver, pushed to the edge of the dresser. Kate slid it into her purse, checked for her lip balm in the pocket. A book. She'd left the fictional detective shaking raindrops from his hat. Kate hesitated, then slid the book into her purse. There was room. Right. She was ready now.

"What about you? Could you survive being stuck with one guy for once? I might hold you back."

A silence followed. "That was low."

Sound of a chair scraping back. "You're right. I'm sorry." A pause. "Then come with me."

"Ian…"

Kate picked up her purse, started down the hall, trying to make her steps heavy and loud. Her heels clicked across the floor.

"Think about the adventure. God, it's incredible the things you can see, discover." Excitement throbbed in Ian's voice. Kate could picture him gesturing as he described, tearing down the kitchen walls with his words, revealing exotic scenes, color, sound. "The smells of bazaars. Browsing through dried fruit, kites, and fireworks. The rhythm of foreign voices. The surprise of encountering old words in new places. The way other climates feel on your skin, the magic in other religions, other beliefs. The aroma of alien flowers beneath your feet when you walk across a deserted hill. Imagine the scenes you could paint. Something new everywhere you turn."

"That isn't me, Ian."

"So what are we left with?" Ian asked quietly.

"You're the only man I've ever met who I've always wanted to say yes to."

"Isn't that enough?"

"It should be, but we both know it isn't."

Kate stepped past the kitchen door. They spun and glared at her. Elaina's eyes shone unnaturally bright. "I'm about to leave," Kate said.

Elaina pushed both hands through her mass of hair. "Let me know what the restaurant's like." She turned to the stove, reached for a wooden spoon, and stirred the simmering contents of the pot. The scent of tomato and basil intensified, steam rising.

Ian avoided Kate's eyes. He cleared his throat. Pinched the bridge of his nose with thumb and finger. Then he let out a breath and smiled at her. "Have a good time."

Kate wondered how long it would be before Ian grabbed his duffel bag and walked out the door. "Thanks."

Elaina tasted the sauce. She frowned. "I don't know. It's missing something."

"Probably salt," Ian said dryly.

If looks could kill, Ian would be a dead man. "Here, Kate, what do you think?"

The sauce bubbled invitingly. Avoiding the bay leaf, Kate dipped a spoon beneath the surface, lifted it to her mouth. Heat, punch of chili powder, sweetness of onion and tomatoes, rich undertone of red wine. "Oregano, maybe?"

"That's what I thought. You've got sauce on your top now, by the way."

Sure enough, there was a smattering of drops on

her blouse, dark against the purple silk. "Oh, blast!" Paper towel. Water ran over her fingers as she held a piece under the tap, dabbed at the stains with it.

Elaina selected a jar from the spice rack, looked over. "I think you're making it worse."

The stains, small before, were now one large, damp spot. Impossible to miss. Wet silk cold against her skin.

The doorbell chimed.

"He's here." Ian was grinning. "Want me to get it? Give you time to deal with that?"

"I'll do it." Kate blotted at the silk one more time, as she walked through the entrance. Took a breath, tried to ignore the flush heating her cheeks, and opened the door.

Gary was looking the other way. Toward the trees and the setting sun, orange sky above the branches, then clouds. There were bruises beneath his eyes. Pale line of that old scar beneath a day's worth of stubble. A muscle jumped in his jaw. He looked exhausted, Kate thought. He turned to her and smiled. "Hi. Sorry I'm late."

Kate tugged the fabric away from her skin. "Actually, I'm not ready yet. The kitchen's straight through there." Kate turned to point out the way, and saw Elaina leaning against the doorframe, watching with interest.

Spotted, Elaina wriggled her fingers at them. "You must be Gary."

For one moment, Gary seemed to hesitate. Then he stepped into the house. "Yes, I am." Music carried down the stairs, a violin throbbing on the lowest string, rising with an upward inflection. Building note upon note.

"This is Elaina," Kate explained. "She lives here, too. And the man carrying plates to the table behind her is Ian, her boyfriend. Have a seat. I won't be long."

Gary looked amused. "Sure. Take your time."

"Come in. We won't bite." Elaina ushered Gary into the kitchen ahead of her. She sent one more glance to Kate, eyebrows raised. Pressed a hand to her heart and pretended to swoon against the doorframe.

Kate stifled a laugh as she hurried down the hall. Stripped off the blouse in her room. What could she wear instead? The red jumper. Not as classy as the blouse, but it would have to do. Kate tugged it over her head. Quick glance in the mirror. Black jeans, high heels. At least it was comfy.

Laughter from the kitchen. Kate followed the sound.

Gary was sitting on one of the chairs with Isra on his lap. The cat was sprawled on her back, shameless as a kitten, pawing at a button on his shirt. Warmth of the stove filled the room. One plate pushed aside to make space for a large book, open on the table in front of Gary. Black cover, unlined sheets, no text. Streak of green along the edge. Kate caught the thick mark of charcoal as Gary turned pages, bold sweep of pastel. Elaina's sketchbook.

"He says," Ian leaned across the table, hands gesturing, "'it's the forks, I tell you.' Only I thought he said something entirely different. Next thing I know, the plane is boarding, and guess who's sitting in the seat next to mine." Expression of horror on his face. More laughter.

Gary glanced up, eyes catching hers. "You look pretty."

The sudden skip to her heart caught Kate off guard. "Thanks." She looked over Gary's shoulder at the book. The paper was heavy, textured.

"These are good." Gary turned the page. "Do you sell?"

"Some. Mostly paintings." Elaina shrugged. "Not enough."

"There's not enough that you part with," Ian cut in. "She gets attached to her work."

Isra shifted, turned, suddenly sat upright and alert, paws tense. Gary stroked a hand down her back, without taking his eyes off the sketch.

The image was laden with details. The pub from the point of view of the bartender, done in blue ballpoint pen. Kate could see the ornamentation on the wood paneling, the photographs on the back wall, the faint smears on the surface of the bar. Two men leaning against the counter, staring into their drinks, into the distance. The booths were full.

Kate almost missed him.

In the left-hand corner of the sketch at a small table was Mr. Wendell. Elaina had captured the bleary expression, the languorous slouch, the surprisingly observant gaze. A dark stain swelled the pen lines. "What's that? Blood?"

Gary looked up. "It doesn't look like blood to me." Easy curve to his mouth, but for one second, Kate thought she saw something else, something cold and hard beneath that relaxed expression. Something that said danger.

"Where?" Ian leaned closer. "That? My guess is it's the remains of a sultry Bordeaux with a velvet finish."

"You'd be right about that," Elaina said.

Ian tapped the sketch with one finger. "Who's that?"

Elaina moved closer to get a better look. Gary pushed his chair back, gave her space.

"Derek Wendell. Why?"

Ian took the book, held it beneath the light. The lines seemed to leap from the page, dark against cream. Red smear fading to brown, looking less and less like wine. "He's the spitting image of someone I ran into in Dublin. His hair was longer and he wore glasses. He had this soft, nasal voice that made you want to punch him. He was bland and blended into the crowd, but gave you the impression of being a total eejit. 'Course, then you felt like an ass for thinking it."

Elaina laughed. "That sounds like Wendell."

"He'd been pumping a friend of mine for information. Ferreting but real polite like, so you wouldn't even notice what he was up to until he got what he wanted."

"What happened?" Gary asked. Isra leapt to the floor, landing with a soft pad of feet.

Ian shrugged. "One day, he disappeared."

"Let me guess," Kate said, "without a clue?" She was getting used to Ian's stories, his flair for drama.

"Yeah. Thing is, this guy I knew? His name was Darren Thatcher."

"Well, then." Elaina went to the stove, took the pot off the heat. "It couldn't have been him, right? It's just a sketch, Ian." Irritation in her voice, seeping through again.

"You're probably right." Ian shrugged, backed down, as though he saw another argument coming and wanted to avoid it.

Gary leaned back in his chair. "Isn't everyone supposed to have a double somewhere in the world? Maybe Darren Thatcher was his."

Seeing Elaina drain the pasta in the sink reminded Kate that she was hungry and it could be a long time yet before she got food. "We should probably get going, Gary."

"Right." He stood. "It was nice meeting both of you."

"Likewise." Behind Gary's back, Elaina shot Kate a wink and a wicked grin.

Kate led the way to the door. Gary helped her into her coat, and she felt his fingers brush the nape of her neck, warm against her skin.

****

That sketch—it caught him off guard.

From their table, Gary had a clear view of the rest of the room. Senses on overdrive, picking up the details. White tablecloths, crisp fold lines. Her skin like cream against the red top. Carafes set dead center, lemon slices floating in water. Waiters carrying on a conversation in French as they moved between tables. He knew it was leftover adrenaline, spiking his blood. Making it hard to concentrate. "Your bookstore could use a better lock."

"What's wrong with the one I have?"

"For one thing, it won't take a pick hook and screw driver to get past it."

"So far, no one has tried." Kate took another bite of her coq au vin, and closed her eyes on a hum of pleasure. "Mmm, this is incredible."

He'd have to thank Percival for giving him the

name of the restaurant. "I'm glad you like it."

"Is that why you started Fenris Securities?" Kate asked. "To keep people safe?"

"People are hard to protect." Only hours ago, he told Adriana's father he'd never forget. Now he was sitting across the table from Kate, watching candlelight flicker across her face. Aroma of veal, shallots and parsley rising from the *blanquette de veau* on his plate. "Tell people to take precautions, they start to feel trapped, do the opposite." Go to a museum instead, to look at a cabinet. "Our focus is on property, things."

"Like my bookstore." Kate smiled. "I thought this was a date, not a sales pitch."

"Sorry, an old habit." He forced himself to relax.

"Looking for weaknesses?" Kate teased. She reached for a piece of bread, broke it in half.

Gary couldn't help smiling back. "Yes."

"What did you do before Fenris Securities?"

"This and that." Give a little, hold more back. Don't reveal too much. "I served with the Metropolitan Police Force, years ago. A probationary constable."

"Really? I can't picture you as a cop."

Gary laughed, felt some of the tension start to ease. "Neither could I. It didn't last. I liked the puzzles, unravelling lies, but I hated the rules. The regulations did more to hinder justice than anything else. What about you? What brought you to England? Don't look so surprised. Your accent gives you away."

"So I haven't picked up that British eloquence yet."

"Canada?"

"Toronto." Kate thought for a moment. "I wanted a change. I missed the house. And I get to spend time with my great-aunt."

"Roselyn Marsh."

Confused. "How did you—"

A mistake. He was starting to lose track of what Kate had said and what he already knew. "It's the oldest house in Willowsend." Half-truths were safer than a lie. "There was an article about it in the paper once." He'd used it for research, when he was trying to figure out why Wendell had picked that house, that town. Gary only hoped they had mentioned her name.

"That's right, she showed me the article." The guarded expression in Kate's eyes lifted.

"The article mentioned something about a tragedy that took place in the orchard. Decades ago now."

She frowned. "I don't remember reading anything like that. What kind of a tragedy?"

"They didn't go into details." When he read it, he'd gotten the impression that someone had pulled strings to keep information hidden. "Probably just a clever journalist trying to hook the reader with an old mystery."

"I'm sure that's it. He even called it the fairy tale house."

"Once upon a time?"

"Right." Kate grinned. "It feels like home now. Though I still miss the snow, maple syrup and my brothers. And, yes, in that order."

Their plates were empty. He didn't want to leave yet. "Would you like a coffee?"

"Yes, please."

Gary signaled to the waiter. "And a crème brûlée, two spoons."

"Gary," Kate said seriously, "I like you."

"And I didn't even have to cook."

"Can you cook?"

"Not unless it comes in a box."

"That's a shame." Kate shook her head sadly.

"One of my faults." Their coffee arrived, steam rising from the cups.

"Ah, but admitting it shows strength of character."

The coffee was smooth and rich. The caramelized sugar of the crème brûlée, crisp and golden.

It was as they left the car, when they were walking toward the house, crossing the grass toward the glow of stained-glass panels, when Gary realized. He never asked about Wendell. Never even thought about it. *You should have taken the bullet.* He could smell earth, overripe apples. Somewhere in the distance, fainter, an undertone of decay.

"So," Kate turned to him at the door, "are you going to kiss me again?"

The jolt of desire took him by surprise.

Kate smiled, head tilted back to look up at him, hands tucked in her pockets. Ends of her hair brushing her collar.

Gary took a breath. Her scent this time, fresh and light.

"You're hesitating." A flicker of uncertainty crossed her face.

Gary snaked an arm around her waist, pulled her to him in one fast move that had her steadying herself, a hand against his chest. He lowered his mouth to hers. Then deepened the kiss, let himself take and take. Greed like fire in his blood, flaring to life, searing his mind blank. And still it wasn't enough. The taste of her was intoxicating.

He stepped back, breath coming hard, though he

wanted to hold on. Hands unsteady.

"You sure can kiss." Kate's voice was shaky.

He stopped himself from touching her again. "Good night, Kate."

Gary watched her enter the house. And he knew he'd just made things a hell of a lot more complicated.

****

The dream closed around him.

The smell of leaf mulch, moss, and dew. The taste of ham and rye. Cold fingers, the dog a darting shape in the misty air, ranging. Quick legs coursing through long grass. Pale tendrils of wood curling onto his father's boots. The flash of the blade, the easy slide and curve of the knife. The dog broke stride, head up, hunting the scent before leaping on.

His father's voice. "Look at him go for that hare, boy. The muscles are what make him look alive. See the way they ripple? The definition? That's strength. Power. Concentrate on the shape of the air around the animal. It's the dark that matters. Look at the shadows, that's what you want to carve away." His father handed him the knife. "Let's see you try."

The animal appeared from the wood, as though it had been trapped inside, waiting for his hands to find him.

Then Gary was in a room, alone. He was choking. He couldn't breathe. He couldn't see.

He was wading through her blood. The room was black, the ground a pulsing burgundy sheet. The air thick.

There had to be a way out. Gary felt his way along, searching by touch. Silence so complete, it was like an absence of sound. The ground sucked at the soles of his feet. A pinprick of light in the distance. Was it real? He heard a whisper, a laugh. Loud in that void. He was too far away still, to hear, to understand what she was saying.

Darkness, denser than the rest, closing in around the edges of his vision. He fought it off. There wasn't enough oxygen. He was losing time. Faster, keep moving. Don't stop. He had to get to her. How long had he been walking?

Glint of silver above. A spider's web, spun a hand's width thick across the ceiling. Was it lower now? He still had the knife. He reached up. The web broke beneath the blade, fine as silk, setting strands floating. The gap he'd made closed over, reforming, thicker than before.

He wouldn't make it. The walls around him were smooth, like concrete. That whisper again. Where did it come from? There were no windows, no doors.

Gary sank down, rested his back against the wall. He listened for her. There was only silence. He should have moved faster. The ripples spread around him.

The light shone, far away. In some distant part of that dark space. But he knew, no matter what he did, the blood would spread, the web would grow. Only a breath or two left.

Gary woke, hand clenched. As though he still held the knife.

Chapter Twenty-Four

Kate found her great-aunt in the garden, spreading mulch around the rose bush.

"I've brought more books for you." Kate set the bag down on the porch. There was a song caught in her head, a clear and bright tune, that had her humming as she closed the store, as she drove home.

Roselyn straightened, brushing sweet-smelling black dirt from her gardening gloves. "Not something with guns again, I hope."

"Abandoned houses this time." Kate could hear the lift to her own voice, that brightness seeping through. "The windswept Cornish coast. A little romance. Secrets a century old." Kate sat on the step, stretched out her legs, angled her face to catch the last of the sunlight. "It reminded me of that article the journalist wrote about this house."

"Which article?" Roselyn straightened abruptly. Her eyes, beneath the brim of the straw hat, were sharp and clear.

"Published just before I moved in. You showed it to me."

"I'm afraid I don't remember the article. Are you certain it was about this house?"

"Positive. I found a part of it online, but it was just an excerpt. Hold on, I bookmarked the page on my phone." Kate pulled up the website, read from the screen. "'The house is remote, standing back from the road, emphasizing its superiority. Perhaps its arrogance is justified; marked by eccentricities, it is unique. Hidden from impulsive scrutiny, it surprises those that stumble upon it, appearing like an architectural gem from the shadows.' An architectural gem," Kate repeated with a grin. She continued, "'The outer sides of the front wall jut out slightly, making an enclave for large, imposing double doors. The building seems to be stretching its arms out invitingly, luring passersby… appealing to the weakness that governs us all. Curiosity. The tower is like a rogue escapee from a long-forgotten fairy tale, rising toward a gray sky. The jagged crack tearing across the stone façade only adds to its ethereal appearance.' That's all. Apparently, the writer mentioned something about a tragedy as well. I thought I might take another look at it."

"If I did have it once, I wouldn't know where to look for it now."

"Never mind then. But what do you think he was talking about? Was there a tragedy that occurred here, on this property?"

"Pure fiction." Her voice was brusque. "You of all people should be able to recognize it, Kate. Then again, you never seem to stop looking for stories." Great-aunt Roselyn smiled. "Insatiable—what do they call it? Narrative curiosity. Isn't that the term?"

"Curse of the voracious reader. Speaking of which, let me know what you think of the books and I'll add your comments to the recommendations in this month's newsletter. Your picks sold well last month." The store newsletter, mailed out to customers once a month, had helped increase sales.

"I'm sure I'll enjoy reading them." Great-aunt Roselyn sounded distracted. "Frost-damage already." She touched one of the limp blossoms, blackened at the edges. "I didn't expect it so soon. The wall should give these roses some protection from the cold, but they face the morning sun. The change in temperature from night to day is too harsh. This one will have to be cut back in the spring." She plucked a darkened petal from the flower. A pause. "Kate, is the house looking neglected?"

Kate shifted, to get a better view. The front door was as imposing as ever. The colored panels in the stained-glass windows bright as jewels. Look closer though, and you could see the wood was flaking, showing signs of wear, some discoloration. The paint peeling around the windows. The surface of the roof was no longer smooth, but beginning to ripple. The shingles buckling, after years of rainwater and melting snow. But it would last, for now. "I suppose it could use some work, here and there."

"Everything that was once new is now old or fading. Things need to be replaced. Modernized. I can't keep up with it. You won't stay here forever. Elaina will leave, maybe go with Ian. And then this house will be empty." Gaze on the withered flowers.

The tone, that melancholy shade to her voice again. "I'm not going anywhere," Kate said. "And soon you'll have another tenant."

"There haven't been any responses to the ad."

"Give it time."

Roselyn dropped the trowel into the bucket at her feet with a sharp clatter. "People don't want one room in an old house anymore. They want privacy. Their own kitchen. A better location."

"We have an apple orchard." Nothing could compare to the scent of apple blossoms in the spring. "What more could anyone want?"

Great-aunt Roselyn smiled. "Better plumbing? At least Mr. Wendell's things are gone now."

Startled, Kate sat upright. She wrapped her arms around her knees. The stone of the step beneath her was cold through the denim of her jeans. "Weren't we waiting to see if a relative would come collect them?"

"Someone was here today."

"Someone came here? To the house?"

"Yes, earlier this morning. He seemed quite affected by Mr. Wendell's passing."

"A relative?"

"A friend. Someone from work. He told me his name. I can't remember now what it was. When he heard no one had been, he offered to take everything."

"All the boxes?"

"Every last one of them. Along with that camera and horrid audio player. I hope he won't listen to it."

"He couldn't have taken everything. I have Mr. Wendell's laptop." That picture, grainy and indistinct. The young girl looking out from behind the glass. Twist of guilt, like she'd stolen something. She shouldn't have looked at the image. "It's in the bookstore."

"Why would you have his laptop?"

"My computer broke. I was using his in the meantime. I was going to tell you." When the moment was right. "His things were there. It seemed like no one wanted them."

"I'm sure, when he realizes it's missing, he'll be back." Great-aunt Roselyn looked toward the trees, just seen behind the house. Leaves starting to turn, the yellow bleeding in. Her expression changed, lost its focus. "Frank will need to pick the fruit soon. I'll have to remind him."

Kate's heart sank. She stood. "Let's go back inside. Come on, I'll help you put the bucket away."

Chapter Twenty-Five

Gary spooned sugar into his tea. Black this time, not herbal. Thank God for that. He could use all the caffeine he could get.

Elspeth looked into the office. She was wearing her coat, a jaunty yellow, purse over her arm. "Right, I'm going home. You should think about doing the same. You're starting to remind me of the pictures in that textbook Jeremy was reading. On forensics."

"Are you saying I look like a corpse?" The tea tasted like syrup.

"Like death warmed over." She buttoned the coat with a smile.

"Thank you, Elspeth," he said dryly. Maybe he did need to catch a few hours kip. "I'll leave when I get this done. Soon," Gary added, hoping it would prevent another lecture.

"Suit yourself, but mind you're human, like the rest of us." Elspeth shook her head as she left.

It took longer than he thought. Drafting, rephrasing. Gary finally hit send on the email. Too slow at writing that last reply. Time to call it a day. He reached for the cup.

"Got a minute?"

Gary jolted at the voice. Tea ran down the sides of the cup, dripped onto the notepad.

Percival was standing in the doorway, one shoulder

propped against the frame, width angled to fit the space. Normally he'd hear Perce walking down the hall, from the first step to the last. Today, he'd missed it, been taken by surprise.

Gary bit back a sigh. He set the cup down. "Yeah, sure. Come in, Perce."

"You met with Harris."

Gary knew Percival would bring it up. The confrontational tone though, that hint of anger, was unexpected. "He came by yesterday."

"Trying to get an edge." Perce was holding a piece of paper in his hand, a smudge of ink on his thumb. Fresh from the printer.

"I imagine so." He knew Perce would keep pushing, worrying at the problem like a dog with a bone. Useful on the job, but Gary was wary of that stubborn glint now. "It's been taken care of."

"Seems to me Harris still has that edge." Percival walked across the room, turned the page around and slid it across the desk toward him. "And, seems to me, you lied. What I'd like to know, is why."

Gary didn't touch the paper. He read from a distance. Legal, several clauses, dense print. *The terms and conditions that govern the contractual agreement between. Agree as follows...* Signatures. One of them his own, heavy curve to the letters, thicker where the ink bled. The date, three years old. "Where did you get this?"

"Attached to an email."

This too, he should have seen coming. "From Harris. When?"

"It came in ten minutes ago." Percival lowered his bulk into the chair across from Gary, sinking down into it heavily. He folded his hands in his lap, leaned forward. "Fact of the matter is, you've been letting me look for someone else, when it was you all along. You were her bodyguard. Why didn't you just say so?"

Gary held his stare. "I should have told you."

"You sent me on a wild goose chase."

He was right about that. "She died on my watch. It's not easy to admit." Fatigue was a dull ache behind his eyes.

"Could you have saved her?" As always, Percival got straight to the point.

"Yes." No hesitation. "I knew something was off. I ignored the warning signs." And there had been many.

"You made a mistake. It happens."

"When you're protecting someone, you can't make a mistake." Gary could hear the snap in his voice. He fought against that flare of anger, got it under control. It wasn't Percival's fault. He'd have asked the same questions and demanded answers. "It takes good intuition and quick judgement to do the job right." Calmer now. That sharp edge gone. "I wasn't concentrated. I screwed up, Perce. At the cost of her life."

"My father was a copper," Percival began in his plodding way. "If there's one thing I learned from him, it's that there's justice, and then there's a different kind of justice. One no better than the other, depending on the situation." Percival said nothing for a moment. At last, he asked, "Is Harris going to be a problem?"

"His daughter died because of me. I'd say he's going to come after us with all he's got." And more.

"File a defamation claim. That would put a stop to it."

Fight it, and there'd be more questions to answer. More people asking them. "We don't have enough proof to present a case. Not enough to justify legal action and all the expenses that go with it."

Perce looked at him with a sharp glance. Like he knew there was more to it than that. Perce didn't look happy, but he didn't argue. "So, we'll wait. See what happens. Handle it on our own."

"But not," Gary said, "with a nine iron."

"A blade to his tire?" Percival grinned, flashing his canines. He picked up the contract. "Seems to me it says confidential, right here at the top." He tapped one broad finger on the line. He took a small silver lighter from his pocket, flicked it on, and held the flame beneath the edge. The flame caught, began to lick up the page. Gary watched its progress, watched it eat away the words, his own signature. The paper turned black, a fine trail of smoke rising. Not enough to set off the alarm. Perce dropped the burning remains into the cup Gary had pushed aside. "I already deleted the email."

"I owe you one, Perce."

"I'm keeping count." Percival leaned forward, his eyes suddenly serious above the half-moon spectacles. "From now on, I don't want any more lies."

"The truth, and nothing but the truth." Gary put his hand on his heart and lied.

Chapter Twenty-Six

"This is my bedroom," Kate told Isra. The cat was lying on the windowsill, back pressed against the glass. A gentle rumble emanated from her. Kate picked up a book from the floor next to her bed, placed it on the covers. "I thought we had boundaries. Our own spaces. Is nothing sacred anymore?"

Kate looked out the window. She ran a hand over the cat's back, feeling the warmth of fur against her skin. "You do like to be near people, don't you?"

Stars, hundreds of them, in the sky. The orchard lit silver. Kate rested her elbows on the sill and looked out. The wet gleam of fruit on the ground, the rough texture of bark had her thinking of folklore and woodland creatures. Of poems about weaving olden dances beneath the moonlight, mingling hands and glances. The heat of the kiss last night still pulsing beneath her skin.

A red glow rose in the air, a slow arc. Small. And real. Not a glow-worm. It was the wrong time of year; the light amber and too steady. The longer she looked, a dark figure began to take shape. A man. There, in between the trees. Staring at the house.

Kate's chest tightened on a surge of fear. She could see him more clearly now. The man raised the cigarette to his mouth. Smoke curled upward. Face like black marble from that distance. Deep-set eyes and sharp angles. If she didn't know any better, he looked an awful lot like the man she'd sold *Laughter In The Dark* to. But why would he be standing outside their house?

Could he see her?

Unhurried, the man stood facing the house, and smoked.

Kate opened the window, letting in the singed scent of tobacco, herbs, and damp leaves. Isra straightened, claws digging into the sill, leaving notches in the wood. Kate took a breath. "This is private property!" How far away was he? Hard to judge the distance in the dark, branches shifting, clusters of stars.

The cigarette fell, or was dropped. Flash of sparks. Red glow on the ground, then that was gone too. The stub crushed into the earth. A cloud passed overhead, sending the orchard into darkness.

He was gone.

Kate made her voice loud and strong, quashing her fear, "I know you're out there! Leave now, or I'll call the police." She waited and listened, her heart loud in her ears. She'd left her cell phone in her purse. Out of reach now, in the living room. Kate thought of matches, of all those trees and what one flame could do, unchecked.

Wind moved through the branches, wood striking wood. Grass rustled beneath her window. Isra sat beside her, every muscle coiled and strung taught.

Spirit or mortal? Did it matter?

Anger coursed through her. Kate closed the window, locked it. The bolt on the front door, she'd check that, too, before going to bed.

Why would he stand there, late at night, looking at the house?

Tomorrow, she'd look for the footprints. The earth was soft. They'd be easy to spot. She'd stand there and follow the angle of sight. Then she'd know what he was looking at. She'd figure out what he wanted. Why he was there.

****

"Okay, what books have you been reading?" Marcus asked.

"I admit it sounds farfetched, but I'm serious." The noise level in the pub was rising steadily. Kate was sitting elbow to elbow with Marcus, so they could talk to each other without shouting. "He looked exactly like that customer. The one who told the kids they should kill someone if they wanted to find a corpse. He was watching the back of the house."

Elaina was tapping drinks and mixing cocktails, her hair twisted up in a ponytail, though most of it had escaped in loose curls. With her almost-black lipstick she looked like a modern film noir goddess. Ian lounged on a stool at the other end of the dark mahogany counter and spoke to her whenever there was a break in orders. They seemed to be getting along better, though having Ian there was a gutsy move. One of Elaina's past conquests could stroll through the door at any minute.

"I found the footprints this morning. Before the rain." Kate took a sip of her wine.

Marcus delicately swirled the olive in his martini before popping it into his mouth. "They're bound to be washed away now." Marcus looked down at his glass thoughtfully. "Elaina normally mixes a bloody decent martini, but it tastes ever so slightly off tonight." He rolled a sip across his tongue. "There's an inexplicable dash too much vermouth." He set the glass down and pushed it away from him. "On second thought, perhaps not so inexplicable. The charms of a carefree drifter can be distracting, even for the most hardened of bartenders. In fact, maybe the man you saw in the orchard was Ian. We all know how your imagination leaps to conclusions. Maybe there's a simpler answer."

"Why would he be out there at night?" Ian was laughing at something Elaina had said, looking like someone who didn't have a care in the world. She couldn't see Elaina kicking him out, not with the way they were looking at each other tonight. She could practically see the sparks flying.

"Maybe he ran out to sneak a fag. Ducking beneath the trees to satisfy his cravings. Remember, Roselyn Marsh quite wisely doesn't allow smoke in the house, only in the tower, to prevent nicotine stains on the wallpaper. Perhaps Ian didn't feel like running up those stairs, a sentiment I can identify with."

Loud laughter exploded in one of the booths. "What, and he was blind and deaf? He would have said something when I shouted. It wasn't him, Marcus. I'll ask later, but it'll only confirm what I already know."

"Look, don't worry Kate." He tugged on her hair. "I could meet you tomorrow after work, help you close up, walk you to your car."

"Marcus." She looked at him with pity in her eyes. Reached over and gave his bicep a squeeze, then shook her head sadly. "I just don't think it would do much good."

"I haven't been to the gym lately."

"You're flexing now. And yet, it's not doing much." She tweaked the muscle.

"When did you become so cold? I can be threatening."

"'Course you can." Kate grinned. "Since you're so full of answers tonight, what do you make of that picture I found on Mr. Wendell's laptop?"

"A budding Mario Testino," Marcus deadpanned. "Stellar work. One can see why he purchased a high-resolution camera. Money well spent. We now know he wasn't using the camera to photograph the flight path of the aquatic warbler. He seems to have preferred portraiture to nature photography."

"You've been rehearsing that speech, haven't you?"

"Guilty as charged."

"The question is, why did he take that picture?"

"Insatiable curiosity. Or an accident. I don't know how many times I've photographed the inside of my own pocket."

A commotion at the entrance of the pub caught their attention.

"Hey! Watch it, woman!" An angry voice exclaimed.

Penelope parted the crowd with her cane. She limped to the counter, wellies squeaking over the floor with each step, every now and then accompanied by the crunch of a peanut shell ground beneath her heel. She pushed between Kate and the man beside her, knocking his nose into his drink, and slammed her open hand onto the counter. "Scotch! An' be quick aboot it."

Elaina rolled her eyes and continued mixing the last order. "You're going to have to wait like everyone else, Penelope. I only have two hands and so much patience."

"Fine then. I'll wait. If room can be foun' tae wait in." She frowned at the little man next to her and prodded him with the handle of her cane, like rags she'd found in the street. "You. Move over."

He set his glass down and scowled. The dome of his head was pink and shiny beneath the ceiling light. Slowly, he slid his three-legged stool over, a fraction of an inch.

"More."

"Madam," the man rebelled, "we'd all like more space, but there simply isn't any to be had." He hunched his shoulders, adopted a defensive posture, held onto his glass with both hands and ignored her.

"No respect." Penelope sniffed and leaned an elbow against the bar. She slanted a glance at Kate out of the corner of her eye. Lowered her voice, "Ye thought this was finished, but ye thought wrang. This story'll fester until it's been aired."

"Are you still on about Mr. Wendell? There's nothing to tell. He died of a heart attack."

"There's mair to it than that. Ye cannae hide it. There was someone in the orchard. That man from the security company, he says I don't know what I saw, but it's a fair way from here to the day I can't be trustin' me own eyes."

"You saw someone in our orchard?" Kate exchanged a glance with Marcus.

"Maybe it wasn't Ian you saw, after all," Marcus murmured.

"When?" Kate asked.

"A night or two before the deith." Penelope brushed beads of water from her sleeve. "And the night of the deith."

"How would you know that?" The hedge was high, the orchard sheltered from view. Or so she thought.

"The mind plays tricks on us, he said. But not on mine."

Kate struggled to keep up. "Who said that?"

"Fenris. Like the monstrous wolf in mythology."

"Scotch, neat," Elaina called, shooting the glass down the length of the slick wood. Penelope caught it with one arthritis-twisted hand.

"You told Gary Fenris someone was at our house?" A knot of unease tightened in Kate's stomach. "He never said anything to me about it."

"He wouldn't want tae, would he noo?" Penelope held her glass to the light and eyed it. "Och, well, Wendell was one for the cards. It's no surprise, he came to an early deith. They say he couldnae pay what he owed."

"Do you have nothing better to do than spread tall tales and gossip?"

Outrage curled orange-painted lips. "Gossip?"

Marcus tugged on the back of Kate's top, in warning. "Kate," he murmured in her ear. "I wouldn't do that, love."

She shook him off. "How do you come up with these stories, these so-called legends? First The Eternal Wife, now you're saying Wendell had a gambling addiction. It's enough! You think Roselyn Marsh has too much. The house, the money. You think love everlasting is an outdated notion. You say she's setting a bad example for young women. You say, look at her, she can't let go. She's living in the past, loyal and devoted to a dead man."

Marcus gave up. "Don't say I didn't warn you."

"It's about time I said something, Marcus."

Penelope tossed the liquor back. She grimaced at the bite of the alcohol, then leaned toward Kate until they were almost nose to nose. "Donna you go shootin' yer sass aboot, lass."

Kate could count the flecks of dry skin beneath the layer of glistening orange. "Why are you so bitter when it comes to my great-aunt? Are you so jealous of her that you have to get all of Willowsend to slander her?"

"Jealous?" Penelope laughed. "O' the widow? Noo. I'm no jealous," she sneered.

"How can you call someone something that constantly reminds them of their grief? She loved her husband. What's wrong with that? You don't know how much hurt words can cause. I want you to stop."

"Ye think she's callit tha' because she mourns her husband?" Penelope snorted, slapped coins onto the counter. "Girlie, ye've go' a lo' tae learn." Penelope pushed herself away from the bar and leaned her weight upon the cane. "I may ha' been the yin to star' callin' her that, but I wasna the last. There's a reason the name caught on, and it's no tae do wi' jealousy. Ye're a smart girl wi' yer books an' big words. Figure it oot yersel'."

"What makes you so much better than her?"

"I ne'er surrendered my life for anyone else's." Penelope limped forward toward the door. "Why is she the Eternal Wife?" she asked over her shoulder. "When ye know, ye'll be callin' her the Eternal Wife yersel'. Ye'll see. There's a reason for everythin', especially an eternally perfect wife."

"How dare she?" Kate seethed. "I'd never call someone that."

His hand closed over hers, squeezed lightly.

"People get envious."

"Great-aunt Roselyn is remembering less, Marcus. She forgets, looks for the dead in the next room. Comes back confused. There's nothing I can do about that, but this is different. She knows what people are saying and it torments her."

"You can't fix everything. Maybe it's time to get some distance. Find your own place and visit her on the weekends."

Kate pulled her hand away. "Weren't you listening? It's getting worse."

"You've lived there for two years, Kate. It's more than anyone could ask for."

"I can't just leave her there alone."

"Because it's safe for you there."

"Apparently it's not that safe."

"You're putting your own life on hold. Before it was just books, now it's that house. You were waiting for Prince Charming then, turning everyone else down. Now you're still safe in that castle."

"I went on a date with Gary."

"Right, and you kissed, so what's next? He'll cut away the brambles and thorns and rescue you, give you that happy ever after? It's time to wake up. That perfect meeting of hearts, minds, and souls—it doesn't happen in real life. You have to take the sword into your own hands."

"You've got some nerve, Marcus, lecturing me when you set the bar so low. All you want is for a man to be easy on the eyes and have the ability to order a decent bloody bottle of wine."

"And you won't settle for anything less than the stars in the sky."

"What's wrong with that?"

Marcus downed his glass. "I love you, but you're living in a fairy tale world. You need to escape while you still have the chance, before that hour of disenchantment comes, or reality is going to break your heart." He levelled his gaze at her. "I don't want to pick up the pieces when it happens. Get out now, Kate. Leave that house and you might be free. The easy route isn't the way to go."

The wine swam in her blood. "The easy route? Who are you to judge me? You still haven't told your father that you're gay. I never thought I'd say this, Marcus, but you're no better than the people who call Great-aunt Roselyn the Eternal Wife. Why do you and Ian both think the house is like Sleeping Beauty's castle? It's just a house." Kate picked up her purse, her jacket. "And I'm not leaving. I like it there. I don't need to be rescued, and I certainly don't want you to try, which is exactly what you're doing right now. So back off. Where did you ever get the idea that I wanted a knight in shining armor to change my life? It's exactly the way I want it."

"Kate." Marcus stood. They looked at each other. He sighed and shook his head in frustration.

Kate turned her back on him and walked out of the pub.

He was worried about her heart? Well, it was a lot tougher than he thought.

Chapter Twenty-Seven

What right did Marcus have to interfere? A tear ran down her cheek, mixing with the rain. Kate turned her face up to the sky. Beyond the roof of the house, thick clouds pooled upon the horizon. Shadows gathered like water in the crevices of the stones. A light was burning at the top of the tower. Elaina must have forgotten to turn it off before she left.

Rain dashed against her umbrella. Kate glanced over her shoulder, but saw only the orchard with its old and twisted trees.

The metal handle, when she touched it, was cold beneath her hand. The door to the tower moved heavily over the ground on a creak of rusted hinges. Kate leaned her weight against it, the soles of her shoes sinking into the moist ground. She opened the door just far enough to get through. A gust of wind tore at her umbrella, pulling it to one side. Kate kept a firm hold on it, managed to close it with a snap. Low-hanging ivy brushed her shoulder as she passed through the stone arch.

The tower smelled dank, of moss and dried paint. The air was clammy with moisture. In the curve of the stairs, Isra sat, her eyes glowing in the dim light. Kate shook her umbrella, scattering water across the stones.

The door should have fallen shut behind her.

Kate turned to look back at the green-tinged

darkness of the doorway. Another surge of wind streaked past, clambering up the walls with an eerie wail that trailed off into the distance above. That sound, like something not of this earth, had the hairs on her arms rising. "What are you doing here?"

Gary was holding the door open. "I don't know. I wanted to see you." He stepped inside and the door slammed shut behind him, a sharp echo. He was wearing dark jeans, a black t-shirt, and a leather jacket. It was no wonder she hadn't seen him.

Rain drummed upon the windows. Isra leapt from her perch. Lightning flashed. The cat was caught in the flare of light, seemed suspended in the air. The next instant, she was on the ground. Her luminous gaze fixed upon them, Isra began pacing tight circles around them, all feline grace and controlled motion.

"Penelope saw someone in our orchard. She said she told you about it."

"She did." That same back-off aura, but this time barely masked by the charm. Something was eating him up from the inside.

"Why didn't you tell me?"

"I didn't think it was important enough to mention." He shrugged it off. "I doubt she could have seen anything from that distance."

"He was here again last night. I saw him this time. He was watching the house."

"And you thought it was wise to be in the tower alone? When anyone could follow you inside." A breath shivered across his lips. "Christ, the cold in here seeps straight through to your bones."

They were alone. Here was the opportunity to take a leap into the dark. It would be her decision. A surge of power tingled over her skin. One step toward him, an invitation, that's all it would take.

Who knew what would happen? She didn't care. This time, it was her move.

Kate took that step toward him, wrapped her arm around his neck, the collar of his jacket damp against her wrist. She felt him tense in surprise. "What are you doing?" He asked, sounding suddenly short of breath.

"Well, I quite enjoy kissing you. I thought we could try it again. And then, I thought we could try the next step too." She could almost hear his heart skip a beat.

"The next step?"

"Sex."

"I —Here?"

"Why not?" Kate grinned, utterly delighted by his reaction. "I've never seen you flustered before."

"I don't think I've ever been flustered before."

"I kind of like it. Dazed and baffled suits you. So, what do you think?"

"I think it's—" he cleared his throat—"it's getting hard to think."

"It's just sex. I'm not asking you to commit murder."

Flicker in his eyes. Then he lowered his head and took her mouth with his. That tingle of contact, the texture of his skin against hers. There was no turning back. It was as though the tightly strung leash of his control had snapped. He took his mouth over her neck, using his teeth against sensitive skin, his warm breath sending her pulse racing. His fingers dug into her hips, pulling her against him. His hands hard and impatient.

He pulled away, asked with a strangled voice, "Are

you sure you want to do this here?"

"I was the one who suggested it. I should be asking you that. Now's your chance to change your mind."

Gary grinned at her. "I'm not going to turn the offer down."

She took his face in her hands and drew him back to her.

The leather of his jacket was soft as butter, the teeth of the zipper jagged as she caught the tab, tugged it down. She pulled the jacket off his shoulders, let it fall.

Tangled together, they stumbled up the stairs, catching at the wall for balance. The exposed stones rough beneath the palm of her hand. He was here, and he was real. This was her choice.

Windows rattled in the panes. Canvases glowed white around them as they sank to the paint-stained floor. The rain outside cut shadows across their skin as they tore at clothes.

Her nails bit into his shoulder as he lingered over her as though time itself had faded. He seemed to be drinking in the very shade and texture of her skin. He lapped at the remnant of moonlight pooled in the hollow next to her hipbone, traced a finger along her collarbone. He ran a hand over her thigh. Sensations building one upon the next. Her breath caught. His eyes on hers, offering more.

She held him close as everything became centered on that moment. The world outside forgotten.

****

He'd let his guard down. Gary hadn't thought of Adriana once, hadn't thought of the crime he'd committed. For a short while, none of it had existed.

He'd felt normal.

They lay on the floor side by side, staring at the ceiling, listening to the wind and the rain. Their breath rasped loudly.

"Wow."

Gary turned his head to look at her profile. "I'd have to agree with that." His heart was thudding in his chest like he'd run a marathon. With the slightest movement, he could brush her fingers with his.

He needed to put some distance between them. He rose and moved to the table against the wall. Pack of cigarettes amidst a pile of loose sketches. He glanced at Kate. She was sitting on the floor, peeling a scrap of paper off her heel. "You're looking pleased with yourself."

"I feel pleased with myself. I'd even go so far as to say smug."

Paper fluttered and rustled in the draught. The wind moaned. Gary picked up the pack, glanced within.

"I didn't know you smoked."

He looked at her in surprise. She was staring at him intently, a different shade to her voice. Like she'd suddenly made a connection. All the more reason to get out of there.

Gary needed something to do with his hands. He dropped the pack back on the table. "I quit a few years ago. It's a bad habit." Wry smile.

"The man in the orchard was smoking, too."

So that flash of knowledge in her eyes hadn't been about him, after all. "What did he look like?" Gary leaned against the edge of the table. "Height, build?"

"I have to put some clothes on. It's too odd having this conversation naked."

"Now that's a shame." He grinned and stayed where he was, amused at the flush creeping up her neck. "I was enjoying the view."

Kate shot him a look. She stood, tugged on jeans, pulled her top over her head, mussing her hair more in the process. "The man, he's not as tall as you are, but close. Lean, bordering on too thin."

"I'm guessing you looked for footprints." She wouldn't be able to resist playing sleuth. That was something he'd learned about her.

"Of course." She brushed it off. "But I'd already recognized him by then."

Gary straightened. "You're saying, you'd seen him before?"

"I sold him a book."

"Describe him."

He'd put her on the spot, but she had an answer in a flash. "Like William Eythe in *The Ox-Bow Incident*. Same jaw line." Certainty in her voice, not a flicker of doubt. The best kind of witness.

"You're sure."

"He might not be able to do William's stunts, but he'd pass for a stand-in. Why are you so interested?"

Gary crushed the cigarette out in a used palette. "I'll take care of it."

"You're not going to lynch him, are you? Sorry, I thought we were making movie references. You'll take care of it, how exactly?"

"It's better not to ask too many questions." He pulled on his jeans, his muscles tense. "Curiosity killed the cat, Kate."

"Is that a threat, or a warning?" She crossed her arms, a stubborn glint in her eye.

"Just advice." He moved around her, careful not to touch her.

Kate stood there a moment, then took a step toward him, her features pale in the washed-out light of the tower. "You seem to have a lot of secrets, Gary."

"Doesn't everyone?"

"Most people don't lose sleep over it."

He bent and picked up his shirt, his jacket. The necklace seemed to burn through the zippered pocket. "It would be wiser for you to stay away from me, Kate."

"You're the one who keeps showing up in places. The café. The hardware store. This house."

He dropped a kiss on her lips. "Try to stay out of trouble. And keep the doors locked."

"That's what every girl wants to hear."

"You've picked the wrong one, if you want roses and promises. I don't make promises anymore."

"That, I'll take as a warning."

Knowing it was the only thing he could have said, didn't make it any easier. "Goodbye, Kate." He left, fighting against a sudden urge to look back, just once.

On the stairs, Gary reached into his pocket, ran the cold chain of Adriana's necklace through his fingers. The raised surface and delicate lines of the embossed orchid. He couldn't allow himself another moment of weakness. He'd make sure Kate was safe, but that would be the end. It would be dangerous for both of them if he let it continue. He was a killer and owed his heart to a dead woman.

Chapter Twenty-Eight

He was hiding something. But what? And how much did it mean to her?

Kate stood for a moment alone in the tower. When she turned off the light, Isra followed her down the stairs, close on her heels. Kate stooped to pick up the umbrella. As soon as she opened the door, the cat leapt outside with coiled muscles, bounding far ahead into the distance.

Mist hovered above the grass. There was the scent of burning wood. Kate looked up. Smoke was rising from the chimney. She could see a glimmer of light in Great-aunt Roselyn's window.

Then Kate froze. The French doors were ajar, leading into the dark kitchen. They swung slightly on the hinges.

Keep the doors locked. A shiver crawled across her skin, accompanied by a growing sense of dread. Had Great-aunt Roselyn gone out into the orchard again, and left the door open behind her? The kitchen tiles would be like ice by now. Why was the ground floor so dark? She listened, but heard nothing.

Kate crossed the terrace, walked past the wrought-iron table, beaded with rain. That same struggle with the umbrella as she fought with the strap that closed the folds. She had her hand on the glass, was about to push the door open, when a blow struck the back of her head.

A flash of red exploded across her vision.

Then everything went black.

****

Pain was the first thing she became aware of. It felt like her head was going to split in two. Kate knew she had to open her eyes. A vague sense of danger nagged at her. There was some reason she should move.

There were stones beneath her. Cold stones. And her clothes were damp.

With an effort, Kate opened her eyes. It was dark and there were stars. Why was she outside? Kate placed her hands on the ground, clamped her teeth against a flare of pain, and levered herself up to a sitting position. She put a hand to the back of her head and winced. There was a good-sized lump, tender to the touch.

Kate concentrated, took in her surroundings. The umbrella was beside her, lying at an angle. There were shards on the ground, too. Ceramic. One of the flower pots Great-aunt Roselyn had emptied and left on the terrace table. She hoped it broke on impact with the stones, and not her head.

Someone hit her with the flower pot. The realization broke through the daze clouding her thoughts.

A wail pierced the air, sending a fresh stab of agony through her skull. A siren? The noise was close. A car being driven up to the house. Police, or ambulance. Kate stood, steadying herself with a hand against the wall. How long was she out?

The pain was beginning to settle into a throbbing rhythm. Staying near the wall, taking one step at a time, Kate rounded the house. Each step made her head ache. Ignore it. Keep moving.

There was a police car in the driveway. The drizzle formed a haze around the flashing light on the hood. What was going on? Fear clutched at her heart. Please, let nothing have happened to Great-aunt Roselyn.

A murmur of voices at the side of the house. Kate followed the sound. Fine rain pricked her skin.

Relief made Kate light-headed. At the door to the basement, Great-aunt Roselyn was standing next to a police officer. She was holding a Liberty print umbrella above her head. The foliage of the Strawberry Thief design dark with moisture. Her posture was perfect, the lift to her head imperious as ever.

"*Coscientia mille testes*," the officer was saying. "Conscience is as good as a thousand witnesses. We'll get the culprit one way or another." Tim's father. Kate was glad to see it was him. Henry's shoulders were hunched against the rain, a spiral notebook in his hand. Blue biro spreading thickly across the damp paper. He looked up and caught sight of Kate.

"What happened?" Kate asked, joining them. Great-aunt Roselyn angled the umbrella so that it covered Kate as well, shielding them both from the worst of the rain. She could see now the window of Mr. Wendell's room. Glass glinted, shards lying between the broken stems of roses. Wind whistled through the opening, whirling petals into the room below. They were scattered across the floor within. Sweet smell of crushed blossoms rising from the flower bed.

"Burglary." Henry had never been one to mince his words.

Great-aunt Roselyn shivered and gathered her raincoat closer around her. Her face was pinched and drawn with worry. "Nothing like this has happened before, Henry," she said firmly. "This is a quiet neighborhood. At least, I thought it was."

Kate leaned against the wall. "Someone broke into our house?" Why? There were no jewels kept hidden in a safe in the study. Heirlooms had been sold over time, to cover property taxes, pay for repairs. The size of the house, though, could have someone thinking there was more, that there were riches within, ripe for the taking.

Great-aunt Roselyn turned to her. "They broke the window of Mr. Wendell's room."

"Used it as an entry point," Henry said.

"There's glass everywhere." Roselyn glanced at the door behind them. Her lips thinned. "My chrysanthemums have been trampled. The roses are looking the worse for wear. My poor beautiful flowers."

"Was anything taken?" Kate asked.

"There was nothing left in his room," Roselyn said. "The burglar seems to have conducted a thorough search. There was so much damage. The mattress cut open, the…" She stopped and pressed a trembling hand to her lips. "They went through Elaina's room. There are things everywhere. Kate, they were in the house. In your room, too. I'm sorry. I feel as though it's my fault. I was upstairs." She closed her eyes as though to steady herself, to regain her composure.

The cold Kate felt had nothing to do with the rain now. "My God."

"Did you hear anything?" Henry asked.

Great-aunt Roselyn shook her head. "I had music playing. The windows were closed."

Henry turned to Kate. "They must have seen the light, and stayed well away from your great-aunt's room. It takes a lot of guts, breaking and entering when the owner is home."

She suddenly took a closer look at Kate. "Are you all right?"

"I think I ran into the burglar." Henry straightened. Like a hound on the scent, Kate thought, fighting a sudden urge to laugh. Was this shock? "I saw the French doors were open. Next thing I knew, something hit my head, knocked me out. I don't know for how long."

"What?" Great-aunt Roselyn put an arm around Kate's shoulders, hugged her close.

Henry studied his notebook. "Mrs. Marsh, when exactly did you notice something was amiss?"

"Fifteen minutes ago. I went to the kitchen to get a glass of water. There was a plate on the floor, broken into pieces. That was when I began to look, and I discovered—" She broke off. "I noticed someone was in the house."

"Around ten-thirty." Henry jotted down the time.

"I took the phone, returned to my room, locked the bedroom door and phoned 999."

"Was the front door unlocked?"

"No."

"It's normally kept locked?"

"Yes," Roselyn said. "All the doors are."

"The tower too?"

"Elaina often forgets to, but the only way to enter the house is through the door into my rooms and that's always kept secured."

"And you, Kate?" Henry asked. "When did you get back? It may help to narrow the time frame."

Kate shifted uncomfortably. She could feel the blush heat her skin. "I got back about an hour or so ago."

Surprised, Great-aunt Roselyn said, "I didn't hear you come in."

"I went to the tower. The light was still on."

"You don't normally spend time in the tower, Kate, and certainly not alone."

"I had a fight with Marcus. I was upset."

"You argued with Marcus?" Roselyn's elegantly arched brows rose. "That is unusual. You're always such kindred spirits."

"Not tonight."

Henry asked, "Did you see anyone on your way home?"

Kate thought back, but the drive home was a blur. Her head ached. "Barely a car went past. I did see someone, Henry, last night."

Fear entered Great-aunt Roselyn's voice. "Where?"

"There was a man in the orchard, watching the house, smoking."

Great-aunt Roselyn exclaimed, turned away from them, her hand clasped over her mouth, her back rigid.

"Do you know anything about this, Mrs. Marsh?"

Roselyn shook her head wordlessly.

"Someone you recognized, Kate?" Henry asked. "Could you identify him if you saw him again? Any defining characteristics?"

"I could identify him." She was sure of it. Kate ran through the same description she'd given to Gary, pausing to let Henry take down the information, adding details when he asked. "I just hope he is connected to the crime and it wasn't a figment of my imagination or a ghost."

Roselyn's face was pale, her eyes wide and wild

with terror. "A ghost?"

Henry put a steadying hand on her arm. "You've had a shock."

"I don't see how I'm going to make this house appealing to potential tenants. Not after this. No one wants to move into an old building that's been burgled and is…" Roselyn's voice faltered, "tinged with death."

"Why don't you pour yourself a glass of brandy, put your feet up? I'm almost done here."

"No brandy. I'll be taking Kate to the hospital." Kate opened her mouth to protest, but Roselyn cut her off with a glance. "A head injury is not to be taken lightly, Kate. We are going to have a doctor examine you, and that is final."

"I could call an ambulance," Henry offered.

"No, really—"

"Yes, thank you," Roselyn said firmly.

Kate watched, resigned, as Henry put in the call.

When he finished, Great-aunt Roselyn asked, "Can I make you a cup of tea, Henry?" Always the hostess.

"That's a kind offer, but this is my last stop. Then I'm off to have a nightcap at home." He ran over his notes. "You'd go around the side of the house," he muttered to himself thoughtfully, scanning the area, "and spot the basement window first. It's appealing as it's out of sight of the road and on ground level. Exit was by way of the French doors. The burglar must have felt secure, been a few steps away from the terrace, almost at the trees, when he heard you come up to the doors, Kate. Startled, he'd turn and—" He raised his arm and brought it down, miming a violent blow. "Well, there you have it."

Kate flinched.

"What did he use as a weapon?"

"It was a flower pot. There were a few on the table, within easy reach."

"I'll collect the shards, have them dusted for dabs. Mind, I doubt there'll be any. Most burglars know enough to wear their gloves."

"Why go through the basement?" Kate wondered. "Wouldn't the ground floor, entering through the French doors, be easier?"

"Easy access, but far riskier. By all appearances, this was unplanned, unpremeditated. A basement is the safer bet." Henry moved forward to take another look at the point of entry.

"Other than these flowers, the rain has washed away any evidence there might have been." Henry hitched up his trousers at the knees and squatted to take a closer look. "Seems as though it was only one person, tops maybe two. One chap's trekked mud across the rooms inside, but he was wearing smooth-soled shoes. Nothing that can be matched with a specific brand. Can't get much from that. Someone else could have been playing look-out but that's conjecture." He stood up, yanked a handkerchief from his pocket and blew his nose violently. He continued, "It could have been a dare. Young lads getting into the liquor. Things escalate. It happens."

Kate thought the damage didn't suit a prank. The level of destruction spoke of violence and anger.

Henry flipped his notebook shut. "I've taken note of the missing valuables. Once you have a chance to go through your own room, Kate, or if you notice anything else that's been taken, let me know." Another siren. "That'll be the ambulance now."

"We'll have to sweep up the glass, hammer boards over the broken window," Kate said. There was plywood in the garden shed, old by now but it would do the trick.

"We'll have Ian and Elaina do that. I'll phone them on the way." Great-aunt Roselyn seemed suddenly overcome with exhaustion. "All anyone will be talking about tomorrow is this story." A fierce glint appeared in her eyes. "Somebody was in my home. I want you to find who it was, Henry. I want you to find them."

There was the strength Kate remembered. She only hoped it would last.

Chapter Twenty-Nine

Gary accelerated to pass the car in front of him, lowered the visor to block the glare from the road. He turned down the stereo and selected the bookstore's number from his contacts. Impatient, he waited for Kate to answer the phone. When he heard her voice, cool and professional, over his car's Bluetooth speaker, he said, "You got injured."

"Gary?"

He slowed at a red light, drummed his fingers on the wheel. The engine purring as it idled. "I heard about the burglary."

"It's barely nine thirty. How did you hear about it already?"

"I picked up a coffee from the café. Henry's wife was there after the school run, telling Neil about the late night her husband had yesterday. Why are you at work?"

"If you didn't think I'd be at work, why did you phone the bookstore?"

"Lucky guess."

"It was just a minor concussion."

"Is that a medical diagnosis or your own opinion?"

"A medical diagnosis." Irritation crept into her voice. "I have a mild head injury. No broken skin, just a bump."

"Must be that hard head of yours," Gary said dryly.

He continued quickly, before she could reply to that, "Shouldn't you be resting?" He checked the mirror, hit the left turn signal and cut across the intersection. A glance at the GPS confirmed he'd make it on time, despite the delay in the café. Updating the security system installed in the office complex would mean running through every aspect with the client, going over the changes that needed to be made in detail. He'd rather go to the bookstore, confirm for himself that Kate was all right.

"I'm only working a half day. I'll be heading home after lunch."

"Any dizziness? Be honest, now." Brake lights up ahead.

"None."

"You're not supposed to read after a head injury."

"Gary, I saw a doctor."

He doubted Kate would listen to medical advice that required her to stop and rest. But he let it go, for now. "What was taken from the house?"

"We haven't had time to go through everything yet, but it doesn't seem like much is missing. A few pieces of jewelry. Small items, easily portable. The ground floor and basement though, cupboards were emptied, pillows slashed." She paused. "It's like they were looking for something."

He wondered if they found what they came for. "Any chance you managed to see who hit you?"

"I didn't even know anyone was behind me until it was too late."

It might have been worse, Gary through grimly. He had told Kate he'd take care of it. He should have acted sooner. Open road now, a field speeding past the window. Gary touched the gas. "All right. Promise me you'll take it easy today."

"I haven't even moved any books."

Gary shook his head. "Well, leave them where they are. Let someone else do that, if it has to be done."

"I'm sitting in my chair, drinking a cup of peppermint tea. I'm feeling relaxed and yet, at the same time, mildly annoyed, which may have something to do with this phone call. But I think it's sweet you were worried about me."

"Good, because I'll be calling again later."

"I can hardly wait." Sarcasm there.

Gary chuckled and disconnected the call.

He had a good idea who broke into the house, who knocked Kate unconscious. Later, he'd pay that man a visit. And issue a warning he wouldn't easily forget.

****

A movement had Kate looking up. Her expression sobered.

Marcus hesitated in the entrance to the store, the door held in one hand, a white paper bag in the other. "Hi."

"Hi," Kate replied warily, waiting to see what Marcus would say.

"I was a horrible friend," he began. "In fact, I don't deserve the mantel of friendship. I have hung it in the back of my wardrobe, pushed it aside with self-loathing. Even now, it hangs there still, sparkling sadly to itself in the dark."

"It does need to be worn with grace."

"We both said things we shouldn't have."

"You started it."

Marcus nodded. "I did. Regret is a bludgeon upon

my soul. Kate, heart of my hearts, light of my life, most kindred of spirits, forgive my foul words."

"Staying at the house allows me to put my money into Fortune's Cove. It isn't easy running a brick and mortar bookstore these days, but I want mine to last."

"I've brought you a scone from the Old Fire-Hall Café as a peace-offering. Please invite me in, but if not, I will leave the bag as a sacrificial offering upon the threshold and suffer the punishment I so deserve."

"You should take to the stage, Marcus. You'd be perfect in the theatre with your flair for the dramatic." Kate hesitated, looked at the bag in his hand. "A scone? With or without raisins?"

"With raisins and warm from the oven." He opened the bag, letting the scent of sugar and flour rise temptingly into the air.

She looked at his hopeful, apologetic eyes and sighed. "Fine. Come in. But I'm still mad at you."

"Duly noted." Marcus stepped into the store, letting the door rattle closed behind him. "I heard about the burglary. In fact, I heard it all from the window being broken with a medieval battering ram to everything being stolen but the antique Egyptian emerald that belonged to Ra himself, which was kept hidden in a secret panel in the walls. How are you?"

"Fine. Taking it easy, as instructed." Kate smiled.

Marcus set the bag down on the counter. "Is there anything I can do to redeem my tenuous, yet stalwart position, as best friend? Or have I forsaken all rights to the term? Destroyed all my chances in a single deluge of callous remarks?"

"Ian did a lot." There was nothing wrong with making Marcus suffer, just a little.

"That's good." Marcus tucked his hands into his pockets. "Any ideas as to who did it?"

"Henry thinks it might have been teenagers."

"Right." There was an awkward pause. "Speaking of Ian, how is the happy couple?"

"I'm sensing some tension. He's still here, anyway."

The rain-faded light showed up the streaks on the store windows. She made a mental note to clean them soon. "So." They looked at each other. Kate's phone vibrated on the counter. She glanced at the message. *Thought your skull was thicker than that! Call me or Ethan if you want advice on booby traps. Happy to pilfer the archives. Will share intel on best techniques, for a price.*

"Ethan or Chris?" Marcus asked.

"Chris. Offering to relive his days as boyhood menace to ensure my safety."

"As all good brothers would."

Kate opened the bag, peeked inside, and caught a whiff of warm buttery baking. "Oh, yum."

Marcus suddenly leaned closer, narrowed his eyes at her.

Kate moved back. "What?"

He caught hold of her chin in his hand. Studied her profile. Stepped back. Scanned her. Then nodded. "You had sex."

Kate gasped. "No." She flushed and avoided eye contact.

"Yes, you did. Who was it?"

Was it that obvious? "I don't know what you're talking about."

"Hm." Marcus snuck a piece of the scone.

"I thought that was for me."

"Liars don't deserve baked goods. Share. It may redeem your karma." He grinned.

Kate narrowed her eyes at him. "Keep your voice down!" At the moment, they were alone in the store, but a customer could enter at any second. She didn't want a stranger overhearing personal details. "Fine. I may have…done something of the kind," she admitted.

"I knew it."

"Stop gloating."

"Difficult." He rocked back on his heels, studying her. "Specifics: something of the kind, or the whole thing?"

Kate stretched luxuriously. "The whole thing."

"Now who's gloating?"

Kate felt a slow, wicked smile spread across her face. "That would be me."

"That's right. The first step is admitting it. It suits you."

"Which one? Gloating or sex?"

"Both." Marcus picked up a post-it from the corner of her desk, flipped it against his palm absentmindedly.

"Be careful with that note. I have no idea what's on it, but it might be important at some point in time." He reached across and stuck it on her forehead. She crossed her eyes at him, plucked it off and slapped it onto the edge of the otherwise useless computer.

"All right, out with it. Who was the lucky gentleman?"

Kate leaned toward him and whispered, "Gary Fenris."

"Blimey, Kate." Marcus rubbed his jaw. "Was it good?" He held up a hand before she could say anything. "No. Stupid question. I've seen how the man walks. Of course it was good. I can just imagine."

"Hey, cut it out." She shot a quick jab to his shoulder. "Some privacy, please."

"Right." Marcus shut his eyes for a second. "Curtain drawn."

"Thank you." Kate broke off a corner of the crumpet.

"Okay, here?" Marcus pointed at his face. "Green with envy. When? Where? How?"

"I really don't think I need to go into the logistics."

"Cute." Marcus waited.

"Okay. When? Last night. Where? The tower. How? All I can say to that is, if you have to ask…"

"The tower?" His eyebrows rose.

"It was spontaneous."

"I'll say." Marcus grinned. "Dare I give voice to my pride?"

"Ha ha, funny man." She reached for the last bit of pastry, but he got there ahead of her. "Hey! What's the big idea?"

"You had sex. You don't get the last piece." He popped it into his mouth.

"Well, some peace offering that was. It seems less selfless when you don't eat most of it yourself."

Marcus tucked a strand of hair behind her ear. "If he hurts you—" he began, his expression suddenly fierce.

Kate cut him off before he could finish the threat. "I'll take care of him myself. I welcome input on creative torture methods, but that's it. The line is drawn."

"I know, but-"

"I don't need you or anyone else fighting my battles for me," Kate said firmly.

Chapter Thirty

There were stains on the floral design. Mud worked deep into the weave of the carpet. In the entrance, the wardrobe door was open, the contents strewn across the floor. Silk scarves, a long black wool coat, hats, all tossed carelessly to the side. Red silk, bright as blood.

Great-aunt Roselyn bent to pick up the coat. Her mouth was a pinched, hard line. She shook out the folds, ran a hand down the fabric to smooth it. "I suppose we should be thankful nothing more was taken, but it's difficult to be positive when faced with this mess. Dirt has been tracked all through the ground floor. We'll have to soap the carpet to be rid of it. And to think a stranger touched our things. It's enough to make me ill at the very thought of it."

Kate could hear the anger in her voice. It matched her own. "I wish we knew who did it."

She was sitting on the stairs, feeling restless and useless. Delegated to role of observer and all because she got hit on the head. Doctor's orders. Annoyed, Kate shifted, stretched her legs out in front of her. The headache was almost gone now. It was hardly noticeable, really. At least this way, she could keep an eye on Great-aunt Roselyn. She was doing surprisingly well, considering everything that happened, but Kate preferred to stay close, for now.

Isra was sitting on the landing above, looking very

much like a replica of the goddess Bast. A fierce protector, the "devouring lady," in the form of a domestic cat. The feline eyes were watchful, the pupils narrow black slits.

"Luckily," Roselyn said, "I managed to extract a promise from the repairman. We'll be first on his route tomorrow. If all goes well, we may have glass in the window by the weekend."

"That's good news."

"It's about time we had some." Roselyn passed Kate an armful of scarves. "Why don't you fold these?"

The silk was smooth beneath her fingers, and Kate found herself relaxing as she concentrated on folding, matching corners to corners. "What was he looking for?" Kate wondered.

"Money, jewels?"

"The gold necklace Mom gave me, it's still there. The drawer was opened, emptied for the most part, but the necklace was left behind. Why?" Her books spread ruthlessly across the floor. Anger flared again at the thought of it. "It would have been easy to take."

There was the fur coat, hanging in the wardrobe. Had he not recognized its value? The vintage Rosenthal china too, what little remained of the set, was still on the glass shelves in the cabinet. All the pieces were there. She'd counted. The smaller items could have easily been carried, tucked into a jacket pocket.

"We must resign ourselves to the fact that we may never know why." A good, clear voice. Great-aunt Roselyn had been like this all afternoon, as though the burglary had robbed her of objects but left her with new-found strength. Roselyn returned hats to their boxes with brisk movements, her focus entirely on the here and now. Kate watched her thin fingers nestle each hat within folds of tissue paper. Feathers, silk, and satin. Beaded jewelry giving off a sparkling light. The whisper of cardboard boxes as lids slid into place.

"Can I ask you a question?"

"Of course."

"Penelope Crawford. Why does she seem so angry with you? So bitter?"

"Ah, well." Great-aunt Roselyn took her time, replacing the box on the shelf. "We were friends once, long ago. She was always the stronger one from the two of us. Determined to do great things, to educate herself. She was disappointed by the decisions I made, and didn't hesitate to tell me so."

"Which decisions?"

"Marrying Frank, for one thing, and then the way I lived my life after the wedding. We were all young, but she had strong ideals. And she's always been quick to judge."

"These are so beautiful." Kate reached for the hat lying near her, the one closest to her bare toes. The straw felt brittle, older than the hats in Great-aunt Roselyn's rooms. "It's a shame more people don't wear hats these days." Tempted, Kate tried it on. The sweep of the brim cut across her vision. The hat felt heavy. Kate had to tilt her chin, and when she did, she saw Great-aunt Roselyn looking at her. Kate gave her a grin. "What do you think?"

"It suits you. In fact, it was your grandmother's favorite. It was mine, but she always used to take what she pleased. Often without asking."

"Were you close?"

"Not like you and the boys. You and Ethan and

Chris have always been peas in a pod, tearing through the house like little savages." The memory had Roselyn smiling. "As soon as I'd hear you say, 'Let's pretend that…' I knew trouble was brewing."

"We can't have been that bad."

"It was always lively, let's just say that."

"She moved to Canada before your wedding, didn't she?"

"Yes. Gone from one day to the next or, at least, that's what it felt like. It broke my heart that she wasn't there. I only realized how much I wanted her to be there when it was too late. To make matters worse, we'd argued only weeks before she left."

"What did you argue about?" Kate removed the hat. The straw snagged in her hair, tugged at the roots as she worked it loose.

"There was a boy. Well, eighteen at the time. My age. He was…different. Sarah said so herself. So strange." She gave the words a mocking twist, full of teenage disgust. The change in her voice had prickles rising over Kate's skin. "He was gangly. Wore old clothes that never fit. Talked too fast, too much. Was too honest, in a way that alienated people."

Contempt and something else in her voice. Sadness. And fear.

"He used to follow me home. I was quite pretty, back then. Everyone said so." Head held high and proud. "He would leave gifts outside the house for me to find. They were always small things. Daisies stolen from a garden, a glass bead on string. I wouldn't touch them. I didn't want to encourage him." A flicker there, in her eyes, and gone again. "But Sarah found one of those gifts and took it. It sounds innocent, but she knew what she was doing. It was a bracelet woven from reeds of grass. I knew she'd taken it. I saw it in her room, but she denied it when I confronted her. He thought I kept it, that I had accepted his token. It was the sign he'd been waiting for. The next gift was a book of poems, the pages marked. Left in the orchard, beneath my favorite tree." She paused. "I was cruel, as so often happens at that age. The carelessness of youth. I left the book in the rain until the pages were swollen and gorged with water."

Kate could see it. The pages thick, the cover warped and damaged. Then black with mold.

"Sarah always wanted what was mine. If the boy had hope, if he could be led to believe I cared, she thought he'd come to the house more often. Sarah wanted Frank to see him, to discover how callous I had been. She wanted to destroy the image Frank had of me. He idolized me, you know. I was on a pedestal. He worshipped me and Sarah wanted to shatter his illusions. I never truly forgave her for it. I wish I had, now. It's easy to sever ties, and so much harder to mend them. When she had that stroke, it was so sudden, I never had a chance." The grandfather clock chimed, counting the quarter hour.

"What happened to him? To the boy?"

"Have you seen the lid for this box?" Great-aunt Roselyn looked around with a frown, suddenly absorbed by the task again.

"Did you see him again?"

Kate heard Elaina's voice then, in the kitchen. "It had to be something I gave to you." Then she was in the doorway, standing hip cocked. Temper flashing. "Ian's watch is missing. He's not torn up about it, but I thought I'd better mention it." Curls tumbled down from the loose bun. Ian was close behind her, holding a glass of water. "That's about all we've discovered so far."

"I'll add it to the list," Kate promised.

Elaina took the glass from Ian's hand.

He leaned one shoulder against the doorframe and watched her as she drank from his glass, both amused and exasperated. "I offered to get you your own, just seconds ago."

"I only wanted a sip." She handed the glass back to him with a grin, brushed impatiently at tendrils of hair falling in her face. "We should have seen this coming. Everyone in town knows Mr. Wendell met his maker. It's not surprising kids seized the opportunity for some petty theft and demolition. There's not a lot of risk, not with the size of the house. Truth or dare, and up the ante. Prove who's the toughest of the lot."

Ian quirked a brow. "And you'd have taken that dare? Risked getting a record, for the thrill of it?"

"For the status, hell, yes. I always chose dare over truth."

"Somehow, that doesn't surprise me." Ian's voice was wry.

"Very funny." Elaina gave him a look. "Anyway, we're calling it quits for tonight."

Getting some rest sounded tempting. Kate's headache was beginning to build again, pounding in her temples, pulling at the muscles in her neck. "I think I will too."

Great-aunt Roselyn sighed, looking around with a pained expression. "I suppose the rest will have to wait until tomorrow."

"We'll have the house cleaned up in no time," Ian told her. "It'll be like it never happened."

"And wouldn't that be nice? If only it were that easy." The wardrobe door closed with a click. Great-aunt Roselyn rested her hand against the wood, her face drawn and weary.

Kate thought of the book left in the rain. The awkward boy. The girl who would later become The Eternal Wife. And felt that familiar tug of an unfinished story. That need for the ending.

Why had Great-aunt Roselyn changed the subject?

Chapter Thirty-One

Ryan Delaney rounded the corner and came face to face with large, scuffed, green dumpsters overflowing with trash. The acrid smell of rotting fruit, old clothes and filth filled the small alley. Somewhere a dog barked. The sound made him jerk, nervous.

He spun to the right. Only bricks, too high.

More wall on the left.

Footsteps fell upon the ground behind him. Measured. Slow.

Trapped.

Delaney gulped. His fingers twitched.

He turned, slowly.

Gary strolled toward him, pavement gleaming wetly behind him in the opening to the road where streetlights swam. Music blared, rose with a pounding beat, the deep bass making the ground shake, then faded as the car drove past. Shadows licked at the walls, slid across his eyes.

A feral grin spread over his features. Pure confidence surged through him, potent as any drug.

"What do you want?"

Gary continued to move forward, his motions lazy. He watched, amused, the other's attempt to cover fear with polite distaste, impatience, the quiver of muscles that betrayed the urge to run. He ignored the question. "How does it feel to be the one followed?" The tone was easy, conversational. "Or do you only get off scaring women? It's not so pleasant when the roles are reversed, is it, Ryan?"

"I don't know what you mean." His eyes darted over Gary's shoulders, across the walls, the space behind him, searching for a way out.

"I think you do." He let a bit of the malice leak out. Adrenaline coursed through his veins, thick and sweet.

"I don't, really." Delaney's hand crept toward his jacket pocket, the imprint of a cell phone delineated through the expensive fabric.

"I really wouldn't do that if I were you." Gary paused a step away. Contemplated the knuckles of his right hand.

The man paused, shrugged. "Okay. All right? We're all friends here. Last time we met, I pissed you off." He tried out his let's-make-a-deal smile on Gary. "I'm sorry. We'll play an honest game next time. No harm, no foul."

"You're weak, Delaney. Lacking strength of character. Integrity. Let's talk about business. That's always interesting. I'm guessing you haven't been doing so well lately, have you, Ryan?"

The cocky grin, slipped, turned sickly.

A guess, but that expression told Gary he'd hit the mark. "Does that have anything to do with your night-time activities? Your creeping around in the dark? Watching houses? Knocking women unconscious?"

"I don't have time for this or your bullshit accusations." He reached for bravado. "I don't know who you are, but I'm a busy man. Call me in the morning. Set up a meeting with my secretary, we'll talk then."

Gary looked up, one quick flash of teeth. "Is that your final answer? Call my secretary?" He sneered. Shook his head. "You're making this almost too easy. I was hoping for a fight. Itching for one."

The man went pasty, laughed weakly. He glanced to the left of Gary, still chuckling in a forced mechanical stream of sound, then abruptly dodged to the right.

Gary rolled his eyes and grabbed the man's collar, stopping him short. "Did anyone say you could go, Ryan? We're not finished yet. Not by a long shot." He fisted the fabric with one quick twist and watched the man's eyes widen. Smelt the nicotine on his breath. "Kate Rowan." He hissed. "Why are you following her?"

"I wasn't. I don't know who—"

Gary shook him once, like a ragdoll. "Why were you at the house?" The man's hands scrabbled at his arms, slid off ineffectually. He whimpered. "We can do this the hard way or the easy way." Gary leaned closer, snarled. "Answer the fucking question. The truth this time."

His Adam's apple bobbed. "She's—" His lips quivered. He pressed them together. Fear tightened the corners of his eyes. Snake eyes. Viper eyes. "She's attractive. I thought I'd ask her out."

"Your wife would like that, wouldn't she?" Sly lying reptile. He saw through the smooth surface. There was panic there that ran deep, was more than the fear of violence. The sallow cheeks, the way the suit hung off him, spoke of weeks of stress. Gary wouldn't solve the riddle tonight, could see he wouldn't get anything out of Delaney. Not then. Not there. He might crumble under pressure, but he wouldn't talk.

No matter. He'd find out the answers eventually. But first he had to make sure the man understood. Give him a concise message he wouldn't forget, he wouldn't be able to shake off in the morning. He wouldn't go back to that house. "Stay away from her and that house. I need you to repeat the words, Ryan."

"I don't know what you're talking about."

Gary shook his head sadly, made the sound of a buzzer. "Wrong answer." He sank his fist into the man's belly.

The man knifed over, doubled up with a noise like a balloon made when the air escaped.

"Come on. Stand up." Gary waited. "Stand up!"

Delaney straightened slowly, one arm clenched over his stomach. "Look, if it's money—"

"Shut up." Quick, like a slap, the sentence shot out. "Use your fists."

The man looked at him, his nostrils flaring with the effort to slow his breathing. "What?"

"Punch me." He hated beating on people who didn't fight back. At least give him the excuse—the satisfaction—

The man threw one wild punch that connected with his jaw.

Gary's head whipped to the side. He licked at his cracked lip, tasted blood. He nodded. "Not bad." He grinned, relishing the lap of pain at the motion. "My turn." He went for the ribs.

The sounds of the fight were dulled by high walls, hallowed by brick and concrete. Something scuttled, moved in the darkness.

The man grunted, fell to the ground. Gary kicked

him, rolled him over.

Delaney coughed, groaned, moving weakly against the pavement. He didn't look so smooth now. His hair was tousled, his shirt dirt-stained and untucked. His clean-shaven face contorted in a grimace of pain.

Gary squatted down next to him, picked up a pebble and rolled it idly between his fingers. "Stay away from her." With one flash of movement, he jammed his arm across the man's throat, pressing against his windpipe, strangling him. The man squirmed beneath him, his eyes torn wide. The quick, instant flash of fate closing in as he saw death in Gary's face. "If you so much as take a step in her direction I'll break your fingers, one by one. If you touch her, hurt her, I'll kill you. And let's not get into what I'll do to you if you go to the cops, tell them about what happened here. Understood?"

One jerked nod, mouth gaping like a fish.

"Use your words."

"Understood," he gasped.

Gary released him, stood. Delaney curled into himself, clutching at his throat.

Gary turned away from the man now a heap on the pavement, walked back toward the street.

"I know what you did." The thin voice, rasping and ragged, almost stopped him in his tracks. For the first time, Gary had a moment's pause, a prick of fear.

His step never faltered. "You know nothing." A coward's last, desperate grasp at power. The need to be left with the feeling of having had the upper hand. It didn't mean anything. What could he know? Just words, thrown out blindly with the hope of striking a nerve. An ill-planned counter.

It had almost worked.

Gary walked out into the city, hugging the warm cloak of violence to him. Knew it fit him well. Too well.

Cardamom, jasmine, bitter almond wafted on the air. Adriana's favorite scent. He took a steadying breath, felt the ghostly fragrance burn his lungs.

Chapter Thirty-Two

The sound of wild rasping breath flashed through Gary's mind. The smell of sweat and fear. The muffled thuds of his fist hitting home.

Early morning sun glared off the path. The wet earth was beginning to warm, and the resinous scent of fir trees hung in the air. Pine needles cushioned the ground beneath his feet. Gary put on his shades and ran faster. Dragging in air, ignoring the stitch in his side. Muscles burning.

I know what you did. Gary couldn't get the words out of his head. They were just a stab in the dark. It didn't mean anything. Delaney couldn't have guessed at the truth.

Still, they crawled beneath his skin, repeated in the back of his mind.

Gary stopped and leaned against a tree, trying to catch his breath. Spots flared across his vision, heart racing.

The memory hit him full force, got him while he was bent double, defenses down. Smell of lemon dish soap from the sink, sharp and bitter. He'd been washing the dishes, his hands submerged in hot water. He'd let the tap run too hot. The water was close to scalding. Their voices raised. Stubborn glint in Adriana's eyes, driving him insane, until he didn't know whether he wanted to kiss her or punch his fist through the wall.

"You're angry," she had said.

"The hell I am." Teeth gritted, he'd fought to keep his cool. She could bring him close to the edge of patience like no one else could.

"Don't try to deny it. Why can't you leave it be?" A glass slamming down. That edge to her voice. "You're always looking for connections, trying to fix things. Sometimes you just have to let it go. Focus on something else. Stop dwelling on it. There are more important things you should be doing. And you know exactly what that is. When are you going to talk to him? Tell him about us, Gary. I hate lying, hiding things from everyone. If you won't, I will."

"We've gone over this. If I tell him, he'll take me off the job. You're safer with me."

"And you say I'm the stubborn one. You'll never figure out who's been sending those threatening letters if you keep obsessing over it. Take a step back. And for God's sake, stop being so grumpy." A smile, her hand sliding up his back, under his shirt. "Just relax, will you?"

Her voice in his mind, it was making it spin. Doubled over, hands on his knees, Gary shook his head. Stress, that's what it was.

Delaney was one problem he couldn't let go of. Not now. Relax. It was easier said than done.

Gary straightened, picked up the pace again, pushing himself harder. Tried to block Adriana's voice out.

It had to be more than the building that connected Delaney and Wendell. Was it gambling? Both addicted to the game? Pebbles gave way beneath the soles of his trainers. Or was it something else? That comment about business going badly had set him off. A deal gone wrong? Or a debt owed to the wrong person. Something that affected those who worked with him, or just himself? Any one of those options might be the pressure point that had Delaney on the verge of cracking. And Gary would be damned if he couldn't figure out what that was.

Adriana was right about one thing. Dwelling on the problem wasn't going to solve it.

"Fine," Gary said out loud. A bird startled from the branch nearby, flew away with a crash of leaves. "I'll go back and buy the bloody paint. Stonewashed Blue. Happy?"

No reply. 'Course there wasn't.

He kept running and thought of Adriana. A memory, but a good one this time. He concentrated and conjured up an image. And there she was, making coffee, wearing his t-shirt, hem skimming long bare legs. Balanced up on her toes because the floor was like ice. "Some Kind Of Wonderful" on the radio, turned up loud. That surprised shriek when he picked her up and whirled her around and through the kitchen. Arms wrapped tight around his neck as she laughed, giddy and breathless and carefree.

For one moment, Gary held onto the sound of her laughter.

Painting the apartment would clear his head. Then he'd figure out the link. He could only hope it would be soon enough.

Chapter Thirty-Three

The shadows hid him like a friend. Gary watched the doorway across the street, waiting. He swept his gaze down the street in both directions. He wasn't taking any risks. There was always the chance he had underestimated Delaney's sense of self-preservation. He didn't think Delaney had the nerve to show up again, but he might be wrong. Better to err on the side of caution.

Kate exited the bookstore and he straightened, alert. She pulled the door of the bookstore shut behind her, the "closed" sign rattling gently with the movement. Night ran down the glass in a swirl of soft shades. Somewhere in the distance he could hear the crystalline staccato of heels on stone.

She tugged at the handle to double-check the latch had caught, that the bolt was thrown. Good girl, he thought.

Standing there, Kate hesitated, threw a glance over her shoulder. Something had set her on edge. She couldn't see him, Gary was certain of that. Kate seemed to gather her courage, then pivoted toward the space between the buildings across the street, toward him.

Their eyes met and Gary froze. Shock flared through him, settling at the base of his skull. How the hell had she spotted him?

He watched Kate glance left then right down the

empty street, shrug her purse higher on her shoulder. With a determined set to her chin, she set off across the road, straight toward him. He wasn't prepared for it. He had underestimated her.

There was no way of avoiding confrontation now. Then she was standing in front of him, looking at him curiously.

"What are you doing?" Kate asked. "To the untrained eye, it would look as though you're lurking." She gestured at him, the dark corner, the street.

Gary weighed his words. "I wanted to protect you. Obviously, not as discreetly as I'd hoped."

Kate looked at the empty street. "Is there some sort of impending danger I don't know about? It all looks pretty safe to me, right now. Is this about the burglary?"

"Look, could we talk about this inside?" The wooden sign above the store looked like sheet-gold in the darkness.

She shot him a glance, but shrugged. "Sure."

Kate led the way across the street, let them into the store. The streetlights cast their glow though the windows. Kate put her bag on the counter and turned to face him.

Gary rubbed a hand over the back of his neck. How best to tell her? Just start. She should know. "The day I ran into you in the parking lot—"

"The day I punched you."

"Yes." Gary gave her a wry look. "Someone was following you that night."

"I know, I could tell. That's why I took a swing at you. I thought it might have been him."

"I got a look at him. Did some research. Got a name to go with the face." Factual, he laid it out. "His name is Ryan Delaney. Age thirty-nine. Your Mr. Wendell worked in the same company. Wendell is the only connection I can find between you and Delaney. He was the man you saw in the orchard. So what do you have that he wants? Or what do you know that he's afraid of?"

"Are you thinking along the lines of a corporate conspiracy?"

"Maybe. I don't know." He didn't have the answers yet.

She licked dry lips. "And you're worried that he's dangerous?"

"He's got one hell of a temper, and the need for control. Gut instinct says yes, he could be dangerous."

"Why didn't you tell me about this earlier?"

"I needed time and I needed to be sure. He might leave you alone now."

"Why? How do you know?"

Gary's knuckles still ached from contact with flesh and bone. "Just a feeling."

"Don't think I didn't notice that split lip you've got." She waited, but he didn't say anything. "Right, silence on that one." Kate dragged her hands through her hair. "All this must have something to do with Wendell. But all his things are gone, except for this useless laptop. I can't access any of his files. They're all password protected."

"Mind if I take a look?"

"Sure, have at it." Kate turned on the laptop, offered him the chair. "I doubt you'll have any luck though."

He knew the man inside out. Chances were, he could get in. He chose one of the folders at random.

Password protected.

"See?" Kate said, leaning over his shoulder.

"Patience," Gary murmured, thinking of possible combinations. Numbers or letters. Date of birth? Too simple. He tried it anyway. No luck. *The password you typed is incorrect.* The words flashed at him. Not surprising that one didn't work. Mother's maiden name? Too sentimental.

"Got any other ideas?"

Her voice jerked him from his train of thought. Gary shot her a look. "If you'd just let me think, Kate."

"Right, sorry." She rolled her eyes, but gave him space, moving a few inches to the left.

He waved her farther away. "A little more." Held up his hand when she was leaning against the edge of the counter. "Perfect. Stay there." He turned back to the computer.

Wendell's game of choice. Poker. Gary typed in Royal Flush. Tried it lower case, one word. And bingo. He was in. A grin spread across his face. He knew the man all right. Expect little, aim for the obvious. Sometimes it was that easy.

Kate moved closer again. Her hair brushed his cheek as she leaned in to look at the screen. "What is it?"

"Images. Not many." Had there been more, then deleted? Or there simply wasn't much in it. The date the folder was created to the date it was last accessed covered two weeks. About six months old. Gary opened the images, one after another. Four of them in total. Lined them up on the screen. "Looks like surveillance photos."

All from the same night, tracking a path through

London. Back of a car, street sign in view. An SUV. Silver paint job. No dents or scratches. License plate out of the frame. Shame, that. The images were blurry. The photographer hadn't compensated for the speed of the car. Odd angle, like the person holding the camera had the other hand on the wheel, caught the image through the windshield while driving. Three of those, all at different points, but recognizable locations. Easy enough to track the progress on a map.

"What do you think it means?" Kate asked.

"Not sure yet."

The last image though, was more promising. A man standing at the door of a building, turned away from the camera. The statue of a winged archer, classical in form and similar to the one on Piccadilly Circus but smaller, seemed to be aiming its bow at the person about to enter. Eros. A gentleman's club, well-known for its architecture and its secrecy. Members were notoriously discreet. The club was old, exclusive, and private. Invitation only. Gaming rooms, glasses of champagne, rich food. Why bother documenting the route, saving it in a secure file?

Panes of glass in the door. Gary zoomed. There. Might be a reflection of the man's face.

Kate studied the pictures, frowning. "What was Wendell up to?"

"We could figure that out. I could upload these to my secure server, check up on where he was." Assign an employee to enlarge the image, sharpen the reflection. Tom could do it. He'd worked his magic on security footage before, pixelated images. These images, they were giving off the scent of hot blood. There was something here, all right. "Don't tell me you're not curious."

"Okay, it's killing me." They shared a look, her eyes going bright with the thrill of the chase. "Do you think it has something to do with Delaney?"

"Might." He'd put the push on Tom. Get the answer sooner rather than later. Gary resisted the urge to take the computer, try to access more files. He'd start with this. Best not to push it. He uploaded the images, and closed the laptop.

"So, should I be carrying pepper spray?" Kate asked. Hands on her hips, feet firmly planted, the stance was all defiance and courage. Eyes sparking with determination.

Gary grinned at her, delighted.

"What's so funny?" She asked.

"Nothing. I'm almost afraid for the other guy."

"As you should be."

The headlights of a passing car swept through the dark store in a blinding arc.

The next instant, Gary had moved, his fingers tangling in her hair. Mouth hard and fast against hers. Her breath caught on his.

The store became hushed, the air thick with time slowed, each moment clinging to the next. Rows of gold-tipped titles, worn covers, uncut pages, and faded illustrations surrounded them. A dense wall of fantasy worlds.

His hands slid beneath her shirt, moved over her ribcage.

Kate grabbed his wrists, stopped the progress of his hands, and pulled back. "Windows."

"What?" His eyebrows rose as he tried to decipher the one-word statement.

"Lots and lots of windows. And I sell children's books."

"You're right." Gary moved back, trying not to smile. "We wouldn't want to shock Winnie the Pooh."

"It's more Christopher Robin I'm worried about." Kate grinned. "He's very impressionable."

"Then why don't you show off your self-defense skills instead. What other tactics have you got?"

"What do you mean?"

"Can you handle the situation if someone attacks you?"

"I thought I had more than proved myself on that point."

"You caught me off guard. That's entirely different. Let's see what skills you've got, Rowan."

Kate crossed her arms over her chest. "You don't have to worry your pretty little head about it."

"Then prove it." He needed to know she could take care of herself, if need be. He couldn't be there every second. And even if he was, things went wrong. There were precautions he should have taken the first time. Delaney would back down if faced by a stronger opponent, but a woman, alone, defenseless... He wouldn't hesitate. That Gary had seen and it chilled him to the bone. An image of dried blood darkening the petals of the carved orchid rose in his mind. "What's your tactic?"

"You're kidding." A single car drove past, the sound of the motor muffled behind glass.

"Put my mind at ease, Kate. Well?" Gary spread his arms, planted his feet, well aware he towered above her. "Give it your best shot."

Kate looked at him skeptically. "I don't want to

hurt you."

He seriously doubted that was even a possibility. "Don't feel sorry for your victim. Don't hesitate. One second of uncertainty is all it can take."

"I've heard all this a million times." Kate rolled her eyes. "I grew up with over-protective brothers."

He'd have to go down a different route. "Well, all I see right now," he paused, "is a coward."

Kate sucked in a breath, her eyes narrowing dangerously. "A what?"

"You heard me."

He never saw it coming. Kate grabbed his arm, her back to him, and flipped him neatly over her shoulder. The next instant, the floor was hard against his back, the jolt of contact radiating through his spine. He didn't even have enough breath to croak a complaint. Jesus Christ. Gary lay on the floor without moving, dazed.

Kate's face floated above him. "Sorry about that. I did warn you. And I was provoked. Don't ever—" she spaced the words out "—call me a coward."

"Believe me, I won't." He groaned. He sat up slowly, hoping everything still moved the way it should.

"Need a hand up?" Kate grinned.

"I can manage." Gary rose painfully to his feet, trying not to grimace. "Where the hell did you learn that?"

"Like I said, I have brothers." Kate shrugged. "I can also tie a sailor's knot and quote *Lethal Weapon* among my many other talents."

"Impressive."

"I know. What's this?" A shiny tangle, disappearing into a crack in the wooden floor. Gleam of gold.

Gary moved, but she was faster. Before he could do anything to intervene, she was holding it, the pendant nestled in the palm of her hand.

"Where did you get this?" Her voice was hollow.

That tone had shards of panic riddling through him. "Get what?" His throat was dry.

She held it up. The chain ran through her fingers. The pendant sparked like fire, catching the light. The orchid swung in the air as she stared at him, demanding. "It was in your pocket."

He could deny it. *I've never seen it before.* Shrug it off. There were ways to fix this, but all of them involved lies, more deceit. Kate waited, eyes dark with distrust.

This was the end.

He spoke. "I stole that necklace from the house."

"Why?" It was a whisper. Her eyes never left his face.

Gary paced, adrenaline and fear coursing through him.

Then he turned to her. "Because I killed him."

Chapter Thirty-Four

"Who?" Kate shook her head, trying to keep up, to hold onto reason. She watched Gary warily as he stood still, his features unreadable. Something about him, the stance, the aura of defeat reminded her of someone else. Of a warrior and an endless battlefield. Death and destruction spilled at his feet. A blind tool of fate, ravaged by the ruin he had caused.

A shiver crawled beneath her flesh. Kate leaned against the counter behind her. Steadied herself.

"Wendell."

Her head snapped up. He said the name like he was laying something revolting at her feet.

"No." Kate shook her head. "He died of a heart attack. Dr. Garreth—"

"It was a heart attack." Shadows created by the window frame stretched across him in long lines, bars of darkness. "An empty syringe, an air bubble injected into the femoral artery stops the circulation." His tone was clinical. Impartial. Above doubt. Beyond denial. "It functions like an embolism. The heart fails, stops beating. A myocardial infarction is the interruption of the blood supply to part of the heart, which causes the cells to die. So, yes, Wendell died of a heart attack."

Kate dragged in a breath. "Why?" Her heart pounded against her ribcage. Her fingers were cold. An air bubble to stop the circulation. It was so simple.

"What does this have to do with the necklace?" It seemed like there was no end to the questions. They raced through her mind, one after the other.

He didn't falter, didn't pause. "I lost someone. Before Fenris Securities, I was a close protection officer, a bodyguard. The CEO of a multi conglomerate had received threatening letters, anonymous, untraceable. I was hired to protect his daughter."

What was it like, knowing you might have to sacrifice your life to save someone else?

"I became…" Now there was hesitation. An almost imperceptible struggle. "Emotionally attached to her and—" His jaw clenched. He took a breath, carried on. "Sacrificed my objectivity." A sardonic smile twisted at his mouth. "I was distracted for one instant. That was all it took. One second. Can you imagine that?" His eyes met hers and the raw pain within them burned her. "I could have prevented it. Should have and I didn't. I lost my focus. She was shot as we were crossing the parking lot. She bled to death and there was nothing I could do."

The scenario unfolded before her eyes, grisly in its detail. The blood spreading.

"I eventually found out who pulled the trigger. Derek Wendell." His lips curled in disdain. "Not his real name, by the way. He was a gambler. Addicted to the game. The adrenaline rush. He got into debt, owed money to the wrong people. They offered him an alternative. Play the role of assassin and they'd let him live. Just like that. In broad daylight, he took her life. Then I took his." He dug his hands into his pockets.

Kate held up a hand. "Let me get this straight. You're telling me that Mr. Wendell was a gambler, an assassin and you killed him? Our Mr. Wendell?"

"Yes."

It was insane. She felt like she'd just stepped through the mirror into an alternate universe, or fallen down a well and hit her head. This was all some extravagant hallucination. The product of too much fiction. Enter next the secret wife, the sinister foreigner with poisoned darts, the body buried at the crossroads and the stash of gold.

"I gave her that necklace. Adriana was wearing it the day she died. It got caught and broke when the medics came. I went back for it, but it was gone. Wendell had it. He picked it up off the ground after they took her away."

"I could go to the police with this." It seemed like the room itself had shifted. Everything had become turned around. Transformed from man to murderer with a few words.

"You could." He shrugged, indifferent. "But remember you'll have a hard time proving it was a homicide. Any evidence would be circumstantial at best. If you're lucky, you'll be able to find a puncture wound on the body. It wouldn't be damning. Penelope thinks she saw someone, but who's going to believe an old woman? At any given moment, I can have two witnesses swear they saw me at the time of death. It wouldn't be difficult to produce an alibi."

Someone laughed. The sound was odd, detached. It didn't seem to come from her. "This is insane."

Gary was standing only a few steps away from her. Waiting for her to say something. It was her move and she didn't know which piece to play, let alone where to place it. Stalemate.

Apprehension curdled the tranquility of the store. The fragile balance was broken by a sound, sudden and loud.

A knock on the store window.

Their eyes locked.

"Expecting anyone?" His voice was calm, but his eyes were sharp and aware.

"No."

A blurred figure peered through the window at them. The shape moved. Tapped the glass with an impatient flick of the wrist. A familiar rap of knuckles.

Kate brushed past Gary and flung upon the door.

Marcus smiled. "Hullo-ullo-ullo." He stopped short at the sight of Gary. Suspicion crossed his features. He looked from Gary to Kate. From Kate to Gary. "Am I interrupting?"

"No." Gary's reply was terse.

"Yes," Kate said.

"I was about to leave." Gary nodded at Marcus and walked past them, out into the street.

Kate grabbed her bag and followed, pulling Marcus along with her. "What are you doing here?"

Marcus shook her hand off and tugged his jacket down, smoothing the sharp creases.

They stood in front of her store, a strange group assembled on the otherwise empty street. One a dashing figure in an exquisitely tailored suit, one a simple bookstore owner, and one a—

"—murderer." Marcus ended the explanation she'd been half listening to.

Kate jumped. "What?"

Gary's shoulders tensed almost imperceptibly. The kinetic energy he exuded seemed to darken, grow denser.

Marcus looked at her strangely. "I was on my way home," he said slowly and clearly, "and caught sight of someone moving around in the store. Thought it might be the wicked gnome slasher or an impetuous book thief, so I stopped to do my duty. What did you think I said?"

"Nothing." Kate tried to shrug off her odd reaction. "Thanks for checking."

"Naturally. We don't tolerate book thieves." He turned to Gary. "I'm the best friend," he explained, suddenly growing taller, and adopting an ever so slightly menacing appearance. His shoulders seemed broader and his brows puckered.

Marcus would choose this moment to don the verbal boxing gloves. She was afraid that, as an opponent, Gary wouldn't stick to cunning wordplay.

"Nice to meet you," Gary replied. His expression open and friendly. He might never have confessed to murder.

Marcus suddenly stepped closer and scrutinized her face. Kate scowled. "She looks pale." It was an accusation.

"Don't be an idiot, Marcus." Was it really surprising that she looked pale after what she had found out? A healthy glow might have been ever so slightly unusual, and flagrantly inappropriate. Or the work of a really decent beauty product.

Marcus shot her a quelling glance. "This is between him and me, Kate. Step back." The command was imperious. Here was the haughtiness and authority of the polished real-estate agent.

Gary shook his head. He had the self-assurance of

an experienced street fighter. He looked amused and mildly irritated.

"I wouldn't, if I were you," Kate warned Marcus.

"That's right." Gary smiled. It was completely unlike the warm, delighted grin that had spread across his features earlier. This one chilled her to the bone. "Whatever you're thinking about right now, don't." He held out his hand to Kate. "The necklace."

Kate let the cool chain slide through her fingers and ignored the way her heart had tightened at the request. "It's yours."

Gary's hand closed around it, concealing that sheen of gold.

For a moment she thought he was going to say something. Then he shrugged abruptly, dismissively. "Take her home," he told Marcus.

"I have my own car."

They ignored her.

Marcus nodded to Gary. "I was going to anyway, if you're not."

Kate rolled her eyes and spun on her heel. They could sort things out themselves. She was going home.

She'd gone three steps when she was brought up short. Gary had snagged her by the back of her jacket.

Kate knocked his hand away. So she wasn't invisible after all. "Please do keep in mind that I landed you on your arse before."

Marcus's eyebrows quirked delicately. "Really, Kate—"

"Beginners luck." Gary's reply was curt. "You're going with him. Don't make this difficult." It was said in a commanding tone, the kind she was sure he used when speaking to an employee.

It irritated the hell out of her. "No."

"Why not?" Marcus looked wounded.

"Marcus, it makes no sense. I can drive myself. If you'd like, you can walk me to my car and open the door for me."

"Good." Gary turned. Began to walk down the darkened street, that efficient stride devouring the pavement. The hand that held the necklace disappeared into his pocket. No goodbyes. Not even a second glance.

"Did I detect a hint of tension in the air?" Marcus asked.

"You're very perceptive, Marcus."

"I do try." Marcus strolled at her side, unusually silent and thoughtful. When they reached her car, he held out his hand for her keys. She relinquished them and he opened the door for her. "Your chariot." He bowed with a flourish.

Kate slid behind the wheel.

Chapter Thirty-Five

"And that's your best shot?" Gary called as he ducked the fist coming toward him. He could feel the air rush past from the force of it. "You're going to have to up your game, Perce." It was late, the gym was clearing out. Familiar smell of locker room sweat hanging in the air.

Perce frowned at him, swiping an arm at his brow. "You'd be on your arse, if I'd landed that punch."

"Maybe, but I'm faster." The trick was to avoid getting drawn into a grappling match. One choke or joint lock from Perce, and that would be the end of their friendly sparring match. Today though, he was leaving it close to the edge. And he could feel the heat of adrenaline pumping through his blood. "Try again."

Perce came at him. Despite the shock absorbing padding, Gary could feel the mat yield beneath the weight of Percival's steps as the man came toward him like a bull dozer. Time to stop dodging. Gary let the next punch connect with his jaw, knocking his head back. He'd left enough distance between them to slow the force of it. It didn't take him down. The blow was buffered by the sparring-glove, but for one second, Gary saw stars. He could feel the rope at his back, the edge of the ring. Thank Christ for the multi-layered foam of the sparring gloves, or Kate really would have something to say about his glass jaw. If she spoke to him again.

Why, she'd asked. Not, how could you? Not, what kind of a person are you? But why.

In striking range now. Perce hadn't yet regained a stable position after the swing. Here was the opportunity he'd been waiting for.

Gary caught hold of Perce's elbow with one hand, and with the other hand got a solid grip behind his neck. They grappled for balance, Perce struggling to fight free. Gary swung out a foot and caught Perce neatly behind the ankle, whipping it out from under him. The leg trip never failed to tip the scales in his favor, despite the difference in their sizes. Take-down. With a colossal thud, Perce was on the ground, flat on his back, and looking immensely surprised to find himself there.

Gary gasped for breath, managed a laugh. The movement had his ribs aching. "Looked to me like you could use a lie-down. Thought I'd help you along."

Perce scowled. "Funny."

Gary reached a hand down, helped Perce to his feet. "Again."

Perce gave him a level gaze. "How long are we going to do this, then?"

Long enough until he stopped seeing Kate's face gone pale with shock. Disbelief. This time Gary landed a punch, felt it reverberate up his arm. Disgust and horror in her eyes. But not fear. At least there was that. He threw another punch, but missed as Perce swerved. He needed her to be safe, but he couldn't get close to her now.

Perce stayed at the other side of the ring, shaking out his arms, keeping the muscles loose, weight positioned on the balls of his feet. "Lost focus there."

Perce was breathing hard, taking the chance for a rest.

"Hell I did." Chin down. Hands up. Gary kept moving, dodging to the side. He braced for the blow. It had him reeling anyway.

"Have you thought any more about Harris? Or are we still waiting?"

"Waiting." For now. He caught Percival with a series of quick jabs that pushed the man back a step, then another.

Perce dodged the next. "Right, so we're letting him take our clients, and—"

Gary caught him with a shoulder to the gut, and kept moving, feet pumping. He kept driving forward until Perce toppled, hit the ground again.

"I'll deal with it in my own time." Gary dragged air into his lungs. Sweat dripped into his eyes.

"You've got a week, before I make it my business."

And he knew he would. "Fair enough." The clock was ticking. "I need a favor."

"I knew it." Perce got to his knees, levered up. The laugh rumbled through him, had Perce's shoulders shaking. He used his teeth to yank off one of his gloves, pulled the second one off. "Buy me a pint and tell me what you need done. I'm not sparring with you again though, not for a while anyway."

"You must be getting old, Perce. All those aches and pains—" Gary dodged the bare-knuckled fist coming his way and ducked under the rope, feeling his legs shake with exertion, the warmth still flowing through his muscles.

Chapter Thirty-Six

That night, Kate dreamt of a battlefield.

The landscape was muted and ravaged, stretching on as far as the eye could see. Tree stumps and discarded weapons, long tapered swords and spears, dotted the field. The ground sank beneath her feet, soggy and spongy, scattered with pools of stagnant water and blood.

The battlefield was empty but for the dead.

The corpses lay amid shafts of dry hay. The acrid smell of blood, flesh and fear mingled with sulfurous swamp gasses. Bile rose in her throat.

An emotion far past terror, far past fury, far past the primal instinct for survival, whatever the cost, tightened her chest. Her senses numbed by the overwhelming force of the feelings in this place.

The battle was over but she could still taste the adrenaline in the air, metallic and sharp like the blade of a knife.

Senseless destruction was spread all around her. It was everywhere. Kate had imagined these scenes of war, historical, human, and magical, but had never grasped the true horror until now. The forms lying around her couldn't have been people, although some small part of her mind registered them for what they were. She took in the scene around her with cold detachment, reconstructing the scenario, registering the scene for what it was. The other part of her mind screamed in primitive, primal fear. Fear for herself. Fear of being destroyed, torn apart and shredded like the bodies around her. Of a sword being driven through her, of being attacked from behind, of being surrounded by the army, the force that did this.

Her movements were endlessly slow. It took an effort of will to lift her arm, to touch her cheek. To confirm she was alive. She wasn't one of the dead.

She stood on that field, felt the ground beneath her, smelt the dirt and the sweat, saw the imprints her feet left in the mud. But she felt intangible, unreal. Like a ghost walking among dead shredded through to the soul so that not even their spirits remained intact. She was a visitor, a specter, in a world she desperately wanted to leave, to flee like an animal. How could she run if she could barely lift her hand? Her mind gave the commands, commanding her body to move, to do something even if it was only to cower on the ground, anything to protect herself, but her limbs resisted.

A breath whispered past her lips into air that had long stopped moving. There wasn't a bird in the sky, nor so much as a caterpillar in the trampled grass. Nothing but decay and the wreck and crash of weapons, the roar of voices lingering in this field of death. Where the faceless dead had been felled, strewn like garbage, and been forgotten.

Then she felt him. A change in the frozen setting. A crackle of power, of life.

She dragged her eyes away from the gore at her feet, and looked at the man standing upon the ruins of war.

And she knew—she knew that this was his world.

The cracked leather, the battered steel of his armor looked like a second skin, as much a part of him as the long lines of his powerful muscles. Fingers caked with brown, dried blood held a longbow lowered to his side. An arrow still rested on the top finger of his bow hand. The lines of his face were lean and hard, his jaw clenched tightly.

Her heart whispered his name.

She knew what his body felt like beneath the steel of his armor. What his lips tasted like.

He raised his eyes, met hers across that endless field of bloodshed and she was captivated by the sorrow she saw in them. He had been a part of the devastation around them and he had survived. Yet, she saw in his eyes the craving for death, his own death, and went cold.

He had survived and yet she knew he would give anything to change that. What made a person wish for an end as gruesome as this? What horrors made torn flesh and splintered bone appealing? What made you yearn for escape in the white heat of pain?

After the first shock of recognition came understanding. No one could live after seeing this, after causing this. The guilt would be all-consuming, another form of torture. She could see it in his eyes.

He wouldn't take his own life. It would be weak. An escape. The warrior would fight, die in battle at the hands of another, and suffer until he did. Accept the pain as toll for that he'd caused. For the blood of loved ones that had run through his fingers to splash to the ground at his feet.

His left hand tensed, once, around the grip of his bow. Even with the distance between them, she could see the strength of the tendons in his hand as his muscles flexed. She was trapped in his gaze.

Something pale shimmered at the edge of her vision. Came closer. An intruder in that broken world, that was theirs and theirs alone. A figure gliding toward them so fast, it was a blur of white silk and blonde hair. One slender arm wrapped around his shoulder, held fast. Strands of long hair twisted around him, swirling even when she had become still. Impassive, calculating eyes appraised Kate. With possessive fingers the woman stroked his hair idly, not a breath escaping those red lips.

"He has a heart of stone." Her voice was cold and clear as the hum of glass. Words stirred the grass, rippling across it like wind over water. Unspoken, yet heard. "Run. Run as fast as you can."

Where could she run to? The ground stretched on forever, the sky above it devoid even of clouds. There was nothing. Nowhere to go. Nowhere to hide.

As she looked into the warrior's eyes, the realization dawned. Even if she had the means of escape, she would choose to stay there with him. There was a bond between them. It held her there.

The woman stared at Kate, issuing a warning with her gaze. Certain of her power.

The warrior shifted his stance, energy strung as taut as the bow in his hand. The woman traced a finger over his ear, down his neck, always watching Kate. The warrior spread his feet, balanced his weight, and raised the bow. He pulled his drawing arm backward in one fluid motion until the hand that held the arrow rested against his jaw. He held the position and aimed, sighting down the shaft of the arrow.

The arrow that was aimed at her.

She felt three figures gather around her without surprise, could smell their familiar scent of paper and ink. One wound his fingers through hers. The other encircled her waist with his arm, a solid form next to hers though without warmth. The third brushed away the tear drying on her cheek.

"Come. Come with us. Love us," they breathed as one.

Kate watched, detached, the warrior across from her, countered his unwavering stare. Watched the bowstring slip from his fingers, pull away from his hand that recoiled to rest beside his neck. His bow arm remained firm, the rest of his body steady, with the flex and snap of the string, the release of the arrow.

She watched his eyes as the iron-tipped arrow shot toward her. Could feel it piercing the air as it flew, fast and true. She watched him, watched its course, without fear.

And awoke with a gasping breath in her own bed as one drowning, clasping at tangled sheets, and wishing blindly that he were still there.

Chapter Thirty-Seven

"Do you think we should ring the police?" Elaina asked.

"What?" Startled, Kate looked up. It was as though Elaina had read her thoughts. Kate was sitting cross-legged in an armchair, a thick hard-covered book splayed across one knee. She had yet to turn the page. A reading light next to her and the twin candles on the low table illuminated the living room. Sunflowers in a vase on the coffee table, ageing now, the flickering flames turning the edges to bronze. For now, she had kept Gary's secret. But how long could she remain silent?

"There's a man loitering outside. I spotted him from the tower. He was staring ponderously at the tires of his Ford Fiesta, hands on hips." Elaina imitated the pose. "When I came into the house, he was still there, sitting in his car."

Kate was suddenly aware of the expanse of glass behind her. She slid the bookmark between the pages, marking her place. "Car trouble?" Or something more sinister? "What does he look like?"

"Tall, big…" Elaina spread her hands to indicate broad shoulders, then trailed off. She shrugged. "I'm not really sure."

"Which side of the street was he parked on?"

"At the end of the drive, where the trees thin out."

"When did you notice him?"

"I don't know." Elaina sounded irritated now. "I didn't look at my watch and make a note of the time on a corner of the canvas."

"Not even a penciled notation?" Kate stood and tossed the book on the chair.

"Should we take a look?"

"Outside?"

"It might just be a flat tire. Would you though? I don't have any shoes on." She wriggled her bare toes, nails painted a shade of brilliant green. "And I'm going to have to get changed soon. Ian and I are going out for dinner. Spending 'quality time together'." She traced quotation marks in the air.

"You're serious? Fine. I'll go see if he's still there."

"It's not your admirer, anyway, that much I can tell."

"What do you mean?"

"This chap came by the pub yesterday, sat himself at the bar and started talking. Asking about you, and if you're seeing anyone. Made it seem like he was an old friend, but I'm thinking, he's a secret admirer. A customer from the shop who has his eye on you."

A chill crept over Kate's skin. "What did he look like?"

"Not my type, but attractive. Well-dressed. Money there, I'd say. Probably a good catch, if you decide Gary isn't the one." Elaina winked.

"What did he want to know?"

"It was just small talk, casual questions. What your interests are, things like that. The pub was busy, so my attention was elsewhere. I do remember telling him how much you like mysteries. He mentioned the burglary. It's the talk of the town, after all. I said you'd solve the case soon, if the cops don't. Nothing earth-shattering."

Maybe she was right. Maybe it didn't mean anything. It was strange though. "Why don't you find the phone?" Kate kept her voice neutral, casual. "Just in case this guy wants to call a tow truck for his car." Or they needed to phone the police. "If I'm not back in five—"

"Yeah, I get it." Elaina said. She threw herself into the chair Kate had just vacated and stretched. "I've seen the movies."

"Make yourself comfortable," Kate muttered as she left.

In the entrance, Kate shaded the window with one hand. Peering out through one of the colored panes, she saw the length of drive, shining palely through the tinted glass. It was too dark, impossible to see farther. There were too many trees. No. She shifted, blocking out the ghostly reflection of the room behind her with the curve of her hand. There at the end of the property, was that the shape of a car? She stepped back.

What was the worst that could happen? The car was at the end of their own driveway, for God's sake.

The kitchen was dark when Kate entered, when she opened the drawer. Glint of knives. She selected one. A carving knife. The blade thin and sharp. The handle felt cool and lay heavy in her hand, but it was well balanced. She gripped it firmly. Better safe than sorry.

Kate walked out to the entrance and opened the front door. Her fingers curled around the handle, the blade flashing.

The porch creaked softly beneath her weight. She waited a moment for her eyes to adjust to the dark. The dense thicket of trees concealed the road. She wouldn't be able to see anything from there.

She stepped off the porch, crossed the grass. A moth, feathery and soft, brushed against her arm. A bird flew overhead with a frightening clash of wings. Her heart pounded, an unsteady, wild rhythm.

Through a break in the foliage ahead, she saw the car. Leaves reflected in the windows, steam clouding the glass. Her palm slid damply on the handle of the knife concealed behind her back. Kate rapped a knuckle against the glass and waited.

Nothing happened. It seemed to simply be a parked car. Her laugh was shaky. Feeling incredibly stupid, Kate spun on her heel.

A whisper of sound, glass against rubber.

Her heart in her throat, Kate turned back and watched the window slide down. The driver just a form in the dusk within the car.

Kate took a cautious step closer. "Are you in trouble? Has your car broken down?"

A tweed-clad arm and leather elbow patch appeared. The man leaned out. A bovine face materialized. It was difficult to tell whether his hair was red or auburn. He seemed to be in his late forties.

Expression unchanged, he looked out at her. "Kate Rowan?" His voice was an impressive rumble of sound.

Shock had her falling back a step. "Who are you?"

"Gary Fenris sent me."

Kate paused. "Prove it."

"He said you'd say that and told me to give you this." He held something out to her. She took it from him cautiously. A slim leather pouch. She opened it. A row of stainless-steel tools within. Five picks and two tension wrenches. "A lock pick set?"

"The handles are reinforced. He said you'd put it to good use."

She smothered a laugh. "Okay. So Gary did send you. Why?"

"Safety precaution."

Kate raised the knife. "I've got that covered, thank you."

On a muffled oath, he jerked his arm back into the car. "I'm just the messenger."

"You must be cold without the engine running to keep the heat going."

"Scottish wool." He gestured at the thick sweater he was wearing beneath the tweed. "Until further orders, you're stuck with me." A grin appeared suddenly. "Save the knife for the Sunday roast. You'll ruin the blade."

The window rose.

Kate rapped her knuckles against the glass again. Waited impatiently. Knocked again. Nothing. She scowled at the car.

How would she explain to Elaina that the Ford would remain parked outside their house for the time being?

The tools though, they were lovely. She fingered the edge of the leather one more time, then slid it into her back pocket.

Walking back to the house, Kate pulled out her cell phone, scrolled through the contacts for Gary's number. The screen was cold against her skin as she typed.—*A bodyguard?*—

A second later, her phone pinged with a response.

—*Yes. Did you get my proof of receipt?*—

Kate wrote—*Thank you for the lock pick set, but I don't need a bodyguard.*—

—*You're stuck with him for now.*—A pause, then another text.—*Be nice.*—

—*For how long?*—

There was no reply.

Chapter Thirty-Eight

Gary had stared down the barrel of a gun before. He could do it again.

Just nerves, that's all. Functioning under pressure, normally not a problem, not for him. This though, this was different. And all because Perce couldn't leave well enough alone.

Waiting, paying his debts that way, was no longer an option now. Time to play his hand. Speed things along. Gary was parked on the street. Up ahead, on the left, was the house.

Car in the driveway. They were home. If they still kept to the same routine, they'd be having dinner. Just finishing up, maybe. Gary met his own eyes in the rearview mirror. It was now or never.

Gary slammed the car door. He stood there a minute, gave the house a good long look. Not the same house. They moved after Adriana's death. Too many memories, too many ghosts. That, he could understand. This house was smaller, the right size for two people, tucked away at the end of a cul-de-sac. Fewer of those little touches that add heart to a home. No dangly charms in the window. No stone dog, mouth open and panting, by the door. Garden less tended. The hedge needed cutting back.

Window to the right of the door. Kettle visible, gleam of a copper pot on the opposite wall. The kitchen. Clear view of the path from there, maybe the front door too, if someone moved close enough, got the angle right. If someone was in that room, they'd know by now that he was here.

Brush of the breeze over his arm, like the touch of a hand.

Gary tightened his grip on the folder, felt the edge of the plastic dig into his palm. Could be he'd get left standing outside. Then he'd put it in the mail slot. It'd be up to them whether they looked at it or not.

Six steps was all it took, and he was at the door. The bell chimed loud enough to hear it from where he was standing, on the other side of the door, echoing through the entrance and on into the distance. He waited. Thirty seconds, a minute. Smell of roasted meat and herbs, a blast of warmth, when the door finally opened.

Harris gave him a hard gaze. It was quick, gone in an instant, but Gary saw that shift, from shock to control. It took skill, but Harris had always been good at keeping himself in check. So Harris hadn't seen him coming, hadn't had time to prepare. An advantage? Gary wasn't sure. Harris was in his shirtsleeves, tie loosened. In for the night.

With a glance over his shoulder, Harris pulled the door closed behind him, kept his voice low. "You've got some nerve, coming here." Resentment there, the force of it held back, but barely. Gary fought the urge to shift his feet.

At least he hadn't shut the door in his face, Gary thought. "You could say that."

"Trouble at the office?" A cold smile, flash of triumph that almost had Gary's own temper rising in response.

"Smooth sailing, don't you worry about that." Gary reminded himself he wasn't there to pick a fight. This wasn't about him.

"You're not welcome here, not in my home. I want you to leave." Gary made no sign of moving. "Now." Harris gave him a shove, hand to the chest. Hard enough to make it clear he meant it. *Back off.*

Gary fell back a step, but didn't rise to the bait. He kept his arms down, loose at his sides. Making it nice and clear he wasn't going to push back. "That's fine. This won't take long. How is Elizabeth?"

"Heartbroken since her daughter died."

Gary nodded, took the jab for what it was. "This is for you. For both of you." He held out the folder.

"What is it?" Harris didn't take it. He crossed his arms over his chest.

Gary had the folder by one corner. The pages riffled. "Emails. From Adriana."

Harris's head snapped up at that. "Which you got, how exactly?" Suspicious, bordering right on the edge of fury.

"She sent them to me." He continued before Harris could get a word in, "Some are about her thesis. Some are about you and your wife, about friends. She always liked to work the dialogue in." And got it right every time. "It's her voice, leaps right off the page at you. I thought you'd want to read them." Gary set the folder down on the empty planter by the door.

Harris hesitated a beat, then picked up the folder, thumbed through the pages. "Why would she send you these?"

Gary waited, let him get there on his own.

Harris read, thumb moving down the lines, turned the page, did the same again. His head came up. Realization dawned. "The way she wrote to you, told you these things. She was in love with you."

"Yes."

"You self-righteous prick." Harris closed the folder, slammed it against Gary's chest. "You thought you'd come here, throw this in my face? It's not enough that you have her blood on your hands. Now you came here to tell me you stole her heart too. Brought hard evidence proving you played her along. Used her."

"No. That's not—"

"You can keep it. Take it and go."

"Elizabeth might—"

"Don't talk about my wife. She saw you coming and you know what she did? She asked me not to open the door. I should have listened. We don't want anything from you. Get the hell off my property before I call the police for harassment."

"I didn't come here to bother you, or to make things worse. I didn't come here to ask you to stop or for your forgiveness. I came here to offer you the chance to end this, once and for all. You said you wanted me to suffer. So tell me how you want it done. I'm too well off? I'll transfer my money, every last quid, to an account of your choice. You want me to lose my business? I'll give it away. Or would you rather put a bullet in me, right here, right now? I won't try to run. This isn't a trick, some con. It's your rules, your choice. This can't go on, you know that. There are people who work for me, who will fight back. And they're very good at what they do."

"Are you threatening me?"

"I'm warning you. So pick a different way. One that will bring this to an end. Don't tell me you haven't imagined killing me, had it run through your head over and over until you can't sleep for the thought of it. I know you go hunting regularly. I'll bet it's my face you see when you take aim. I'm sure you've bought an unmarked gun, paid cash, one that can't be traced, just in case. This is your chance. Take it."

"I'm not going to lie. I've thought about killing you. Wished for the opportunity to do it and get away with it."

"Your life hasn't been the same since she died? So remove me from the equation. Maybe then you'll have some peace."

"Death isn't good enough for you." Harris stopped, his expression unreadable. He looked at Gary, shook his head. "Jesus, you actually mean it. You'd let me take that shot, wouldn't you? Seems to me it takes a certain kind of man to do that. A troubled man. One who's already suffering. Why else would you be standing here now? Tell me one thing, did you love her?"

"Yes."

"Did you treat her right?"

"I tried to. I hope I did."

"I'm going to keep these emails, and we'll leave it at that." Harris held out his hand for the folder. "As far as I'm concerned, this is over. But trust me when I say I don't want to see you again, ever. Stay away from me and my wife."

"Of course." There wasn't anything else left to say. Gary turned, walked down the path. He didn't look back. He'd need a stiff drink tonight all right.

When Gary got to his car, he tossed his phone on

the passenger side seat, sat there for a moment, hands on the wheel, waiting for his heartbeat to slow. Fragments of those emails running through his mind. Long breathless paragraphs of excitement. Those short ones he hadn't included in the folder, *shall I bring wine*, that were all his. *Can't wait to see you.*

Green light on the phone, caught his eye. Gary unlocked the screen. One missed call. Tom. One new email, Tom again, image attached. About time. Gary clicked on the email app, opened the message.

Best I could do. Did some digging. Got intel for u. May need a raise for this. T.

Cheeky little bollock. Let's see if he earned himself one. Gary began downloading the attachment. Felt that thrill hit as he watched the progress bar speed toward hundred percent. He was close now. The answers within reach. It was like a drug, potent and sweet, straight to the blood stream.

The image filled the phone's screen.

The reflection in the pane of glass was still grainy, but Tom had worked his magic all right. Despite the shadows, the low quality, the face was recognizable. Delaney.

And there was the link. Wendell had been tracking Delaney. Now that was interesting. And it had Delaney running scared. Whatever Delaney was up to, Wendell had been gathering evidence on him.

Blackmail?

Gary pulled out onto the road. He kept the speed steady, pushing the limits but not over, passing cars where he could, taking the shortest route back to the office.

He needed to talk to Tom. Find out more.

Chapter Thirty-Nine

"I need tea." Kate hoisted herself onto the barstool and planted her elbows on the counter.

It was nearing eight o'clock in the evening and the Old Firehall Café was populated by only a smattering of customers. Cutlery clinked and voices murmured gently. The air tasted of baking.

Nearby, Tim and Will took up the table for four. They each had a battered backpack at their feet and their outer layers bundled across the extra chairs. The surface of the small table was sprinkled with a layer of crumbs. In the center was a thick slice of Neil's chocolate fudge cake, along with two coffee cups, two plates, and two detective novels. They ate in glum silence. Even the brim of Tim's baseball cap seemed to be drooping.

"You look like you've had a rough day," Neil remarked.

"It's been quite a week so far. I've still got some accounting to do at the store. I only came by for sustenance. I'll have an Assam tea to go. And a chocolate chip cookie."

Neil began measuring tea, then glanced at the boys. "Another milk, lads?"

Tim nodded, his chocolate stained lips set in an unhappy line.

"No luck with the gnome mystery yet?" Kate asked

them sympathetically.

They exchanged a glance. "No."

They ducked their heads and turned their attention back on the cake. Tim and Will never passed up the chance to discuss mystery, murder, and intrigue. Something was wrong. She looked from Penelope to the boys, and suspicion dawned.

The door to the café banged open. The pleasant murmur of voices and clinking cutlery cut off abruptly. A fork fell to the floor.

Ponderous footsteps crossed the room to the sofa. Fabric and wood strained, groaning beneath a massive weight. Along with everyone else in the room, Neil had his eyes trained on the corner of the room behind her. Kate didn't have to look to know who it was.

She sighed. "Make that two cups."

"Sure." Neil handed her the tea.

She paid for the drinks, her eyes on the boys. "Thanks."

Tim and Will watched her approach their table with uneasy expressions. Tim swallowed abruptly, choked on a crumb, scrabbled for his cup, and downed the rest of his milk.

Kate set down the drinks between the books and the cake, spun a chair around, transferred its contents to the other and straddled it. She rested her elbows on the chair back and leaned forward. "I've got a few questions for you." She lowered her voice to an appropriately conspiratorial whisper. "About the case."

"What do you mean?" Will shifted and tugged at the collar of his t-shirt.

"Just confirming some facts. Getting things straight." Kate smiled. "Mind if I take a look at your notebook for a second, Tim?"

Tim watched her warily. Will hesitated.

Tim kicked him lightly under the table and nodded. "Do it."

The book was tugged out of a bag and slid across the table to her.

Kate flipped the worn cover open. Scanned the notes scribbled in a loose scrawl, the pencil almost etched into the paper. "You've narrowed the time of Sleepy's demise down to the hour between four and five o'clock p.m. Right?"

"Right." Will rocked back in his chair. It swung before balancing precariously on two legs.

"And the garden was unwatched from four o'clock on." She looked up, waiting for verification.

"Yeah," Tim agreed reluctantly.

"Both of you were at Penelope's house from the time school ended until four forty-five."

"You can ask Grandma. She looked at the clock. She'll tell you the same thing."

"A water-tight alibi." Kate nodded, blandly. "Then you walked back to the house afterward, arriving within about ten minutes, and discovered the corpse."

"Uh huh."

"Did anyone see you on your way home?"

Tim and Will exchanged an uneasy glance. Tim said, "I'm sure there was someone outside at that time."

Will leaned toward Tim and whispered something. He raised his eyebrows and waited. Tim thought for a moment, then nodded.

"Neil," Will announced finally. "He was signing for a delivery. We waved to him."

"That should be easy enough to check up on." Kate

turned. "Neil?"

"Yeah?"

"Last Friday afternoon, do you remember seeing Tim and Will on their way home from Penelope's?"

"Sure." He grinned at them.

"What time was that?"

Will sucked in a breath through his teeth. Tim clamped a hand over his arm in warning. They tensed. The chair rotated slightly in the air.

"Now, let me think." Neil frowned, thoughtfully. "A delivery, you say. I can check the time." He pulled a small calendar out from beneath the counter, thumbed through it. He ran a finger down the page, tapped it. "Four thirty."

There was an expectant, tension-filled pause.

"You're certain the delivery wasn't late?"

"No. I looked at my watch when they arrived. Spot on, as usual."

"Ah ha!" Kate said, triumphant.

Will yelped, all four chair legs crashed to the ground. Will shot forward, bracing himself with both palms against the edge of the table. His breath came in little staccato gasps, and he had flushed scarlet to the tips of his ears. Tim hunched his shoulders.

Kate paused, lowered her voice. "So, in fact, you must have left Penelope's around 4:20 and therefore had ample time in which to get home, distribute the fake blood, set the scene and clean up afterward. It's convenient having a witness who can't see and refuses to wear glasses. Easy enough to convince her you were leaving at five. Or did you change the clocks beforehand?" She leaned forward. "Am I right?"

Will nudged Tim in the side. "She knows," he

whispered.

"It doesn't prove anything. It'll never hold up in court."

"It doesn't have to," Kate said. "The only person I have to convince is your father."

Shocked silence.

Tim nodded, defeated. "You're right, Kate. We killed Sleepy."

"*Conscientia mille testes*," Kate murmured, remembering Henry's words.

Tim leaned forward, suddenly intense. "But we didn't kidnap him!"

"Who did?"

"I'm not naming any names." Tim shook his head, a stubborn set to his jaw. A miniature martyr in denim.

"Okay."

"I found out who had him, and...kind of...bribed him," he looked at her uncertainly, trying to gauge her reaction to this further piece of criminal activity, "to turn the gnome over to me."

"You bribed him?"

"You don't know what some people will do for chocolate," Will told her with a grin.

"Dairy milk?"

"Marshmallow cream. What are you going to do, Kate?" Will asked, his face pale beneath the last faint traces of summer sun.

Kate thought, making them wait. It wouldn't hurt for them to suffer a little. "I thought you said only bad guys killed people, Tim?"

"Sleepy isn't a person, Kate."

"That may be so, but you both know what you did was wrong. You concealed information, bribed someone, staged a murder, lied, and misused the power of the divining stick. Those are serious charges."

"We just wanted to practice investigating," Will explained.

"Turns out it's no fun when you know who did it." Tim slowly removed his hat. He stared at it sadly. Tugged at the strap, fingered the brim wistfully, then tossed it on top of the books. "I don't deserve the cap."

"We're going to go to jail." Will moaned and dropped his forehead to the table.

Kate's mouth twitched. She hurriedly rubbed at her nose.

Tim crossed his arms over his chest and waited bravely.

"Okay, here's the deal." Kate made sure her expression was suitably sober. "You have twenty-four hours to confess your crimes to your father, Tim. I want both of you to go together and explain everything." Two hopeful pairs of eyes lifted to her face. "If you don't, I will, and I'm sure he won't be happy to hear it from me. You are going to clean up Sleepy as best you can, and re-touch the areas that are ruined. I want the gnome better than new. And you have to apologize to Penelope. Got it?"

"It was my idea." Tim drew himself up in his seat. "I'll go alone."

"No way." Will shook his head vehemently. "I'm coming with. We're in it together."

They did a solemn, complicated handshake and nodded. They looked like two front-line soldiers about to face enemy fire.

Kate rose. "And Tim?"

He looked up, his expression resigned.

"Keep the cap." Kate grinned. "You'll make a great detective someday, so long as you don't play both parts. Let someone else be the villain."

He shrugged and tugged at his ear, embarrassed. A pleased smile crept over his face.

Kate grabbed the tea and paused next to the sofa on her way to the door. The man glanced at her.

"Come on, then. Time to close shop."

She handed one of the cups to the large red-haired man. He lumbered to his feet. "Elegantly handled, Rowan," he said.

"Thank you. Are you sure you don't have anywhere else you'd rather be?" She asked hopefully.

"Yes."

Kate slanted her eyes at him.

"No, I'm not leaving," he said placidly.

"Fine. At least tell me your name."

"Percival."

"Well, Percival, how long do you think this relationship is going to continue?"

Silence.

"You are a man of few words."

Percival shrugged and blew on his tea.

Chapter Forty

"Tell me what you've got," Gary said.

He'd given Tom the biggest work space available, but still Tom had managed to fill every inch of it. Five screens, storage boxes rowed on shelves, some filled with hard drives and spare parts, packages waiting to be unboxed containing gear to test and games, though Gary was willing to turn a blind eye on that one. Wires everywhere. Some looped up and taped against the back of the desk, others running the length of the floor. The room hummed. Gary picked his way through the tangles, grabbed a chair. He swung it around, straddled it backward, and waited. The cup in his hand was hot, steam rising.

Feet on the desk, Tom had the keyboard on his lap, fingers flying, headphones on. Noise cancelling. Tom kept typing with one hand and held the other up, eyes never leaving the monitor. "Hang on." He finished what he was doing, hit *enter* with a flourish. Shifted the headphones to his neck. Gary could hear it now, a blast of heavy metal. Tom shoved one foot off the edge of the desk, used the momentum to swivel his chair, and faced Gary. "Hi." Tom rubbed his hands through his hair, eyes bleary. Too long staring at the monitor. He sniffed the air. "Coffee?" He looked at the cup Gary was holding.

"Double espresso." Gary passed it over.

"Thank Jesus. Elspeth brought me juice earlier. For the vitamins." He drained half in one go, Adam's apple bobbing in his thin neck. "Hot," he gasped, sucking air in. "But good. You got my message."

"Yeah, thanks. You said you did some digging."

"You were right about the location. About it being a gentleman's club. I got a friend to run the name through a government database, see what he could get on it. You never know, right?"

"And?"

"Thanks to him, I've now got access to phone calls, investigations, forum posts, and I'm loving it. All that information just waiting to be had. I know we're skirting the line here, but I figured you wouldn't mind. Just get the job done, right?"

"Right. So long as we don't end up on someone's radar screen."

"We're good. He owes me one."

"What did you find?"

"It took a while, since I couldn't refine the search to narrow the results. But I got a hit. Boy, did I get a hit. It's flagged."

"What does that mean?"

"The club. It's under current investigation from the lads at the top. Surveillance, maybe even a sting op."

"Under investigation?" That had his attention. "Do we know why?"

"Nope." Tom laughed. "Jesus, the face on you. I'm only takin' the piss. I wasn't about to stop there, was I? It only whet my appetite."

"Good lad."

"The name of the club got another hit, in the dark web. It was mentioned in a forum post."

Finding the information by trolling beneath the surface of the public internet. There was a reason Tom had the rep he did. He didn't give up until he got results. "What kind of posts?"

"Sex." Tom's eyes glittered in the blue light of the screen. "I'm talking S&M, full on shades of gray, but with girls, the younger the better. For those who like a little violence. It's all done by word of mouth, for those who can pay. I found one post that mentioned the name, before it got deleted. I scrolled past and by the time I backtracked, it was gone. On the front of it, it's a traditional club; high-backed leather armchairs, books, and whiskey. Most of the members probably don't even know what goes on in those other rooms. Those that do get shown the other side have to jump through hoops to get access. They'd have to pass a careful screening and prove their loyalty."

"Seems like someone's got their eye on them now, though."

"Yeah, someone's looking to put paid to their antics and best of luck to them. It's nasty stuff. This got something to do with a new client?"

"A favor for a friend. I said I'd look into it."

"Well, your friend had better be careful. Whoever is involved in this won't want any of it to see the light of day. Dirty secrets like this, people will do anything to protect. Commit murder if they have to."

And Delaney already felt threatened. "Thanks, Tom."

"So, about that raise..." Wide grin, teeth white in the dim room.

"We'll talk about it later. Good work."

Tom was right. Delaney had one hell of a secret to

keep.

Gary should have put two and two together sooner. The MP3 player hidden in Wendell's room. The password-protected folders on the laptop. It was all about sex. Wendell would have used any opportunity to get ready cash. Stumbling on this would have been risky but, done right, he could have bled Delaney dry.

The burglary. A sign Delaney was getting more and more desperate, heading toward a full-on panic. If he confided in someone, asked for help, he'd be getting pushed to solve the problem, and solve it fast.

I know what you did. Had Delaney assumed Wendell had something on him, too? That Gary was also being blackmailed? If that had been the case, that comment would have given Delaney an edge, a hold over him.

The club was under investigation, but that didn't mean arrests would be made anytime soon. Didn't guarantee Delaney was even a target.

So he'd do it himself. He'd lure Delaney away from Kate, take the focus off her. Get Delaney to come after him instead. And then he'd strike. The thought of it surged through Gary, hot and dangerous and fast. Had his pulse racing with it.

He needed to talk to Percival, warn him things were about to escalate.

Chapter Forty-One

The view outside the window of the bookstore was obscured by Percival's broad back. The faint strains of a whistled Bach aria were muffled by glass. Kate peered suspiciously at the innocuous broad shoulders spanning her window. At least he hadn't deterred customers.

Mrs. Sulley frowned thoughtfully at the man standing outside as she pulled out her wallet. "What's your policy on loiterers, Kate, dear?"

"Only those with red hair allowed."

She took the bag Kate handed to her. "You know him then?"

"A passing acquaintance. He enjoys the fresh air."

The bell jangled above the door as she left.

Kate flipped the sign in the window to CLOSED. The last rays of light drifted across the shelves. Outside, the street was fading into soft grays. Kate set the paper cup from the Fire-Hall Café on the counter within handy reach. She turned on the CD player and sank into her chair. It bobbed gently as she sat and straightened the stack of books she'd chosen to write blurbs on for the website.

I killed him. Headlights arced past and for an instant Gary was standing across from her again. Confessing to murder.

Kate turned up the volume. Maybe the music

would help drown out the relentless echo of his words. There wasn't much she could do about the image of the lifeless body sprawled on the stairs, a parking lot and blood spreading across pavement.

A figure approached the shop, just a dark silhouette against the light. It was impossible to tell if it was a man or a woman.

Percival took a step forward and engaged the figure in conversation. She shrugged and turned her attention back to the laptop.

****

"Bookstore's closed," Percival grunted.

"I see that." The voice was cultured and smooth. The man's face was drawn with worry, but easy to recognize. In better shape than Percival had thought, but not a threat. Percival kept his expression neutral. He waited to see what the man would do.

"Please," the man said. "My mother has collapsed behind the store. She's taken a bad fall. She needs help. I can't lift her on my own. My car is parked right over there." He gestured at the shiny, low-slung vehicle. "I need to get her to the car so that I can take her to the hospital."

So he was going to play it like that. Percival hesitated, thought it through. Glanced behind him at the store. Be discreet, Gary had said. Shops were beginning to close down the length of the street. It was calm and still. Nothing had happened all day. Things were about to pick up now though. He wondered how far it would go. Better safe than sorry.

"It won't take long. It's just around the corner," the man pleaded.

Percival was beginning to enjoy himself, letting the

man play out his act. So far, it was weak. He'd not be getting any standing ovations. There wasn't enough urgency in his voice to have the ring of truth. "Fine." Percival set his cup on the ground.

"She's right over here." The man led the way down the alley next to Fortune's Cove.

The sounds of the street became muffled. Their footsteps rang against the pavement, cold and hard. Out of sight of anyone passing. Back door of the bookstore sealed. Thick walls. Perfect. No point getting trapped in a dead end. Percival stopped.

The man turned back, looked at him questioningly.

Percival planted his feet, centered his weight. An obstacle, impossible to get around. "Make your move, Delaney."

Percival could see the shock hit. Using his name had caught him off guard. Percival could see Delaney reworking the plan in his head, running through his options. Percival had his eye on the man's right hand, watching the fingers twitch, waiting for them to form a fist, but he reached into his jacket instead. Gun? Unarmed himself, Percival tensed, ready to dive if the shot came.

Delaney's hand appeared, metal winking. A wheel brace. Inconspicuous. Easy to get a hold on, to measure the force. Delaney hefted the weapon, curled his fingers around it, got a good grip and raised one eyebrow. A smile playing around his mouth. He too was enjoying himself.

An uneasy feeling settled over Percival's shoulders.

Delaney moved like lightning. The blow caught Percival beneath the jaw. The metal rang, vibrated, with the impact. Pain exploded up Percival's jaw and through his head. His teeth ached with it. The swing was solid, plenty of force behind it. The blow would have taken down a lesser man.

Percival's eyes rolled in their sockets but he didn't budge. He omitted an ominous, rumbling growl of pure fury. The sound emanated from his chest, sonorous and menacing.

The other man blanched and fell back a step.

Percival followed, baring his teeth. His hands stretched out.

A phone suddenly rang in a jacket pocket. They froze and eyed each other.

Fueled by adrenaline, Delaney spun and ducked. They broke into action again. Delaney lashed out, the metal whistling through the air. He missed. Percival's fist fell upon his temple, cut across his forehead. The wheel brace skittered over the ground, rolled beyond reach.

Delaney scrambled to his feet. Percival could see fear in his eyes now. Arms flailing blindly, Delaney landed a wild punch. The phone rang again.

Sweat ran into Percival's eyes. His ear rang shrilly. He didn't see the next blow coming until it was too late. Knuckles connected with bone. Once. Twice. The pavement suddenly seemed uneven. Blood ran from his nose. Percival blinked. He looked at his opponent, dazed and surprised. The ground tilted beneath his feet. He groaned, an involuntary sound of dismay.

The man side-stepped as Percival crashed to the ground. Percival's gaze skidded across the empty sky above. His head reeled. His eyes rolled toward the blurring figure.

Delaney was left standing. He breathed hard, swiped a hand over his face. Smoothed away a thin trickle of blood seeping from a cut above his brow with the pad of his thumb. Grimaced.

Delaney straightened his clothes and walked toward the street.

In the alley, the phone rang on unanswered.

Chapter Forty-Two

Hinges creaked as the sign swung slowly above the door. The bell jingled.

Kate looked up. "Sorry. We're closed." She took in the perfect suit, the gleam of polished shoes, only slightly marred by recent scuff marks. The angular, almost gaunt face with the fine bones and cold eyes. The scent of cigarette smoke. The fresh cut above the left eyebrow, and the bruise purpling around it. He might have been handsome if his sharp mouth had relaxed into a smile rather than the unforgiving line it was now. Kate closed the laptop. She pushed back her chair and rose slowly. "You bought *Laughter in the Dark.*"

"I'm flattered you remember, Kate." His voice was like syrup. "I must admit, I am partial to Nabokov."

Her fingers pressed against the edge of the counter. Kate watched him closely. There was an underlying aura of menace the pleasantries couldn't conceal. It set her on edge and made her wish the street beyond the glass didn't look so deserted. So dark. Where was Percival? "We're closed."

"I realize that." The latch clicked as he locked the door behind him.

"What are you doing?" Her voice was sharp. She pressed her hands flat against the counter to hide a sudden tremble.

"I thought we could have a conversation." He glanced over his shoulder to see what she was looking at, then turned back, a smile curling his lips. "Don't worry. We won't be disturbed. It's such a quiet area. Everyone safe inside their homes. The streets empty. I've always found the small-town mentality within the heart of the city is under-appreciated."

Kate's hand inched toward the store's phone. If she could dial 999 or speed-dial Marcus, someone would come and—

"Leave the phone, Kate." The command was a gentle, caressing whisper. It was more threatening than a shout would have been.

Kate paused and reluctantly held up her hands. "What do you want?"

Delaney tucked his hands into his pockets. At ease. He strolled toward a shelf of books, idly scanning titles. "We could have been friends, Kate." He glanced at her over his shoulder. "You're very beautiful. Erudite and brave."

His words made her flesh crawl. "Yeah, well, you make me sick. And don't even think of coming closer, or you'll be wishing you had the physique of a Ken doll."

Fury twisted his features. She watched the struggle as he held onto control. Then he relaxed. "We'll see if your opinion doesn't change. I've been watching you, Kate. In the parking lot."

White curling fog. Dusky shapes.

"In the orchard."

The amber glow of a cigarette. Herbs and damp earth. A wraith of smoke rising around his features.

Her breath came more quickly. She licked her lips.

She had to keep him talking. She needed time to figure out how to get out of the situation. Time to think. "I saw you." It felt safe behind the cash register, but the counter was a useless barrier and she'd get penned in if he made a move. She'd be trapped in an instant.

"Yes."

Kate inched around the counter. How the hell was she going to get herself out of this? All she had were books, a laptop, a pencil. The tip wasn't even sharp.

"I thought it was enough to be rid of Wendell, but then you went snooping around. Where's the computer, Kate?"

She stopped short. "What computer?" He was only a few steps away.

"Wendell's computer. It wasn't in the house, so where is it?"

Involuntarily, her eyes darted to where the laptop sat on the counter. She could have kicked herself.

"Is that it?"

She didn't answer.

"It is." Anger drew his features together. Blood began to ooze from the cut again.

"You were the one who broke into the house." Smashed the window. Ransacked their room.

"A highly distasteful and ultimately fruitless endeavor."

The floor glowed like the flame of a candle in the last dying rays of light. The buildings across the road all but invisible. The streetlight flickered to life and shone through the windows behind him, transforming his face into a dark mask that reminded her horribly of the grotesque, smoke-wreathed figure in the orchard. His eyes narrow and unblinking, reminded her of a reptile. Cold-blooded.

The store had never seemed so small. There was nowhere to run. She'd never make it fast enough to the back room, and if she did and got out, she'd only end up in the alley. If she could get past him, to the front door she might have a chance. By now she knew the interior of the store would be lit up like a stage for those outside. But would they be able to interpret the situation for what it was? Would she be able to signal for help? Her thoughts raced. "Why do you want the laptop?"

"The innocent act isn't endearing and you don't pull it off very well. You know why. You saw the pictures." A muscle throbbed in his cheek. His pale, tapered fingers curled into a white-knuckled fist, the bones clearly outlined beneath the stretched skin. The gold band on his ring finger cut into his flesh. Some of the honey drained from his voice. It was suddenly coarse and ugly. "There are important people involved in this. There's a lot at stake, Kate. It's not just me. Those pictures, they make it look worse than it really is. Wendell should have left well enough alone. But he always wanted more. I had to end it. He was a greedy bastard. I abhor greed. It's so weak."

She was trapped with her books. An aura of déja vu clung to the motes of dust drifting through the air. She had lived the scenario before, only this time the heroes were trapped within the covers, sealed inside dust jackets, and she wouldn't wake to find it had all been a dream. She was on her own.

"Despicable." He flicked off the light, casting them into darkness.

For one moment the store was impenetrable. Sheer, primitive terror rose up inside her. Then her eyes adjusted to the dark.

He took a step forward, a shifting shadow.

Kate drew back. The counter pressed into the back of her thighs. Even if she tackled him now, used the element of surprise, she couldn't unlock the door fast enough to get away.

"Poison was purely self-defense. A favor to humanity."

"Hold on. What poison?" What was he talking about?

"Aconite in the pickles. So easy to add it to the jar. It seemed like a miracle that he died of a heart attack the next day. Your great-aunt has such a lovely voice by the way, made sweeter by her words. A heart attack. But I pieced it together. His death was too perfect, too convenient. Someone else had a grudge against him, but one who was more merciful than I would have been. It was only a matter of research. Fenris had the strongest reason to eliminate our friend, and had the knowledge, the training to do so."

Wendell knew how to make enemies. How could they have been so misled by him? "I swear I haven't seen anything. If the pictures are on there, they must be in an encrypted file. I know nothing about computers. Ask anyone."

"Do you really think I'm going to believe that?"

"Take the laptop, if you want."

His hands clenched. She could see sweat beading at his hairline. The desperation, the excitement, the anticipation in his eyes. "After your boyfriend attacked me in the alley I almost gave up."

"My…boyfriend?" Kate's thoughts reeled.

"Fenris." A fury so violent it didn't seem human

radiated from him. His pupils dilated. "But the pain wore off and I was still alive." He spread his hands. "And I know his secret. It isn't something you can hide. He murdered Derek Wendell, while I'm innocent of the crime. I hold the winning hand and the game is almost up. If only I'd been able to destroy the pictures. It's a pity really. Such a waste. But"—he smiled—"I'm afraid you know too much."

Fear was like a vice around her lungs, an iron clamp. "You don't want to kill me. You would no longer be innocent. Your hands would be stained with my blood."

"I don't plan to kill you. The fire will take care of that." A smile, sick with excitement, twisted his mouth into something that resembled an animal snarl.

"Fire?" The word was a whisper. It seemed to caress the rows and rows of books lined on her shelves like a malevolent hand. The paper. Flammable. All the words. The stories. Fortune's Cove, destroyed by smoke and flames.

"I thought it would be a fitting way for you to die. Along with your books."

Chapter Forty-Three

Gary tried his phone for the fourth time. No answer.

He thrust the phone into his pocket and lengthened his stride. His heart pounded. Adrenaline sizzled through his veins, his muscles. It all felt too familiar, too much like the scene that haunted him. It should never have come to this. The past rose up behind him, a lurking, shifting shape in the night, urging him to go faster. Nightmare visions swirled through his mind. Wounded. Trapped. Frightened or dead already. Why the hell wasn't Perce answering the damn phone? He'd been powerless the last time, had watched her blood run through his fingers.

He hoped to God he was wrong. But the dark apprehension, the sense of foreboding wouldn't let up. The fifth time he listened to the machinated whirr of the voice mail, the dispassionate, robotic voice took on sinister tones that drove straight to his heart.

The street was dark, but for the dim pools of light cast by tarnished lamps and the occasional passing car. Fear twisted in his gut. Cold sweat pricked beneath his collar. The wooden sign cast a long jagged shadow on the wall. The bookstore looked deserted.

****

Kate's breath rasped painfully. On the stereo, a sixties song with a beach theme played incongruously, into the strained silence.

Delaney's eyes flickered. "Surf's up? Really? How can you listen to that?"

"I don't know. Maybe because I don't have the soul of a sadistic pyromaniac with Machiavellian tendencies?" Panic made the words tumble from her lips. Words that might have been better kept to herself.

His hand lashed out and cut across her face in a vicious backhanded slap.

Pain blazed and flared hot across her cheekbone. Kate gasped. Her eyes stung. She blinked, caught her breath. Now she was angry. Seriously pissed off. "You shouldn't have done that."

Kate thrust her hand upward, palm first. It connected with a sickening crunch and his head snapped back. Delaney clapped a hand to his nose. Blood ran through his fingers, over his chin and dripped onto his starched white collar, staining the fabric. His eyes were round with disbelief. "Bitch!" He looked at the gore on his fingers before wiping his arm across his upper lip. "You broke my nose."

"You hit me, pal, I hit you."

His hand snagged in her hair, yanking her head back, forcing her to look up at him. The tendons in her neck strained against the force. Her hair felt like it was being torn out at the roots. She flinched, but looked at him steadily and noted with satisfaction that the blood still ran freely from his nose.

****

Gary approached the store, scanning the perimeter. The glass reflected the street behind him like the surface of a mirror. He cupped his hands on the surface, his breath fogging up the glass.

An Excuse for Murder

What he saw within had his blood running cold.

The man's back was to him, but his shoulders were curved forward and straining with barely restrained violence. Kate was pressed against the counter, her head yanked back, trapped by the hold he had on her hair, the vulnerable line of her neck exposed. She glared up at the man, equal parts fear and defiance in her expression.

Gary's vision went dark at the edges. His muscles went rigid, then loosened and warmed. His nerves sang.

He tried the door handle. Locked. That wasn't surprising, only horribly inconvenient.

Gary hammered his fists against the door. "Kate!" His voice was a hoarse shout.

****

For an instant Delaney's grip on her hair loosened. Kate didn't hesitate. Her fingers scrambled over the counter, searching, then closed around cardboard. She smiled.

And flung the contents of the paper cup into his face.

He let go abruptly and cursed. Delaney swiped at his eyes, the hot liquid running down his face, dripping from his hair.

Kate dodged past him, toward the door, stumbling on legs stiff with tension. Her eyes met Gary's through the window.

Then a hand clamped over her ankle as Delaney threw himself after her. She hit the floor, pain flaring as her elbows met the ground. Kate twisted, writhing, and lashed out at him with her foot, aiming for his face.

He ducked. "You fucking little bitch," he hissed, and yanked her toward him. He loomed above her, drew back his hand, his fingers curling into a fist, dark intent in his eyes.

Kate drove her knee upward, into his groin. Direct contact.

From behind them came an explosion of sound. Debris rained over them. Splinters of glass pricked her skin.

Delaney's eyes rolled back and he wheezed. He tumbled off her, knees curling involuntarily to his chest. He rocked back and forth, whimpering.

Kate clambered to her feet, staggering slightly, and breathing hard. "I warned you," she gasped.

Chapter Forty-Four

Kate brushed her hair out of her eyes and stared at Gary standing in the doorway. Blinked. It took a moment for her to register exactly what she was seeing. "You broke my door down?"

Then she couldn't say anything because with two strides, Gary had pulled her into his arms in a bone-crushing embrace. His heart raced against hers.

Kate gasped. "Ribs! Careful with the ribs."

He loosened his hold a little, only to run his hands over her, down her arms, over her face, lingering gently over the angry red mark on her cheek.

"I can't believe you broke my door down!" Kate complained, straining to look at the destruction over his shoulder. "I was handling it."

"Whose blood is that?" His voice was clipped as he gestured at her t-shirt. "Yours or his?"

Kate looked down at herself. "His. I think." She suddenly felt queasy. "I look terrible." Her ears started to buzz as she gazed the red splatters on her top.

Gary took one look at her face before lifting her so that she was sitting on the counter. He stripped off his jacket and wrapped it around her shoulders.

"I'm fine," Kate said through suddenly chattering teeth.

"'Course you are." He pulled the lapels closer around her. Held on for a second before letting go.

A moan from the man balled on the floor made him turn. Gary tugged his belt from the loops and secured the man's arms roughly behind his back. Delaney cried out and struggled, but Gary's hold on him was like iron. He lashed Delaney's arms behind his back with the leather belt. Then he grabbed a fist of Delaney's hair and yanked the man's head backward.

Delaney's eyes were wide with terror.

"I should have killed you when I had the chance," Gary growled.

He towered over the man and looked like he would give anything to finish the job right there and then. "Gary—" Kate said involuntarily.

The muscles in his arm strained. Then he released him and Delaney's forehead smacked back onto the floor.

"Hey!" Delaney yelped and rolled onto his back, his face contorted with fear and pain.

"You're not worth it." Gary stepped over him, disgust on his face.

He glanced back at Kate. Whatever he saw in her eyes seemed to cut him to the bone. "You thought I was going to kill him?"

No. Yes. "I wasn't sure." Quiet. Truthful.

"Why would you be?" Gary looked down at his hand, his eyes shadowed and unreadable. "Why is his hair wet?"

"It's tea."

Gary snorted, half amusement, half disbelief. "There's no avoiding tea when it comes to you, is there? Where's Percival?"

"I have no idea. He wandered off a little while ago."

"That doesn't sound like him." Gary frowned. "I can't believe Delaney risked coming here."

"He wanted the laptop."

Delaney glared at them in sullen fury.

"What is that noise?" Gary suddenly blurted, looking around the store for the source. Then asked, "California surf songs?" His voice was incredulous.

"It's not nice to judge." Kate turned the music off and the store was silent.

"Murderer." Delaney spat at Gary. "What do you think is going to happen when the police come? I'll tell them everything."

Gary opened his mouth to reply but Kate cut him off. "Tell them what?" Her cheek throbbed painfully. "What do you really know? How did he kill Wendell then?"

"I don't know. Some sort of poison. I know he did it. One look at him and they'll know too."

"That's your proof? Any cop worth his shield will laugh in your face. Give it up. Face it. You're the villain here, Delaney." She grabbed a roll of packing tape sitting at the far end of the counter. She tossed it to Gary. "Shut him up, will you? He's giving me a headache."

"With pleasure." Gary tore off a strip and plastered it over Delaney's snarling lips. He straightened. "You're going away for a very long time, Delaney."

"Whoa." At the sound, Gary and Kate turned to look at the entrance.

Tim and Will stood in the broken doorframe, staring wide-eyed around the store, taking in the mess, the trussed-up figure on the ground. Tim turned to Will. "I told you Kate was awesome."

"Even after I cracked your case?" Kate asked dryly.

"Yeah. If anyone could figure out we'd done it, you could. You know how it works."

"It?"

"Mysteries."

"Crikey," Will breathed, gazing at the scene with blatant admiration. "She clobbered him."

"Completely." Tim stepped into the store and peered down at Delaney's nose knowledgeably. "That's a gusher."

"Is he dead?" Will asked curiously from the threshold.

Delaney scowled back at Tim furiously, his shoulders working as his wrists strained at the belt tying his hands together.

"No." Kate clapped a hand over her mouth, to stop herself from laughing. If she started, she didn't think she'd stop.

Through the window, a figure staggered into view. He grasped at the broken frame and stumbled into the store, his shoes crunching across broken glass. One hand was cupped to his chin.

"Percival." Gary greeted his employee with relief, but his voice was brisk when he continued. "Where the hell were you?"

The large man maneuvered past the boys with barely a glance at Delaney and stopped in front of the counter. He addressed a spot in front of Gary's feet. "I didn't judge the situation properly and sacrificed the entire assignment. I should have seen it coming." He muttered the formalities in an unhappy slur. "Shouldn't have been so damn cocky." Suddenly his expression changed. "The tosser clipped me one in the alley!"

"Really?" Gary glanced at Delaney with a faint hint of respect in his eyes.

"With a bleeding wheel brace. I'll tender my resignation tonight," he rumbled.

"The hell you will. You did your best. Can't ask any more than that. Just don't let it happen again."

Kate watched the exchange curiously. Turned out Gary was more forgiving when it came to other people's failures than his own.

"Now make yourself useful and ring up the police." He glanced at Delaney. "And an ambulance."

"Yes, sir."

Chapter Forty-Five

Blue and red lights pulsed and flashed over faces and shelves, shimmering through the windows in ghostly hues. Percival stood on the pavement outside, doggedly refusing to let anyone through. He crossed his arms over his chest and shifted slightly on his heels. If Gary wasn't completely off the mark, Perce was quietly whistling the Prelude to Wagner's *Lohengrin*.

Gary stood to the side and watched. It was only a matter of time before Kate revealed the truth.

"Let me get this straight." Marcus leaned against the counter next to Kate and blinked slowly. He had arrived at the store in record time and hadn't left her side since. "Ryan Delaney is married, but was a member of a gentleman's club that provided costly services catering toward nympholepts with a propensity for violence. Our pseudonymous friend Mr. Wendell—gambler, weak-willed and morally challenged scoundrel—gathered evidence of this unfortunate fetish in all its digital, inkjet glory and reaped the benefits of his fortunate happenstance for a year, using and losing it to finance his love for the game."

"Right."

Marcus continued, "Finally Delaney snapped, and spiced up the old pickle stock with deadly flair. When lo and behold Wendell's vitality was arrested by a timely heart attack as he was unscrewing the very lethal concoction meant to sever his mortal coil. Coincidence or fate, Delaney thanked his lucky stars, before being seized by the fear that those documents of shame would return to haunt him again by falling into the hands of another—specifically yours. He followed you to see what you knew. Luck was on his side yet again when he cleverly convinced Roselyn to turn over Wendell's belongings to him. However, there was no laptop. Knowing there had to be a computer on which the pictures were stored, he broke into the house to search for it, only to come upon an empty room. There is no longer so much as an incriminating crumb of pulverized potato crisp dust or an empty can of cheap beer, let alone negatives of the blackmailer's prized photographs. You came upon him and he bopped you over the head. Fearing for your safety, Gary cornered him in an alley, appearing from the darkness like a well-dressed vigilante, and gave him a two-fisted warning, impossible to misinterpret. Our desperate villain, however, was not easily frightened, or simply daft beyond all belief—"

"Pissed off."

"Or that. Either way, he decided to seek you out, throwing caution to the wind. Our villain performed the ultimate faux pas and entered your store after closing, bent on—"

"Burning my store to the ground and killing me in the process of taking the laptop back."

Marcus blanched. "Quite so. Destroying evidence, the cretinous poltroon."

Kate laughed, then winced. Every muscle had begun to ache. "Poltroon?"

"A coward."

"I'll have to remember that one." She rubbed chilled fingers against her jeans. Her voice sounded detached, as if she was watching something from a long way off that had nothing to do with her. Delayed shock.

"With your usual panache, you beat him to a bloody pulp," Marcus finished. He looked like his mind was reeling.

Gary said, "Money and fear are strong motives, and he had both."

"This could only happen to you, Kate." Marcus gazed blankly at the entrance to the store. "When exactly did he break your door down?"

"He didn't. That was Gary."

Marcus's eyebrows arched to an impossible height and shot a glance at him. "What?"

"The door was locked from the inside and Gary broke it down. I had it covered. I don't need anyone to save me or Sir Percival over there."

"That's a matter of opinion," Gary said dryly. Tonight proved that she did need to be protected. The hero just wasn't meant to be him.

Marcus looked from the gaping doorway to Gary and back again. "I'm impressed at the valiant attempt nonetheless."

The store had quickly filled with a small crowd. Tim and Will had their backs pressed up against a shelf to the side, hoping to remain unnoticed. They gazed at the activity with unabashed delight. "The door is shattered," Tim murmured. "Kate is going to be so mad."

Dr. Garreth stood in the center of the store, feet planted firmly, hands on hips, and scowling. His head swung from side to side, taking in the situation with open disgust. When he dropped his leather satchel at his feet with a bang, splinters of wood and glass rippled outward across the floor.

A figure jogged across the road toward the store, was about to enter the store when an arm, the size and width of a tree branch blocked the way.

Jeremy glared at Percival. "I'm with the doc."

"Credentials," Perce demanded.

"Ow! God damnit!" The exclamation exploded through the store.

Delaney was on his feet, hands cuffed behind his back, and was scowling and swearing furiously. Henry held onto him with one hand while a strip of packing tape dangled from the other. He looked at him patiently.

"You have the right to remain silent. Anything you say can and will be used against you in a court of law." Henry rattled off Delaney's rights as he marched him to the door.

"You're arresting the wrong person." Delaney spun suddenly, staring straight at Gary. "He's the one you want! He killed him!" He all but spat the words at him. "He killed Wendell!"

Tim and Will gasped. "So cool," Tim whispered on a sigh of sheer bliss.

"Ace," Will agreed.

Gary's face remained impassive, giving away nothing. He could feel the tension radiating off Kate.

Henry looked at Dr. Garreth questioningly. "It would mean a lot of paperwork, if what he's saying is true."

Dr. Garreth stared at Delaney. Then he slapped his thigh and broke into raucous laughter. "That's a first!" He wagged his finger at Delaney. "Trying to turn a natural death into a homicide. If the fellow died of anything other than a heart attack than I'm John bloody Wayne. Better stage a postmortem because I must have missed the bullet." He shook his head in disbelief. "Anyone want to exhume the body? Be my goddamn guest."

"But—"

Henry pushed Delaney roughly toward the door. "I don't want any more stories from you. Wait until the lads at the Yard hear about this," he muttered happily. "Ha! Always bragging about gang wars, brawls, and murder. This'll wipe the smirk right off their faces. *Culpam poena premit comes*."

"Huh?" Will frowned.

"'Punishment presses hard onto the heels of crime.'" Tim translated the Latin without a second thought, it being obviously a well-worn phrase in the Smith household. Something casually used over the mashed potatoes and gravy.

Tim suddenly squinted at something over Will's shoulder. He gasped, eyes alight with excitement. He stretched on his toes and gingerly removed a book from the shelf the way an archeologist would remove a fossil from the earth. He brushed over the cover, then held it aloft for Kate to see, a triumphant grin crossing his face.

From where he was standing, Gary could see the blue and brown cover, with bold white typeface and two boys deciphering mysterious symbols carved into a stone slab.

"*The Mystery of the Mayan Warrior*," Will breathed reverently. The boys sat on the floor, backs to the shelves, and Tim flipped the cover open. They leaned over the book in anticipation.

Delaney limped past them as Henry led him out. Jeremy stared openly at Delaney's blood-stained face and his crooked nose. "What happened to him?"

"Kate did," Gary said.

"Blimey." Jeremy shook his head pityingly. "Let's patch you up then, shall we?"

"Jeremy," Dr. Garreth barked. "Take care of his face. And twinkle toes," he added to Kate, "you'll need to be treated for shock. You can go to hospital with us via ambulance or by a designated driver of your choice. Take your pick." He hefted his bag, glanced once more around, harrumphed, and followed Jeremy out.

Marcus jingled his keys in his pocket. "I'll take you."

"No one gets in there," Percival rumbled suddenly. He braced his hands against the doorframe, blocking the way.

Neil simply pushed the other man aside with one hand as if he was brushing aside a curtain, and barreled his way through. In the other hand, he was carrying a take-out cup from the Old Firehall Café. Percival had met his equal when it came to size and stature. After a moment's shock, Percival swung around, stretched one giant hand out, and grabbed a fist-full of Neil's shirt.

"It's okay, Percival," Gary said.

Percival released his captive abruptly.

Neil glared at Percival before crossing the room. He shoved the paper cup into Kate's hand. "Hot toddy from the café," he said gruffly. "Thought you'd need it."

Kate cupped her hands around it gratefully. "Thanks, Neil." She took a sip.

Rubber soles clomped over shards of glass and wood. Percival pushed the intruder out onto the sidewalk and barricaded the doorway with his bulk. "No."

Thwack! A cane sliced down and whacked him sharply on the forearm. Percival's broad back tensed. "Ye'll move aside. Noo!"

"No."

"Remind me to give Percival a raise after tonight," Gary murmured.

The cane poked Percival in the side. He growled and his fingers tightened on the door frame.

There was a tense pause.

"Who doo ye think ye are, blockin' my way? I'll no tolerate it! Not from anyone, least of all a knuckle-headed lout like you."

"I bet he was after a book." Tim peered at the destruction, keeping a firm hold on his own find. "A book with a secret code that was sold by accident and he needed it back. To find the treasure."

Will nodded solemnly. "Diamonds?"

"What else?"

Will suddenly dug a fist in his pocket and came up with a handful of wrapped candies.

Tim studied them for a second, then chose a green-colored one. He picked a piece of fluff off, thoughtfully unwrapped it and popped the candy into his mouth.

"When are you gonna tell your dad?" Will asked, rolling the candy around his mouth.

"When he gets home. You can come over." Tim paused. "It's Mum I'm really worried about," he confessed.

"If the bairn can get in, then so can I!" Penelope

snarled.

Percival swung his head around and looked toward Gary with a pained expression on his face.

Gary shrugged.

"Percival is a brave man," Marcus said without tearing his eyes away from the scene in the doorway. "That is one job you couldn't pay me to do. Not for all the money in the world."

Kate laughed. "I agree. You can call Percival off now, Gary. He's suffered enough for one day. I still don't know why you thought I needed him to protect me. The villain just limped out of the door in handcuffs thanks to me."

In a flash, Gary grabbed her wrist and yanked up the sleeve of the jacket, revealing the long shallow gash running the length of her lower arm to her elbow.

"Hey!" Kate tried to pull back.

"Then what the hell is this?" Gary clenched his jaw.

Marcus took a quick step forward, animosity emanating from him. "Let go."

Gary released her abruptly. "That was luck. You could have been killed. Has that thought even registered with you?"

"Yeah, it has, but I'm fine besides some scrapes and bruises. You can't save everyone, Gary."

"Obviously." Gary fought to keep his voice distant and dismissive. "I should go. There's enough going on here. You don't need me, Kate."

"Hold on—"

Gary continued out the door as though he hadn't heard.

****

Kate shoved the cup of tea into Marcus's hands.

"Kate—"

"I'll be right back." She hopped off the counter, skirted around Tim and Will, avoided Marcus's questions and poked Percival firmly in the back. "I need to get outside."

Percival glanced at her warily, simultaneously managing to keep the street in view. "I'm not sure about that."

"See how Delaney walked out of here?"

He nodded grudgingly, suspicious.

"That could be you if you don't let me through. Got that?"

He stepped aside.

"Thanks."

Penelope stood on the pavement, peering at the police car, the ambulance, the broken door frame, the jagged glass, and Percival. Her lips were pressed together tightly and her eyes were bright, razor-sharp, and piercing. She stomped her cane on the ground imperviously. Judgment had been passed. "Girlie! What'll be the meanin' of all this fracas?"

Kate shoved past her.

Penelope gasped in outrage. Percival reached out and grabbed hold of the cane just as she was about to charge after Kate. She swung around on him and bared her teeth. "What do ye think ye're doin?"

They glared at each other.

Kate sprinted to catch up with Gary. "Hey!" She grabbed his arm and brought him up short. She stepped in front of him and blocked his path. The blue light of the cop car throbbed over his features. The air felt cool and slightly damp on her skin. She handed him his jacket. "You forgot this. Why do I have the feeling that you're walking away for good?"

Gary paused, his jaw set and his eyes unreadable. "I watched her get shot. I watched you hit the floor through a sheet of glass, covered with blood."

"Not my blood. Well, mostly not."

"It doesn't matter. The point is that I could have prevented it. Instead I set everything into motion."

"Delaney would have killed Wendell if you hadn't."

"And that makes it better?"

The words hung suspended between them. Emotion caught at her heart.

"Kate." A breeze twisted past, tugged at their clothes before sliding away through the buildings and on. "You don't trust me. You don't know me. You think you do, but you don't." A wry half-smile teased at his mouth and fell short of his eyes. He stepped closer and looked down at her.

Her heart clenched painfully. "Don't put words in my mouth." The scratch on her arm stung. "You're a better person than you think you are, Gary. I hope one day you'll realize that."

"I said it once and I'll say it again. I can't give you promises. I don't have any left," he said simply.

Kate hugged her arms around herself. "So this is it?"

"I know what loss is, Kate. I still miss her. I see her every time I close my eyes."

The confession rang in the air, lingering on like the clash of bells.

"There's no competing with a ghost."

He laced his fingers through hers. Raised her hand

and pressed a careful kiss to her wrist, above the wound. It tingled up her arm, hummed through her pulse. "You of all people should know that the girl in the fairy tale never ends up with the killer."

"This isn't a fairy tale."

"I'd have to agree with that."

"You offered once to be my partner in crime. What if I need your help solving another mystery?"

Gary grinned. "I'd wager a tenner it won't be long before you stumble on another mystery. We'll see what happens then. We might have to discuss it over dinner."

"There's always a way to lay the ghosts to rest, Gary."

"If you discover the secret, let me know. Stay out of trouble, Kate."

"You too." Kate lifted her chin. This wasn't the end. She'd see him again.

Gary walked into the darkness and the night, thick with the scents of autumn.

He reached into his pocket for the necklace. His fingers closed around the pendant.

An Excuse for Murder

Chapter Forty-Six

"There are too many ghosts in this house. Perhaps it's time to stop holding so hard onto what's been and gone."

Great-aunt Roselyn's voice startled Kate from her thoughts. They were sitting at the kitchen table. On that table were two wine glasses, a bottle, and a wooden bowl full of freshly picked apples. Beyond the glass, dusk softened the forms of the trees until they were only shadows in the dark.

Kate noticed with surprise that her glass was empty. She reached for the bottle. The tinted glass was dusty, the flavors of the wine old and rich. A vintage Merlot. They had decided this was the right occasion to uncork it, after everything that happened. Kate poured, refilling both their glasses. The wine gave off a dark fruit-scented perfume. "What do you mean?"

"There are so many memories trapped in these walls."

"You're not thinking of selling, are you?"

"No, I don't think I'd have the heart to sell. Not now. But each day, it seems to be getting harder. Sometimes the past seems more real than the present."

"It would be a big change, living somewhere else. Starting fresh though, it might be good for you."

"At my age, Kate, one is no longer able to start fresh." She gave a wry smile.

Was this the moment to ask? "Great-aunt Roselyn, what happened to the boy you told me about? The one who brought you those gifts."

"He died."

The statement was blunt, startling. The words seemed to take on a physical presence in the room, like they'd filled the space with the very force of them. "How?"

"He took his own life."

Suicide. A shiver ran through Kate. A branch tapped against the window, a soft scratch of sound. "And you found his body." Now it suddenly all made sense. That fierce whisper after Mr. Wendell died. *Not again.*

"Yes, I was the one who found him. Out there." Roselyn looked toward the window, and the orchard. "Hanging from a tree. I saw his feet first. They twisted slowly to the left. Stopped. Swung to the right." Her voice was quiet, flat. "And stopped. Then I saw his eyes. The eyes I'd loathed were open and staring. The branch was moaning, straining beneath the weight. The sound that tree made, it was almost human." Roselyn took one of the apples from the bowl. Held it cupped in her hand. "Have you seen the way the apples glow red in the sunrise? Every shade of crimson visible, every bruise, the very texture of the veins in their leaves. The grass was damp on my ankles and scattered with apples. I'll never forget it." She returned the fruit to the bowl.

"That's why you said, 'There will be no more death in this house.'"

"A foolish statement, really. But I never expected to witness another death, not here in this house. So, you see, I know how hard it is to find the dead, to be confronted with the loss of a life. It leaves a mark, alters you."

"You were so young."

"So was he. To make matters worse, it was my fault."

"From what you've told me, it sounds as though he was already troubled."

"Oh, there was certainly a pre-existing inclination. He had a sensitive temperament that often bordered on depression, and he had a tendency to romanticize death. The poems he read seemed to affect him deeply, influenced him. He seemed monstrous to me, that disturbing intensity. But he had a good heart. Better than mine. His only fault was to love too much, whereas mine was hate and contempt."

"There's a fine line between love and obsession." The orchard, the gnarled trees and fruit-laden boughs were almost black beyond the window. "You can't blame yourself for what he did."

"Can't I? I was eighteen and scornful. Sure of myself. Confident I was worth loving and always would be. Spoiled, even. And quite heartless." Roselyn took a sip of her wine. Her face was pale but her voice, when she spoke again, was strong. She met Kate's eyes and explained, "I detested him. He was awkward. Shunned by the others and mocked. He watched us all too closely. His heavy-lidded eyes repulsed me. When he told me he loved me, I was horrified, afraid the mere fact of it would somehow contaminate me, too. I turned him down, again and again. More cruelly each time. I laughed at him. Threw away his gifts. I hurt him. He became angry. Then desperate. Made threats and cried in a way that embarrassed me."

"Did you tell anyone about it?"

"Of course not. I was too proud. His infatuation was mortifying, but also flattering. He adored me. And I enjoyed hurting him. It was so easy. It was intoxicating to have such power over another person. To be able to transform joy into despair with a single word or a glance." She sighed. "It all seems so long ago now, so foolish. After I found his body, I knew what guilt was."

"Did Frank know what happened?"

"No. Hardly anyone did. The boy's parents didn't want people to know that their son had committed suicide. They wanted to keep the scandal hidden. My parents were only too happy to keep quiet."

"But Penelope knew."

"She began planning ways we could leave, how we would make something of ourselves, have careers. Then Frank asked me to marry him. I knew he would. He loved a version of me that was safe, that I could maintain. And so I said yes. I stopped wishing for more. And, from then on, everything I did, every decision I made, was for him. Penelope was furious. She couldn't understand why I did it."

"She still can't."

"I know what the others see. A stereotype. But I knew my place. I chose it. I took care of him. I made this house a place of tranquility for him to return to. And I never complained or questioned his judgement. I made him happy and that was all I wanted."

"Was it worth it?"

Great-aunt Roselyn smiled. "I like to think so. I also had high expectations of him. I wanted him to build me a fortress of words. Speaking of which."

Roselyn took an envelope from her pocket. It was yellowed with age.

The letter Frank wrote before he died.

"You're so much stronger than I ever was, Kate. Perhaps it's time to take inspiration from you." She reached for the fruit knife in the bowl. Removed the cover and slid the blade beneath the flap of the envelope. She held the knife there, about to make the cut, and hesitated. Kate leaned forward. Roselyn looked up and they exchanged a glance, recognizing the thrill of that moment. Kate could feel her heart race and found herself wishing for magic. For a miracle from beyond the grave. For words that would give strength again. The diamond on Roselyn's finger seemed to kindle, to flash with a cold flame.

The knife sliced through paper.

Then the letter was in Roselyn's hand. Folded twice. The crease still sharp. Kate watched as she peeled the edges of the paper apart, carefully, slowly. The edges clung to each other. Then Kate caught a glimpse of faded blue ink. The letters sprawled across the page, large and rounded. Not many words. Half a page of lines, maybe less. Would it be enough?

Great-aunt Roselyn looked once more out at the orchard. Then she read.

When she had finished, she lowered the letter, and smiled. She smoothed one hand over the page, touching the letters.

"Is it what you'd hoped for?" Kate asked.

"Both less and more." She paused, folding the letter along the creases. "Sometimes it's the silent words, those that are left unsaid, that mean the most."

****

It would take time before she stopped checking the doors were locked. It was when she was making sure the bolt was thrown on the front door that she saw the light on the porch. The cigarette smoke. Kate tensed. Someone was sitting on the porch, on the top step, watching darkness settle on the base of the clouds. The cloud of smoke hanging in the air, turned to silver in the light.

Kate pushed aside visions of gloved hands and concealed weapons and opened the door, braced. Then she saw the cascade of curls and relaxed. "Elaina." She moved closer.

Elaina was sitting on the step, knees pulled up to her chest. Insects whirred around the bulb. The night sky seemed to be pressing down upon the roof, the tower. Elaina brought the cigarette to her lips with one paint-stained hand. Were her fingers trembling? She could paint Isra's fur with minute strokes of the brush. Her hands never shook. But there was an unmistakable tremor in them now.

"He'll come back." Smoke scraped over Elaina's voice.

"Ian?" Kate sank to the step beside her. Every part of her body ached, but she refused to let the pain get the best of her. "You decided not to go with him." The air was damp, carrying a chill with it.

"He always comes back."

And she'd draw his face, over and over, until he did. "Have you ever wondered what would happen if we left this house?"

"All the time." Elaina's grin was quick and sharp. "But the rent is so damned decent."

They sat there in silence, despite the cold, watching

the smoke unfurl, pale and ghostly. The walls rose up behind them. Moss-covered stones permeating the air with their scent, mingling with the perfume of old roses and grass. The trees rustled, like tranquil giants, with the creak of dry wood.

Chapter Forty-Seven

"You have reached your destination," the GPS chirped at Gary. He hadn't needed to program it. He could have found the cemetery blindfolded. He'd planned out the route often enough. And now he was here. After forty-five minutes of ignoring opportunities to pull a U-turn. Driving too fast over jolting roads, the evening sun in his eyes.

The car idled. Gary stared out of the window at iron gates caught in the glare of his headlights. Dew clinging to the ragged hawthorne hedge, brambles sparking like silver. A rusted bicycle leaned against the fence. Blue paint peeling away, exposing the metal underneath. A wooden sign warned that littering, smoking, and dogs were not allowed.

The gate was open.

It would matter sweet fuck-all if he went in there or not. No one would know if he turned the car around and left. The dead don't watch the living from some palace in the sky. Christ, he hoped they didn't. The idea of his father staring at him with a judgmental sneer from behind a spiritual one-way mirror was downright terrifying.

He'd never visited the grave. A bodyguard who got his client killed didn't get invited to the burial. He'd accepted that with a who-the-hell cares shrug. She should have been intangible molecules in the sunlight, swirling away on a current of air, not trapped in a casket underground.

Gary got out of the car, slammed the door too hard. The sound ricocheted, loud as a gunshot. A muddy track edged with bindweed led up to the open gate. Pebbles crunched under his shoes. Then his hand was against cool iron. His heart rate kicked up a notch.

A wide swathe of turf led between the plots. Gary walked past a chapel of rest. Marble crosses. Rusted circles of iron, caught in the fading light. The trees bordering the cemetery seemed to draw closer. There was something secretive about the graves.

He could feel the electric current of it at the base of his spine, before he saw the name. A granite gravestone, three feet high, and hard to miss. Gary zipped his jacket against the cold and watched the shadows spread.

"I forgot flowers." His voice sounded strange in that still place. "Probably should have brought some. I was never good at that." Leaves rustled in the distance.

They don't need to be long-stemmed roses. Just a memory, something she'd said. Close, like a whisper in his ear. Bright and teasing. *Sunflowers, daisies, something you can pick off the curbside.*

He laid words at her feet instead. "I killed him." It was no more than a sigh. Gary tipped his head back, looked up at the branches, outlined against the dark sky. This time, there was no reply. Not even a memory.

He felt like a fool, standing above her grave, hands in his pockets, waiting for God only knows what. Too solid, too warm.

It was time he told her. "I've met someone." It felt like a confession.

Moths whirled white around him. Long stems of grass brushing against the grave stone.

A word about the author…

As an avid reader and writer of crime fiction, Vanessa Westermann's ideal day would be spent plotting fictitious crimes. Vanessa is a former Arthur Ellis Awards judge and has given a talk on the evolution of women's crime writing at the Toronto Chapter of Sisters in Crime.

Vanessa's book review column entitled "Vanessa's Picks" was published in the monthly newsletter of a popular Toronto mystery-specialty bookstore from 2012 to 2016. The column was developed into a blog, featuring literary reviews and author interviews.

While living in Germany, she attained an M.A. in English Literature and went on to teach creative writing.

She currently lives in Canada and is working on her next novel, while drinking copious amounts of tea.

Readers can find her blog at:
www.vanessa-westermann.info
or follow her on Twitter @VanessasPicks.

Thank you for purchasing
this publication of The Wild Rose Press, Inc.

For questions or more information
contact us at
info@thewildrosepress.com.

The Wild Rose Press, Inc.
www.thewildrosepress.com

To visit with authors of
The Wild Rose Press, Inc.
join our yahoo loop at
http://groups.yahoo.com/group/thewildrosepress/

CPSIA information can be obtained
at www.ICGtesting.com
Printed in the USA
LVHW042357261119
638675LV00018B/626/P